Interactive Press

Black Books Publishing

Twice winner of the Western Australia Premier's Award for Digital Narrative and the Queensland Premier's Award for Poetry among other distinctions, David P Reiter has been recognised internationally for his ground-breaking creative works.

Hemingway in Spain and *Nullabor Song Cycle* began as text works and later were extended to films. *My Planets: a fictive Memoir* began as a physical book and an enhanced CD but then, in collaboration with the Banff Centre for the Arts in Canada, became the ground-breaking *My Planets Reunion Memoir* <http://ipoz.biz/myplanets>, an interactive website in which text, film, audio performances, classical music, astronomy, and animation converge on a journey from separation to reunion of biological families.

In his latest hybrid work, David creates a hybrid satire of not only independent publishing but many aspects of contemporary and futurististic life in which memory and focus can be measured and discarded in nanoseconds. Seemingly arbitrary hyperlinks invite/distract the reader into visual and auditory experiences larger than any physical covers can contain.

Dr Reiter is Publisher/CEO at IP (Interactive Publications) and lives in Brisbane with his wife, two children, and a geometrically expanding menagerie of irreverent pets.

Interactive Press
Brisbane

Black Books Publishing

a novel

David P. Reiter

Interactive Press
an imprint of IP (Interactive Publications Pty Ltd)
Treetop Studio • 9 Kuhler Court
Carindale, Queensland, Australia 4152
sales@ipoz.biz
ipoz.biz/IP/IP.htm

Printed in 12 pt Cochin on 14 pt Avenir Next.

National Library of Australia Cataloguing-in-Publication data:

Author: Reiter, David P. (David Philip), author.

Title: Black books publishing / David P. Reiter.
Publisher: Carindale, Qld. : Interactive Publications, 2018.
ISBN: 9781925231670 (paper)
                 9781925231687 (eBk)
Subjects: Fiction.
                 Novels.
                 Satire.
                 Publishing.
                 Independent Publishing.
                 Microblogs.
                 Instant messaging.

Also by David P Reiter:

Just Off Message	Kiss and Tell	Real Guns
Timelord Dreaming	Paul and Vincent	The Greenhouse Effect
My Planets: a fictive memoir	The Gallery	Global Cooling
http:ipoz.biz/myplanets	Sharpened Knife	Tiger Tames the Min Min
Nullarbor Song Cycle	Letters We Never Sent	Tiger Takes the Big Apple
Primary Instinct	Triangles	Bringing Down the Wall
Hemingway in Spain	The Cave After Saltwater Tide	
Hemingway in Spain (film)	Liars and Lovers	
Changing House	The Snow in Us	

for those who succeed enough to satisfy themselves
in spite of the tide of opinion

ACKNOWLEDGEMENTS

This work relies on associative links to work that is freely accessible on the Internet and acknowledges its sources via URLs provided in hypertext and footnotes that were accurate at the time of publication. The author expresses his gratitude to the authors and artists of those referenced works sources and hopes that this incidental promotion will give rise to new audiences for all concerned.

The author also wishes to thank the many people who provided inspiration and valuable feedback during the composing and the endless stages of refinement of this work, which only served to remind him of the poetic justice served up when the roles are reversed occasionally from infallible publisher to an author reminded of his clay toes.

Doubtlessly, with a work like this that satires an industry with a proud feudal history there will be those who will interrogate for imperfections in our own critique, and I am glad to take full responsibility for any that go viral. Nevertheless, as a certain First Peoples Tribe I respect but of which I am certainly not a member points out, it is necessary to embed at least one imperfection in a completed work so as not to offend the gods. And so it is here.

I leave you in the capable hands of my [slightly?] inebriated central character, Dylan Cashew. Feel free to share your thoughts with him (and the universe): http://bit.ly/2FoCO8B

CONTENTS

PART 1: EXODUS

And when the people came upon the Red Sea and found that all six lanes outbound to the Promised Land were clogged with plastic waste, the Lord said unto them, 'that'll teach you to put your faith in Google Maps!'

Chapter 1: What Have I Done?

DYLAN CASHEW DID NOT WANT TO BE THERE. There were many other places in the world he also did not want to be, but this staid room, this pen-etched desk, these monotone unpolished tiles and four unforgiving walls comprised a standard by which all other places Dylan did not want to be could be judged.

From a coalmine canary's perspective, it was not all bad: the room had a window. But mostly bad: the window was Photoshop black, peering out as it did to the cropping lines of an airplane hangar. So dark in fact that he could see himself and his unkempt hair slightly better than the assorted aircraft below.

His first few days as Assistant Technical Editor, Aerosystems Establishment Canada. *What have I done?* Things were bound to get better, if they didn't get worse, which was more likely since things had a way of bottoming out before scampering for the light of day if they didn't have anything more pressing to do at that warp of space-time.

'It could be worse,' a voice in an East Midlands accent said out of nowhere.

Dylan wheeled around from the window, his gaze probing the recesses. 'It can't be!'

'The indefinite pronoun should never be used to refer to an Author of Note,' the voice chided.

'Where are you?'

'In your head – until you give me permission to metabolise.'

'*Metabolise?* That's a new one on me.'

'I'll take that as a yes, then?'

'You said we were finished in Edmonton!'

'Because you gave up.'

'Not on writing – just writing about *you*!'

D. H. Lawrence – or rather a hologram very much like him – came into view.

Dylan blinked. Then winced. Then winced again.

'I had high hopes for you,' said D. H. 'It's not too late to admit you were wrong.'

'There's my future to think of,' sniffed Dylan.

'Oh, is that all?' scoffed D. H.

'*Now* who's using the indefinite pronoun carelessly?'

'Not to mention my wife.'

'Teach you to get married so young.'

'I'm twenty-three years old, D. H.'

In that frozen instant between galaxies, Dylan had accepted that talking to a holograph was not only acceptable in the circumstances but perfectly natural.

'Too young to know better,' D. H. nodded. 'I was nearly thirty before Frieda and I got married. I already had three novels, a book of poetry and a play notched on my belt by then.'

'Well, la-de-dah for you.' Dylan paused for effect. 'Of course I knew all that.'

'We were on a roll,' said D. H. 'And then you had to go and spoil everything!'

'I didn't have a choice,' Dylan stammered. '*She* proposed.'

'Caught off guard, eh?'

'No. Well, yes. Yes – and no!'

There was a knock at the door, so D. H. took his cue and vanished.

A tallish man in a tweed jacket, definite threadbare pants and sporting a bright tie that cried out for attention, leaned in and looked around.

'To whom were you talking to – just now?'

Dylan broke into a controlled sweat.

'I'm sorry, Mr Lehmann. I forgot to mention that I occasionally talk to myself when... my blood sugar gets low.'

Mr Lehmann was Dylan's superior, the Chief Editor who had interviewed him back in Edmonton, and, to Dylan's amazement, had actually offered him the job. Lehmann was an ex-pat Austrian, whose Germanic accent was so slight Dylan could either assume he'd been living in Canada for many years or had embarked on a deliberate campaign to camouflage his roots to blend in with the natives. Lehmann had greasy hair that would have suited him to a bit part in a 50s black and white film by a struggling Norwegian director. And his way of speaking with overdrawn inflections on the wrong words reminded Dylan of auditions he'd imagined attending in his student days but never quite did.

'*That's* fine,' said Lehmann, straining to sound reassuring, as if out of a rules book. 'It's a lonely job – editing. Until you learn the ropes.'

Dylan eyed the sheath of papers Lehmann was clutching to his chest like an injured pigeon. 'Is that for me?'

'Yes,' said Lehmann. 'Your first *report* – on the Mirage.'

'Let me guess. It's an aircraft?'

'Quite so. *Pride* of the Armée de l'air[1].'

D. H. materialised behind him. 'Ah, yes, the Mirage – ancestor of the Rafale[2]. Now there's a bitch of an aircraft!'

Dylan glanced nervously from D. H. to Lehmann, but the latter was none the wiser. Still, Dylan waved the hologram away. Since he had no way of sneaking into D. H.'s parallel universe without an iris scan, he had no idea what a Rafale was.

'I'm sure you'll find the draft report interesting,' said Lehmann, setting it down on the desk, pressing the creased corners flat again. Lieutenant Rousseau will report here at 10am tomorrow to review your edit.'

---

[1] http://bit.ly/2CfCll2
[2] http://bit.ly/2BZz0N8

Dylan gulped. 'What if I'm not ready?'

'Chop, chop,' chuckled Lehmann. 'There's plenty more where this came from. *Dead*lines, deadlines!' He backed away, straight through D. H. 'Feel free to *ring* me about any queries.'

Two hours later and Dylan's hair was so disheveled that it was looking neat. And only three pages into the twenty-odd page document.

'Arrgh!' he declared, thrusting it aside and glaring at his coffee cup. 'More caffeine. Better yet, make that jet fuel!'

'Life is a travelling to the edge of knowledge, then a leap taken[3],' said D. H., leaning over his shoulder.

Dylan shuffled pages. 'What? Where did you read that?'

'I didn't read it – I *wrote* it.'

Dylan slammed the report closed. 'Congratulations. Another one of your memorable throw away lines to keep the critics guessing?'

'Not so memorable as it happens if you didn't recall it.'

'I wish I could *leap* over this report,' said Dylan. 'Now I know why no one else wanted this job.'

'Ah,' said D. H. 'But you must have been chosen from a cast of thousands. Or at least a few word-mongers after a pay cheque.'

Dylan nodded. 'I'd prefer to believe the former. But I could tell I was probably the only one who applied.'

[It seemed like only yesterday, and it actually was well before yesterday – if you discounted virtual time...]

Dylan, in an ill-fitting suit and an even tighter tie, grasping his résumé, waiting for a door to open at the appointed time, expelling the previous, and doubtlessly better qualified, candidate. The door opens seconds later, but no one emerges, just the long and impressively narrow nose of Lehmann, followed soon after by a face that invites

---

[3] http://bit.ly/2zEinjG

him into the interview room.

Awkward seconds limp past as Dylan tries to remember the pose he should strike on the padded interrogation chair according to *The Idiot's Guide to Successful Interviewing*[4].

The question he's dreading – what's your background in aeronautics? – never comes. Instead, Lehmann mumbles on about the small town near the Base where most of the civvies live.

'Everyone knows everyone else's business,' he explains. 'Which isn't a bad thing if a bear has broken into your house.'

[Bears are the stuff of legend for Dylan, not quite Disney-style but close.]

Like all experienced editors. Lehmann picks up on the slightest whiff of ambivalence. 'You've never encountered a bear?'

'No,' says Dylan. 'But I'm happy to offer it an escort out if one strays onto my property.'

'You've got the job!' exclaims Lehmann.

'Are you sure?' Dylan says. 'I'm inexperienced!'

'Great,' says Lehmann. 'No one likes a know-it-all!'

'I'm terrible at parts of speech. I… I can't remember the difference between a misplaced and dangling modifier![5]'

'Even better. Pilots hate dealing with elitists and their jargon.'

Dylan decides to use his ultimate weapon. 'What possible connection is there between my research into D. H. Lawrence and technical reports?'

'None,' Lehmann says. 'But that's beside the point.'

'Which is?'

'The job is yours!'

'You see?' Dylan said, as if D. H. was still there, which apparently he wasn't, at least not in this particular universe.

---

[4] http://bit.ly/2E2SJbO
[5] http://bit.ly/2E1xC9P

'I was the only sucker stupid enough to apply for this job, so how could I send Lehmann back empty-handed?'

Clearly, D. H. had lost interest.

Thirty or even twenty years on, Dylan would seek sought solace in YouTube or Snapchat, but the only electronic keyboard within shouting distance now was across the hangar in the steno pool. He felt exposed in his stale little office behind his splintery desk with only a laminate of papers to defend him against anyone who slipped in to check on his progress.

He stared at page three yet again. It actually wasn't that bad. Three-quarters was occupied by a figure and table and the rest with descriptions of the innards of a Mirage instrument panel that made no more sense to him than a menu written in Polish.

'You look fine to me,' Dylan said, patting the page. 'A+, in fact. Moving on to page four!'

He winced when he turned the page: it was solid text. In fact, one unbroken paragraph.

'Ah, ha!' he declared, teasing it with his red pen. 'A violation of Rule 1 – readability!'

He scratched two diagonal lines, almost at random, but close to a third and then two-thirds down the page. He felt a surge of joy that only an editor discovering god-like power for the first time could feel as he shattered the sound barrier of an extended paragraph.

He went on like that for hours. Until his head hurt. Until every page had a minimum of six red marks. Why six? It seemed a magic number, like Three Wise Men + Joseph, Mary and Joseph, or the Holy Trinity x two.

Not that Dylan was the slightest bit religious. He was yet to find himself in a foxhole, but it never hurt to be prepared for the End of All Days[6].

Lieutenant Durand was his first pilot, and the report

[6] http://bit.ly/2DlXHiT

with Dylan's minimum of six red corrections on each page belonged to him. Durand was tall, with a tidy crew-cut and blazingly clear blue eyes. And yet he seemed nervous as he eased into the chair across from Dylan.

Dylan cleared his throat. Not because he needed to, but because he expected that was what an experienced editor needed to do to put an author just slightly off his game.

'Pardon,' Durand said, thickly accented. 'My English… is not the best.'

'Why do you bother, then?' Dylan asked. 'You could have written in French!'

'But no. The Major would not allow it. Oh, but you are joking, yes?'

'I never joke about such serious things,' Dylan said, perfectly straight. 'Except when I have to!'

It took a few seconds for that to compute and then sink in for Durand.

'I wish I could just *fly* the Mirage,' said Durand, 'and not have to write about it!'

'Me too,' Dylan replied. 'I mean, the bit about flying.'

Something got lost in the translation. After every page of discussion, and sometimes in between, Durand would come back to his joy of flying, how it had been all he had every wanted to do since witnessing the first Moon landing[7], how he was happiest when his plane was at full throttle and he was feeling ever so slightly light-headed from the speed.

Dylan would nod sagely at every corrected word choice or mended comma splice[8], as he expected an editor should do while listening to an author in confession mode. Their discussion gathered its own momentum, until, finally, on the last page, Dylan realised, to his horror, that he'd just accepted Durand's invitation to take him up in a test flight in his Mirage.

---

[7] http://bit.ly/2zDqEop
[8] http://bit.ly/2CdLDkm

'Thank you so much, Dylan,' he said, bursting out of the chair. 'You have made my report… how do you say, *glow?*'

'Just part of the job,' said Dylan, still in editorial mode.

'So what time will be best for you?'

'Time?'

'To suit up – for the test flight?'

Dylan gulped. 'Oh, that. I didn't think you were serious. Or rather that I was serious – about doing that.'

'Come on,' said Durand. 'Of course I was serious. I want to share it with you. The thrill of speed.'

'I tried speed reading[9] once,' said Dylan. 'I came in last.'

---

[9] http://bit.ly/2Cgmfu8

Chapter 2: Flights with a Difference

DYLAN CASHEW WAS CONVINCED HE'D LOST HIS MIND. He had to be stark raving mad – or some such similar cliché.

'I *must* be stark raving mad,' he affirmed, already strapped into the co-pilot's seat behind Durand. 'Otherwise I would be on the ground with the rest of the boring, sane people. Or merely sipping jet fuel!'

Somehow D. H. managed to squeeze in next to him just as Durand fired up the engines and started speaking in code to the control tower.

'Nice outfit,' said D. H. 'You could start a couture[10] for editors.'

Dylan squirmed a bit, especially as the engines revved and they began to taxi toward the runway. 'It's tight,' he said, pointing down at the strap between his legs. '*Very* tight.'

'The better to archive your precious bits in case you're ejected,' smiled D. H.

'How do you know so much about jet aircraft?'

'I wasn't buried yesterday,' sighed D. H. 'And I do know how to google.'

The plane made a right turn until it lined up on the runway.

'What's gargling got to do with it?' Dylan said, breathlessly, digging his fingernails into the armrests. Of course, he'd never heard of Google at that point in space time, let alone its ambitious verb.

'Wheee!' shouted D. H. 'This is a lot more fun than flying in a Tiger Moth. Up, up and away!'

Within seconds they were hurtling along the runway. Dylan was tempted to close his eyes against the rush of

---

[10] http://bit.ly/2C3rLn9

ground, shrinking ever so quickly, but then he thought, better the fate he could stare straight in the eye than the one that came at him out of a black hole.

'We're about to go upside down,' said D. H. 'Brace yourself!'

'How do you know *that*?' screamed Dylan, bracing himself just in case.

'Time-travelling does have its advantages,' said D. H., as the plane not only went upside down but went into a double roll[11].

It was all a blur of sky, glaring sun, and green and brown earth from then on during which thoughts of survival rather than parts of speech flooded through Dylan's mind. Of course, D. H. made himself scarcer than scarce between the rolls.

'Coward!' shouted Dylan.

'No, you're not,' said Durand, turning back to him.

'JUST… keep your eyes on what's ahead,' said Dylan, about to part with whatever he'd had for breakfast.

Durand laughed rather demonically, and even lifted his hand from the throttle for a second or two, before levelling them out.

'Want to take the controls?' he shouted back. 'I can tell you what to do.'

'No thanks, Houston,' whimpered Dylan. 'Can we please land now? Pretty please?'

By the time he arrived at the Officers' Mess that evening, Dylan had concluded that there must be a Higher Order of Chance if not a god looking after him, and, further, that his existence had purpose beyond finishing his PhD on D. H., though what that purpose might be still eluded him.

Of one thing he was certain: it did not involve near or actual space travel at supersonic speeds.

Lehmann was waiting for him at the bar.

[11] http://bit.ly/2CbBhnH

'As your superior,' he said in subdued tones. 'It is my responsibility to buy you your first drink and introduce you to the female officer of your choice. Thereafter, you're on your own.' He said this with all the warmth and sincerity of a sociopath.

'Scotch and ginger, thanks,' said Dylan.

'Good choice on both counts,' said Lehmann, signalling to the bartender what appeared to be a double. 'Follow me – I have just the Scot for you.'

Just a little ways down the bar stood a slim brunette with light brown eyes that lit up even more when she saw Lehmann and Dylan on their way over.

'Mr Lehmann,' she grinned. 'A pleasure, as always. And what do we have here in tow?'

'Hillary, allow me to introduce my assistant editor, Mr Dylan Cashew.'

She screwed up her eyes and stifled a laugh. 'You're having a go – *Cashew*?'

'Don't blame me,' said Dylan. 'They say my father was so nuts about my mother that he changed his name!'

Hillary nudged Lehmann with a finger in the chest. 'Dismissed, Captain Lehmann. I think Mr… Cashew is more than able to hold his ground in present company without your support.'

Lehmann seemed more than happy to shuffle off to a party of officers not far away.

'You'll get used to him,' Hillary said after him. 'He's *very* Germanic – but a good bloke nonetheless.'

She had a way of pursing her lips that Dylan did his best not to find attractive – at least until he knew whether or not a burly Major mate was in the vicinity.

'And what do you do here, at the Base?' he asked, taking a gulp of his drink.

'I'm a Public Relations Officer,' she replied. 'Or rather *the* Public Relations Officer since two weeks ago when my senior split.' She sighed. 'It's an odd position to hold at a place that prides itself on keeping everything secret, don't you think?'

Dylan had to laugh. 'So you just go through the motions of relating to the public?'

'While propping up the bar? Yes, I suppose so. But when our esteemed Commander has to report to his superiors in Ottawa, I'm the one who prepares his briefing notes. Under-employed most days, but when I'm needed I'm indispensable.' She paused, ever so slightly. 'But the answer to the real question in your mind is no, there is no Mr McEwan here, though there was once, by a name other than mine, who wanted to merge mine with his, which I was tempted to do since he was a baird[12] and owned a huge property up on the moors. Actually, no, I made the whole thing up.'

'The whole story, or just the bit about the baird and the moors.'

'Lehmann better watch his back,' she smiled. 'You're quick. Everything up to the baird and moors. He had his ambitions, but they weren't as permanent as that.'

To make the long story shorter [after all, this *is* a book about the joys and psychoses of publishing, not a soppy romance] they had several drinks, seconds and thirds at the food bar, and then several dances to the military band. Dylan had thought himself all thumbs on the dance floor, but the heady fuel of a third and four scotch with a Scot made it all happen in a fashion that didn't call attention to itself or to others who really *could* dance.

Before the sex scene that didn't happen, at least not before the next lunar eclipse, Hillary and Dylan shared a cab back to Frigid Lake, a tiny town not far from the Base where most of the civilians lived. It was an imperfectly round body of water, very deep in the middle, so deep that it reminded

---

[12] http://bit.ly/2lkPO67

Hillary of Loch Ness[13], minus the Monster, or perhaps not.

'Often I wake up in the wee hours *hearing* things – off the lake,' she said, as they pulled up in front of the house she shared with three other civvies.

'Things?' repeated Dylan, doing his best to resist the temptation to suggest they have a coffee, only because he thought the question might be expected of him, after they had hit it off so well at the Mess. 'What sort of... things?'

'Oh, you know. Trees creaking in the wind that occupy the same audio channel as a beast surfacing from the depths.'

How extraordinary, thought Dylan. I may be falling in love, at least with her bizarre imagination.

'You'd be lovely to have insomnia with,' he blurted out. 'No, I mean, would you like to make a coffee for me as we listen for... the beast?'

She stared at him as if he were a bar of only partly melted chocolate discovered at the bottom of her handbag. 'Yes, she said. 'I mean, no. I have roommates, you see. And we have a pact not to bring dates home after midnight unless we are quiet and go straight to bed.'

At that moment, Dylan was feeling nostalgic for the back seat of the Mirage in mid-roll. But he knew he had to say something, anything, to head off the sex scene that didn't happen. It was just like D. H. *not* to appear when he needed him most.

'And this bed of yours...' he began, straining for something to finish off the fragment.

'They call it a super-single,' Hillary injected. 'Spacious for one, convenient for two – for conversation, or sipping sherry.'

He had no reason to believe, from her tone, that she had anything beyond that in mind.

'You're my last fare before I knock off,' the cabbie said from the front seat. 'Make up your mind – your place, his, or mine!'

---

[13] http://bbc.in/2IlF8nM

Any potential for this to turn from the sex scene that didn't happen to the one that did dissolved as she kissed him lightly but ever so lingeringly on the cheek and then dissolved out the door.

D. H. assumed her seat. 'That was a close call,' he said. 'Driver, drive on!'

'You know he can't hear you,' Dylan muttered into his sleeve.

'What was that?' said the cabbie, turning back to him again.

'I said drive on!' Dylan and D. H. said in unison.

'Treat them mean[14] to keep them keen,' D. H. said. 'Or should that be *think* them keen and treat them mean?'

'I never liked your poetry,' Dylan said.

The cabbie winced but drove on. It was probably just the booze talking.

The shack outside of town that Dylan occupied was Lehmann's idea of a joke when he offered it as a temporary place Dylan could have until he found something more suitable than a Canadian version of the hut by Walden Pond[15]. But it suited Dylan to a tee.

It was pitch black after the grumpy cabbie had disappeared back up the bumpy road, and that was just the way Dylan liked it. He lay down on the driveway and imagined the starry, starry night that would be there if it weren't overcast, and, seconds later, pelting down with rain.

He lay there for a time nevertheless, at least until the splotches of rain became pools on his forehead. He struggled to his feet, stumbled to the front door, rummaged through pockets for his keys, cursing himself for forgetting to leave on an outside light, which he couldn't have done anyway since the bulb had burned out and Dylan hadn't changed it since every night since the two days ago he'd moved in had

[14] https://ind.pn/2DnBvVL
[15] http://bit.ly/2DoFFwC

had a full moon reflecting off Frigid Lake, so what was the urgency?

'Here, let me help,' said D. H. nudging past and opening the door with a twist of his keyless hand.

'I had – *have* – the key right here,' Dylan grumbled, brandishing it.

'I think you'll find that that is the key for your *car*, which is safely, though distantly, back at the Base,' smiled D. H.

Too late, Dylan found the right key and brandished it somewhat less assertively. 'Do not think I am... inbriated!'

'Why would I think you were inebriated?' said D. H. before adding, 'Though that would have been your best excuse for not bedding the girl!'

'I'm not like that,' said Dylan, switching on and off all the wrong lights until he found one leading to the bedroom. 'May I remind you that I am an Assistant Technical Editor, and there are protocols to be followed in all things, which I have accomplished without shirking.'

D. H. leaned against the bedroom door. 'Would you like me to tuck you in?'

Whether or not he asked D. H. to do that or not, in the wink of a asteroid Dylan was fast asleep and dreaming of canoeing Frigid Lake with Hillary in search of the Beast. The Moon was playing tag with passing clouds and the lake seemed to swallow their paddles with each pull at the water. Now and then, they would share gulps from his flask of scotch, which brought them midway across the lake in no time.

It was then that they heard it.

Or thought they heard it.

A low-pitched gurgling, accentuated by a rumbling just beneath them. The *It* was surfacing, with an insistent roar that sent the Moon ducking for cover. Was it the Loch Ness on a work visa? Dylan and Hillary dropped their paddles and cringed together against the horrid exhalation of air that was geysering to the surface.

It was then that Dylan woke up, alone, in his bed. No sign of Hillary or even D. H. And yet the sound, like a wooden cargo ship grinding against rocks, was real.

Still unsteady, Dylan staggered to the galley kitchen, which overlooked the lake. Where there should be moonlight reflecting off calm water was a bulk that obliterated all light. *What rough beast?* was on chorus mode in Dylan's mind.

In spite of his fear, he threw open the outer door and inched his way down to the lake's edge. Towering above him was a wall of ice three times higher than the cabin, trying to grind its way ashore.

And no sign of Hillary.

He could hardly wait to trade notes with her again.

Chapter 3: His Kingdom for a Teaching Post

DYLAN TOOK HIS ENCOUNTER WITH THE ICEBERG PERSONALLY. After all, it had an entire lake it could have terrorised and yet had chosen his innocent inlet. He was not superstitious about most things but then nocturnal icebergs were not most things.

Maybe it was a sign, a omen, a RuneScape[16] portent.

Or maybe he needed to upgrade his plonk from cask to a corker at least a screw-top bottle.

At two in the morning that was the only thing that made the remotest bit of sense.

'I am on *salary*,' he announced to the iceberg. 'You need to show me the respect due to an Assistant Technical Editor on a modest but enduring pay cheque.'

The iceberg groaned like a character Edgar Allen Poe might have created if he'd ventured further north in his obsession with untimely murder.

'What was that?' Dylan snapped. 'I don't speak Icelandic!'

The iceberg was silent.

'Blue whale[17] got your tongue?'

A gust of wind came up from behind Dylan, and seconds later the iceberg started to retreat from shore.

Dylan shook a finger after it. 'Teach you to mess with Dylan Cashew, Prince of the Arctic!'

He had to admit that a report on retrofitting a new pilot ejection chamber module for Harrier aircraft was not as stimulating as a third double shot of caffeine after a sleep-interrupted night. But there he was, almost knee-to-knee with

---

[16] http://bit.ly/2CfHYoQ
[17] http://bit.ly/2li7jDW

the report's author, a crusty major on leave from Scotland to conduct and complete the research.

'Hopefully in my lifetime,' quipped the Major, pointing at the many instances of red editorial marks on the first page.

'Oh, those,' Dylan said. 'They're mostly for show.'

'For... show?'

'My supervisor rates my productivity by the instances of red ink per page. Between you and me, some of them make perfect sense, while others will magically vanish between now and the next draft.'

The major stared at him as though he was from outer space then suddenly burst into laughter. 'They told me back home about the quirky sense of humour Canadians[18] have, but I haven't experienced it until now!'

Dylan was on the brink of saying he was actually quite serious then just laughed. 'Yes, funny, isn't it?'

The truth was exactly that: Lehmann was suspicious of an untouched edited page.

'There's no such thing as perfection the first time around,' he'd said, reviewing Dylan's first major edit. 'If you don't find anything to fix, we become surplus to requirements. And our masters are always looking for ways to cut costs. The typing pool is a case in point. Women are good at typing, men are not. Imagine a future when men have to learn to type their own reports. Women would have to go back to being mothers!'

Suddenly, Dylan saw the logic behind a blizzard of red marks.

Dylan was decidedly junior in the ranks of civilians working at the Base. Lehmann had been there from the outset when the Establishment was first established. While the Forces might have preferred to hire Canadians someone in the higher echelons had decreed that an injection of foreign contractors would give the Establishment more

---

[18] http://bit.ly/2C0awDj

credibility with their client countries: especially the UK, and a smattering of other European countries like France, Germany, etc. That someone knew someone who knew someone who was looking for a posting abroad from the Mother Country, and that particular someone was Lehmann, who knew of a few other crones who were likewise inclined, and so it went.

Dylan was not the first Canadian to be hired once the foreign contingent had a firm foothold, but he was certainly in the minority. There was Clem the accountant, who only awoke around the end of the financial year and during Annual Report time. And then there were the women in the typing pool[19], who were nearly invisible during working hours and more so after that since they didn't have officer status and couldn't access the Officers' Mess. Elsewhere in the ranks there were several UK men who had come more for the fishing in the nearby lakes than the work, plus a few Indian admin types who seemed grateful for the opportunity to work in uncrowded conditions.

While Dylan's pay wasn't grand, it was adequate enough to be content with and even get used to. For the most part, he was left to get on with it, whatever it was from day to day, which sometimes wasn't much, but at least enough for the most part to look busy whenever Lehmann came by, or one of the officers dropped in purely by accident or just to be sociable.

He was happy to go home to his rustic cabin in the evenings, which he gradually furnished with more than the necessities of bed, dining table, mini-stereo and matching beanbags. It had a brilliant outlook across the lake, especially at sunrise, and now that the weather was truly warm, and all thoughts of icebergs could be dismissed as rumours, he decided to make a peace offering of a used canoe, which he parked a respectful distance up from the water, to the lake.

---

[19] http://bit.ly/2E30j6g

That very evening his old Mazda died, and the only mechanic in town shook his head at its prospects.

'Time for the scrapheap,' he grunted.

'But...' was all that Dylan could manage. It was true he'd bought the car third-hand from another student who'd travelled back and forth to Toronto in it at least twice. He considered calling a tow truck to haul it back to the cabin but then accepted the offer of a lift from the mechanic who gave him a crisp fifty dollar note to take the car off his hands.

'Shouldn't an editor be driving an Audi anyway?' the mechanic said, dropping him off.

'What's a Audi?' Dylan replied, revealing that he was no better versed in prestige cars than D. H.

That very evening Dylan decided he needed to aspire to greater things – and salaries – than was typical for junior editors at the Establishment. Perhaps this was a result of his ever-diminishing stash of scotch, which began as the lifting of a glass in tribute to Molly the Mazda's impending date with a metal compacter – or whatever those thingies were called that whisked you off to recycling Nirvana[20] – but eventually led to the impulse to ring Hillary.

He nearly tripped over a chair leg in his haste to get to the phone, only to find D. H. had snatched it from the table. Had Dylan not been into his third scotch by then, he would have remarked on the almost surreal quality of a figure of his demented imagination lifting a physical object. In the circumstances, he accepted it as believable as a five-dollar note surviving the ravages of a washing machine.

'I wouldn't if I were you,' D. H. said, holding the phone behind his lower back, which didn't conceal it at all since he was, as usual, opaque as a shower screen.

'Wouldn't what?' Dylan said.

'Calling a lass at your stage of inebriation is inadvisable because it will almost certainly lead to a sexual act – or at

---

[20] http://bit.ly/2pGk00A

least an attempt on your part to commence one.'

'I wish...' Dylan said, making a half-hearted lunge for the phone, which D. H. easily evaded, 'you didn't string so many words together to make your point!'

'Or worse.'

'That's better,' Dylan said, hesitating before making another unsuccessful lunge for the phone. 'Though I still don't get your meaning. What could be worse – or better – than a sexual act when I'm half-pissed?'

'More clever men than you have been cornered into a marriage proposal in such circumstances,' said D. H.

'Is *that* all you're worried about?' Dylan said. 'I have neither the means or the inclination to get married – at least until my novel-to-be wins the Booker. Besides, we haven't even had sex yet!'

'You need to reread *Women in Love*,' said D. H. 'And get back to writing my dissertation.'

'You mean *my* dissertation?'

'Whatever,' said D. H., dimming to translucent.

It might have been the impressively strong scent of her perfume, or the sight of the unopened bottle of scotch Hillary produced from a brown paper bag, OR the warmish brown of her eyes, but things were looking quite promising to Dylan as she set their glasses side by side on his distressed coffee table.

'Your directions for getting here were dodgy,' she said, pouring. 'I might get lost – if I have to go home in the dark.'

'Well,' said Dylan, inserting himself into a novel that was definitely not *Women in Love*. 'I'm sure we have enough scotch to last until sunrise!'

Even so, he was determined to prove D. H. wrong – at least about the marriage bit.

'I meant,' he hastened to add, 'That I can sleep out here – on the couch.'

'This pathetic two-seater?' she said, downing her glass and tilting it toward him. 'You really need to expand your horizons beyond the op shop![21]'

'About teaching...' he began, refilling the glass with fingers he wished weren't trembling.

She cocked her head. 'So... that wasn't just a ruse to get me here?'

'No,' he said. 'You'll see, at first light, that Molly is definitely gone – past tense.'

She shook her head. 'Don't tell me that you named a car wreck after a James Joyce character.'

'Not a car *wreck*, a wreck of a *car*,' Dylan corrected, straining to come up with a quote but failing.

She toasted him. 'You do wear your scotch well. I doubt that I will be so articulate after three rounds. But I'm willing to try!' Her glass was empty again.

Dylan sighed. 'I do want to talk about the other thing – teaching. I need to hear from someone that it's not a crazy idea, objectively speaking.'

'It's *not* a crazy idea,' she parroted. 'Did that sound credible? But why teach?'

He painted the dream for her, finding a teaching job at a university somewhere, anywhere, in the Yukon if necessary, if there was such a thing as a university near the Arctic Circle. Why else had he done years of academic studies if not to teach?

'You could write,' she offered. 'Or go into publishing maybe. Once you earn your stripes as a technical editor?'

He put up his hand: The Force was definitely not with him. 'It's all too easy,' he said. 'Red pens at sunset, for pilots and engineers who'll always be grateful to you for making sense of their words, only too happy to shout you drinks or even dinner at the Mess, sucking you into the easy life, a down payment on an... Audi, perhaps, and then, before you

---

[21] http://bit.ly/2lhipsX

know it, a mortgage on a house safe from icebergs.'

'Icebergs?' she laughed. 'In the Yukon?'

He pointed to the kitchen window, and beyond to the darkening water. 'Icebergs: they're closer than you might think.'

To make the long seduction short, after they'd finished a decent portion of her bottle of scotch, and he couldn't remember in which unpacked box he'd put his, he led her into the bedroom, set her at the bottom of the bed while he brushed out toast crumbs, etc., from the sheets.

He had every intention of leaving her there and making do on the two-seater, but the instant he had her settled she grabbed him by the elbow and pulled him down on top of her.

'Keep me company,' she murmured, adding, 'I find it hard to get to sleep in a strange bed!'

And with that, she passed out.

Dylan had obviously already spent too much time at the Base because all he could think of, as he lay as lightly as possible across her chest and temptingly close to her bosom, was whether it would be right and proper, or even defensible, to take off her shirt and jeans – to make her more comfortable. Before he made his escape back to the living room.

The scent of her perfume – Scottish heather, or whatever the closest native flora smelt like, was making it hard for him to decide what to do. He eased himself up on one elbow and, convinced that she was totally out of it, slipped off her top. She sighed, as if it were all part of a deep REM waterfall[22].

To his horror, there was nothing below the top except her pert breasts, with their nipples at attention as if in response to a stiff breeze.

'A fine mess you're in now!' muttered D. H., lying beside her on the other side of the bed.

---

[22] http://bit.ly/2CeFYKY

'Oh, God,' said Dylan. 'Should I try to put her blouse back on? What if she wakes up?'

'I'm sure times have changed from my day,' said D. H. 'But this does look like an... open invitation.'

'To do what?' Dylan demanded. 'No, I couldn't possibly. Not that I could, even if I wanted to, after so many drinks.'

'You're probably right,' said D. H., sliding a holographic finger down between her breasts, circling each nipple before giving it an ineffectual tweak.

'Stop that!' Dylan said.

'It's not like you've taken her *pants* off,' murmured D. H., gazing pointedly at the top button of her jeans. 'I wonder if she has anything on under that!'

'STOP IT!' Dylan demanded. 'No wonder *Lady Chatterley* was banned!'

Whether the scotch or exhaustion finally caught up with him, Dylan couldn't remember anything after that. The first thing he knew was waking beside her with the first Shakespearean flush of dawn crossing her cheek. Her breasts were still exposed, and shock and horror, her pants were strewn across the bedside table. Fortunately, the sheet covered her from the waist down.

For his part, he was also naked, though he could tell his penis had run for cover, seeking anonymity in clumps of the sheets. His toes went in desperate search for his undies, which were nowhere to be found. He sat up carefully and scanned the floor around the bed but could not see the undies, at least not on his side of the bed.

There was only one other place they could be. His commando toes penetrated the space on her side of the bed, but, just as they found their mark, his knee grazed her thigh, and she awoke.

'Oh my god,' she said breathlessly, yanking up the sheet to cover her breasts. But then she lifted it again to check her nether regions. 'OH MY GOD!'

'I can... explain,' Dylan said. 'Actually, no, I can't. Sorry!'

'Did you...' she stammered, grabbing for her pants. 'Did we?'

It might have been simpler if D. H. could have reappeared at that instant, in the flesh, and explained what had happened, how a see-through author had managed to remove their clothes and prompted whatever might have happened afterwards.

Dylan did his best to avert his eyes as she hastened into her clothes, but didn't, quite. She had an exceptionally nice bottom.

Abruptly, she turned back and ripped the sheet off the bed. 'Ah, ha,' she said, pointing. 'Who's been a naughty tadger?[23]'

Dylan didn't recognise the word, but its implications were clear enough. 'I swear...' he began.

'Well,' she said, cocking her head. 'Go on, then. Do we need a bible or a forensics kit?'

'I wouldn't,' he said, digging himself in deeper. 'I mean, I couldn't have.'

She bent down and sniffed, actually *sniffed* the sheets. 'No,' she said. 'Unless it was an immaculate one. But your intentions were clear, weren't they, you and your wee tadger?'

She slapped his penis rather hard, startling back when it rose in defence of the estate.

'Beg pardon,' she said, and then adding, in slight admiration. 'Oh!'

Which merely provoked his penis further.

She narrowed her eyes. 'If we had – and I'm accepting your word that we haven't – I'm only saying I would not have been entirely opposed, or perhaps even in consensus... if you'd asked, as I'd been half-hoping, that we'd made a start to that ultimate... objective.'

---

[23] http://bit.ly/2BLw6ai

Dylan had reached a new low on the planet of ridiculousness. There he was, wearing nothing but a three-quarters hard-on, while she, fully dressed, lectured him like a puppy. He reached for his undies, in vain, because she snatched them away and tossed them to the far corner of the room.

'Thank goodness it's Sunday,' she said, taking off her top again. 'Our Lord's Day of Rest. Now where were we when that last glass of scotch so rudely interrupted us?'

Perhaps it was going back to bed for the second time in twenty-four hours that made all the difference in Dylan's decision to go into teaching. Hillary thought it was a curious idea, even after he managed a second orgasm, which was another first for him, at least with a second person in bed with him at the time. Stars had crossed if not collided, and teaching would be a new galaxy for him, one whose light appeared at a moment of emergency when he was on the brink of dark matter that meant inescapable boredom in a steady pay cheque.

Several cups of coffee and a diminished headache later that same afternoon, Dylan invited Hillary to go canoeing with him across Frigid Lake.

'I think all that sex has gone to your head,' she replied. 'Frigid Lake is dangerous. A storm can come up out of nowhere and sweep you into a vortex. Sensible people paddle along the shore.'

It said something about her, Dylan concluded, something positive and daring, that she agreed to go, despite the fact he had no lifejackets.

They set off under a perfectly blue sky, with the slightest of head breezes. Hillary sat in the front and knew what to do with a paddle, which was probably just as well he thought if they ran into trouble. The other side of the lake was invisible, beyond the curvature of the Earth, and only a few minutes into the trip, Dylan began to wonder if maybe they had taken on too much.

'Where would you like to teach?' Hillary asked, leaning into her paddling.

'I haven't thought that far ahead,' said Dylan, 'but certainly not at a big university.'

'Why not? That's where the best students are.'

Dylan smiled to see she was more interested in the quality of students than the money a professor might receive. 'I know what it's like at places like that,' he said. 'Publish or perish, and more politics than teaching.'

'If you want to avoid all that, maybe you should stay here. At least with pilots and engineers, what you see is what you get.'

'True,' he said. 'But there has to be more to life than correcting punctuation. I'd like to find a place where teaching is more important than your list of publications, where I can deal with students as individuals rather than numbers.'

'Then you'd better start looking,' Hillary said, angling her paddle so it sent a spray of water back at him. 'To get that idealistic streak out of your mind once and for all.'

'You think it's a bad idea?'

'Not necessarily. Most people think that Atlantis[24] never existed, but it only takes one discovery to make the myth real.'

Dylan was sure she had a connection in mind, but, just as he was about to ask what it might be, they were hit side-on by a wind gust. Suddenly the lake was choppy, and swells were heading toward their bow. The far shore was still beyond the horizon.

'What now, my Captain?' Hillary called back, paddling with all her might.

'Mid-course correction,' he said, already steering the canoe so the swells were behind them. 'Let's head for town!'

---

[24] http://bbc.in/2I91KZg

The town of Frigid Lake was more than three kilometres by road from the cabin but only one kilometre by water, so it was entirely feasible for Dylan to do his shopping by canoe rather than by the now deceased Molly. Had they headed due East from the cabin they would have arrived by now, so Dylan calculated that they were at least a kilometre out from shore. It didn't help that a dark cloud had materialised overhead with a threat of thunder rippling the air.

'At least there's no lightning,' said Dylan, putting his back into his paddling.

And then there was, inconveniently in front of them but at least well above the water, accentuated by a resounding clap of thunder overhead.

'If we never make it to shore,' Hillary called out, her breathing strained, 'To my list of unfilled wishes let me add not having had a chance to wear your ring.'

Dylan hoped they would, if only he could ask, with more breath at his disposal, if she was serious.

The canoe was half filled with water by the time they landed, slightly off course, at the town park rather than at the dock. The park was called Minasoo, in dedication to the monster fish that supposedly lived in the deepest waters of the lake and, as legend had it, whipped up a storm when fishermen it dislike fished the waters.

Hillary pointed to the sign. 'Just as well we didn't meet Minasoo out there,' she shivered.

'Maybe we did,' Dylan said, nodding back at the steel-grey waves of almost oceanic size that were crashing ashore. He bowed to the sign. 'Sorry, Minasoo – won't happen again!'

After they dragged the canoe out of reach of Minasoo's henchmen, they headed for the pub.

The barman took one look at them and smiled. 'Are you tourists?' he asked.

'No,' Dylan smirked, 'Just stupid locals!'

The barman tossed him a set of keys and nodded toward

the stairs. 'That'll get you into the first room on the left. You'll find fresh towels and a heater. No hanky-panky or I'll have to charge you for a day.'

'Charge us,' Hillary said. 'I'm too tired to go home tonight!'

Chapter 4: Those Who Can't, Write…

AND SO IT WENT AT THE ESTABLISHMENT FOR THREE MONOTONE YEARS while Dylan waited for his chance to get his dream job. He scoured the academic newsletters, the Saturday want ads in the major dailies, and even pestered his former academic supervisors for any tips they might have about jobs that never reached the public eye.

All the while, he saw how the other civilian staff at the Base seemed to grey ever so slightly in complexion over time, how the chit-chat at the Mess and at cozy parties they had off-Base came to resemble minimalist art at its most tedious to the point where he could predict who would get what from Secret Santa. While it was easier and certainly cheaper for him to give away reprints of D. H.'s early novels that D. H. always seem to have on hand at holiday time in the vain hope that Dylan would finally return to university to complete his dissertation, he realised by the third year that he too had become *predictable*.

There had been a flicker of hope in the second year when an ad appeared for a drama teacher at Medicine Hat College. Dylan read the job description several times with trembling fingers, dizzying himself with the possibilities.

'*Medicine Hat?*' Hillary said when he'd had enough alcohol at the Mess that night to mention it to her. 'Is that a real place?'

Dylan fished out from his pocket a scrimped up page that he'd torn out of a road map with a red cross on the minuscule dot that was Medicine Hat. 'There – you see. It's a… city. Well, almost.'

'It's in the Badlands,[25]' she said. 'You're more likely to

[25] http://bit.ly/2pFYnO2

rub shoulders with dinosaurs than decent drama students. Besides, what do you know about drama?'

Dylan lifted a limp finger in what was supposed to approximate a sign of victory. 'Ah, ha – how soon they forget.'

Hillary scratched her head. 'Oh, you don't mean...'

'Yes, I do! The season of *Say Who You Are*, directed by yours truly.'

She nodded. 'You mean that decidedly amateur production, which played to half empty houses when there was absolutely nothing else of artistic or even social importance to compete with it on the Base?'

'Half *full*,' he corrected. 'And more than half on the second and third nights.'

'Counting the complimentary tickets,' she said. 'The very play you had to act in as well when one of the leads dropped out because of that rare skin disorder that was probably just a figment of his angst-ridden imagination?'

'Wayne could never remember his lines anyway. And the audience laughed at him rather than at the script.'

'Even if they do invite you for an interview,' she sighed, 'and even if they are hard up enough to offer you the position, why would you go there?'

'For a foot in the door,' Dylan insisted. 'The longer I stay here the more I feel this invisible hand of permanence wrapping its fingers around my throat.'

She narrowed her eyes. 'It's not that bad. You have a lifetime supply of red pens, a window with insider view of a top-secret hangar, subsidised *everything* at the Mess, and my company at a campground of your choice under the stars. They probably haven't even heard of an Aurora Borealis in Medicine Cap.'

'Hat,' he corrected.

'Gotcha!' she cried. She took his hand, turned it over and traced his lifelines. 'A man who doesn't see when he's got it good…' She lifted his fingers up and kissed them. 'Who clearly needs another drink!'

And she was off to the bar.

Dylan had to admit that he got on with her, even when they weren't in bed. She'd helped him replace his worn-out furniture, bluffed her way with the used car dealer to get him a deep discount on a replacement for Molly, extended his repertoire beyond fish and chips and canned spaghetti and rekindled his interest in camping. What a weekend they had had fishing for dinner then sleeping out under the stars, watching the Aurora Borealis till the wee hours with mulled wine.

Yet, here they were, months on after that near encounter with the Minasoo, but what were they?

When she returned with their drinks, he sighed.

'Get this into you,' she chided. 'It'll all be better then.'

'If I get this job, will you come with me?'

She looked at him. 'As what – your stage manager?'

'I'm serious!'

She traced his lips with a finger. 'Dylan Cashew, are you proposing to me?'

He tried to nip the finger twice, missing both times. 'What if I am?'

'Excuse me, aren't you the same man who recently called marriage a farce?'

'Only in the hands of people who don't respect it.'

'You're embellishing.'

'No, I'm *refining to suit the context*. That's what editors do.'

'Well, Mr Director, we have two possible scenarios: you and me here, or you and me – question mark – in Medicine Hat. The first one I can handle – if you put a ring where your mouth is. The second one, I'd have to think about.'

'Don't know why I'm bothering, anyway,' Dylan said.

'Bothering with what?'

'Medicine Hat. I'm sure they'll have their pick of bi-polar

directors from Hollywood.'

'I think you mean Broadway?'

'Naw. Broadway's never heard of Medicine Hat. But Hollywood thinks it's a Canadian spin-off of a spaghetti western[26].'

She downed her drink. 'You're already practicing, aren't you?'

A week later, he got the call. Medicine Hat wanted him for an interview next week. The voice on the other end of the phone line sounded like Marlon Brando in *Apocalypse Now*[27].

'We've got two hundred bucks to get you to and fro,' Marlon grunted.

There were no flights from Frigid Lake to Medicine Hat, Marlon informed him, only one daily from Edmonton, and no easy connections back. They would pay for his return flight from Edmonton or for fuel if he chose to drive.

'Your choice,' Marlon said, as if anticipating the darkest place on the set of *Apocalypse Now*, which hadn't been filmed yet.

Dylan knew the back roads and could probably make it to Medicine Hat in less than a day, but it would be nice to have company.

'No,' said Hillary, over the phone.

'Why not?'

She lowered her voice. 'You might be able to sneak a few days of sick leave, but they're on to us: if I take the same time off we'll both get docked. And you'll get further behind in your car repayments.'

'Have you ever read *The Heart of Darkness*?'

'Of course. We had to do it for our O levels. Why?'

'I think it would make a great movie,' Dylan said. 'Starring Marlon Brando.'

'He's gone to seed,' Hillary said. 'Ever since *The Godfather*.'

---

[26] http://bit.ly/2lisbeo
[27] http://bit.ly/2FTFZFr

'You're right,' said Dylan. 'Don't know what I was thinking.'

It occurred to him then that D. H. might be adding telepathy to his time-shifting powers.

Hillary didn't change her mind, so Dylan decided to go solo, driving due south. He wasn't sure it was going to be much of an advantage when D. H. appeared in the passenger seat, fumbling with his road map.

'Medicine Hat?' said D. H. 'Here it is. Smack in the middle of… some place called The Badlands. I didn't think Canada had deserts.'

'It has the Arctic,' Dylan said. 'And that's rather deserty.'

'Hmm,' said D. H. 'Is it anything like Taos[28]?'

'I don't know – I've never been there.'

D. H. smiled. 'I'd never been to Taos before I arrived, then I never wanted to leave.'

'But you did,' Dylan remarked, taking his eyes off the road for an instant, long enough to drift over to the middle of the road and be honked at by a truck coming in the opposite direction.

'Careful!' shouted D. H.

'Yes, yes,' said Dylan. 'I saw him. I can't be expected to concentrate one hundred percent on the road when I'm talking to a ghost.'

'Respect!' snorted D. H. 'I am so much more than a ghost!'

'You died in Europe,' Dylan added. 'That should have been the end of the story.'

'But Frieda brought my ashes back to Taos.'

'How romantic!'

'Not really. She thought by mixing my ashes in with the concrete of the so-called memorial they built in my name that I would forgive her philandering. She never did understand *The Plumed Serpent!*'

'Nor did I,' said Dylan. 'So this is some kind of DIY Limbo

[28] http://bit.ly/2BLW4KP

for you, coming back to second-guess the living?'

'Keep your eyes on the road,' said D. H. 'Or you'll be joining me there, in body as well as in spirit.'

It was then that D. H. noticed the letter wedged between his seat and the gearbox. He pointed at the logo on the envelope.

'Nice design, though not a word in Latin,' he remarked. 'But what's with the blank open book at the top?'

Dylan glanced at it. 'Tabula rasa[29]? A college without preconceived notions?'

'Or a place devoid of creativity. An intellectual desert?'

'You're not going to talk me out of this. It may be my only chance of getting into teaching.'

D. H. put the envelope back. 'I wrote seven plays, bang, bang, bang. It wasn't hard, but I didn't give a jot about any of them.'

'Is that why you never turned up at any of the performances?'

D. H. nodded. 'Theatre is so… public. At least with a poem or a story, if it gets published to silence, you can make of it what you will. With a play you have to face your audience with your pants down!'

'If I get the job, maybe I could produce one of them. You could float in through the door and watch from the back row.'

'Very funny. Well, if you get the job – which you won't – my favourite is *The Widowing of Mrs Holroyd*[30].'

'Isn't that the one based on "Odour of Chrysanthemums"?'

'Of course. Nicely footnoted.'

The road had just come to a dead end.

'Where the hell are we?' sighed D. H., opening the map again.

'That's rich,' smiled Dylan, turning around the car, 'coming from a lost soul!'

---

[29] http://bit.ly/2mTYYab
[30] http://bit.ly/2pLD1Pd

The interviewing panel was all male, but they made it pretty clear from the outset that they were looking for a woman to fill the position.

'Some of my best friends are women,' said Dylan. 'Does that help?'

All three panelists just stared at him.

'Where did that come from?' the Chair finally said.

'I can take a hint,' said Dylan. 'Especially when it isn't subtle.'

And that was pretty much that.

D. H. was waiting for him back in the car.

'I should have worn a dress,' said Dylan, strapping himself in.

'I told you so,' smirked D. H. 'Though if you *had* worn a dress you would have got full marks for originality.'

'However dense they might have been,' said Dylan, firing up the engine. 'I think they would have caught on – eventually.'

'Never mind,' said D. H. 'The air's so dry here that you'd have to be drinking constantly to keep up your sanity. What now, my Prince?'

'We drive back… home, such as it is. Militarily-speaking. Better fasten up if you don't want to die a second time.'

'Sorry,' said D. H., already fading. 'You've already exceeded your mentoring time for the month. I'm out of here!'

'But I need someone to keep me awake.'

'Then pick up a hippie,' said a voice, somewhere above the roof of the car. 'In a dress!'

It was well past midnight by the time Dylan drove onto the path down to the cabin by the lake. Every pothole he hit reminded him that the trip to Medicine Hat had been a total waste of time. How could he have imagined that his destiny was to mount feminist productions for audiences more interested in panning for gold or digging up dinosaur bones?

To his amazement there was a car glistening in the moonlight at the cabin. It was Hillary's. There were candles lit all around the living room, but most of them close to burning out.

'Hey,' she said, opening the door for him. 'I... wasn't sure when you'd get back, so I made some dinner in case you're hungry.'

Dylan managed a smile. 'Thank you. But how did you get in?'

She narrowed her eyes. 'You may think you're creative in all things, but hiding your spare key under the front mat isn't one of them. How did it go, with the interview?'

He nodded at two glasses flanking an almost full bottle of scotch.

'Sorry,' she said. 'I made a start there for you.'

He gave her the outline rather than the full story.

'That's a relief,' she said. 'Here I was, practicing my *sorry I can't see myself there even with you* speech, but I am sorry for your sake that you didn't get it. Here, drink up, because I may have tidings that will cheer you up.'

She poured, he tossed it back, she poured again.

'So what's the good news?' he asked. 'Lehmann's carked it?'

'What a dreadful thing to say!' she winked. 'No, it could be better than that.' She pulled a scrap of paper from her pocket and handed it over.

It was an ad for another teaching job. This time in British Columbia.

'It's you,' she said, and then squeezed his hand. 'And it could be me, too!'

The more he read, the more excited he became. '"Lecturer in Modern Literature, preferably British specialization",' he read aloud. '"An interest in Creative Writing would be an advantage".'

'That's definitely you,' she said.

'D. H. will be pleased,' he said, forgetting himself.

'Who's D. H.?' she said, springing on it. 'Your piece on the side?'

He laughed. 'I can hardly manage one let alone two. Besides, I like your expensive taste in scotch.' Then he remembered. 'But did I hear you say "it could be me", meaning you?'

'They call it "Beautiful British Columbia",' she said, producing a brochure from her bag. 'And I'm sure it would be even more beautiful with you!'

'So let me get this straight. If I apply and get the job, this is a proposal?'

'More of a confirmation, bud. I've got your proposal on tape.'

'What if I don't get the job? Are we back to being just drinking buddies?'

'You'll get it.'

'But what if I don't?'

She hesitated. 'Well, then, there's no rush, is there?'

The truth was that Dylan had never heard of Penticton[31], British Columbia, let alone been there, but when the call came from the Head of Department offering him an interview in a week's time AND a free return flight from Edmonton, he decided to do some research. But where? The Frigid Lake library was only open three days a week and had little more than romance and science fiction novels and a few scraggly picture books for preschoolers, while the Base Library was all scientific and engineering books, monographs and journals.

He was just about to ring the long distance operator when D. H. appeared.

'Going West, young man?' he asked.

'I don't suppose you've heard of Penticton?' Dylan asked.

'Yes, of course,' said D. H, waving up a holographic map.

'What *is* that?' Dylan gasped.

---

[31] http://bit.ly/2IIQQie

'Haven't you ever seen a map before?'

'Not a see-through one.'

'Better than that outdated one you travel with. I don't suppose you've heard of Google either.'

'Nope.'

D. H. sighed. 'You will soon enough. I guess it's hard for you to keep up if you've never been there.'

'So what the hell is Google?'

D. H. emitted a space-time[32] grin. 'It's a search engine.'

Dylan scratched his head. 'Is that anything like a *jet* engine?'

'Faster. Much faster. Nearly at the speed of light.' He paused. 'But I'm getting ahead of yourself by a few years. ANYWAY, Penticton is much larger than Frigid Lake, and it has a lot going for it: swimming and fishing in the summer, skiing in the winter, and wine-tasting all year round.'

'I'll pass on the high energy sports,' said Dylan. 'But the wine tasting sounds OK! What about the college? Will I have much competition getting on there?'

'It's not exactly Oxford. But if you must teach, and you want to be outside the big cities, you could do far worse than Penticton.'

'Without dropping names,' winked Dylan. 'I'm up for it!'

There was no way that Dylan could make it to Penticton and back in a single day, and he knew he couldn't plead sick leave, so he'd have to front up to Lehmann about his plans. He waited until the end of the day to catch Lehmann in his office.

He might just as well have confessed he'd been confirmed for the next moon landing[33].

'A teaching post?' Lehmann said, dropping his red pen onto the report he was editing. 'Why on Earth would you want to go teaching?'

---

[32] http://bit.ly/2zEXCER
[33] http://bit.ly/2BNoBju

'It would be *university* level,' said Dylan. 'Not secondary.'

'Nonetheless. You know what they say: those who can't do *write*, and those who can't write *teach*!'

Dylan tried to keep his cool. 'And where does editing fit on that scale?'

Lehmann pointed his nose skyward. 'It's a calling. To make the world a more perfect place, safe from the dangers of split infinitives and the chaos of run-on sentences.'

'Well, I answered the call,' Dylan said, feeling his nails digging into his palms, 'and years later I'm still an Assistant Editor.'

'And a much improved one – from where you began,' said Lehmann. 'Much appreciated by engineers and pilots alike.'

Pour it on, thought Dylan. 'Yeah, I've deeply appreciated all you've taught me.' Back at you, he thought, I can splatter out the flattery as well as the next guy.

'I suppose you'll want a reference?' sniffed Lehmann with a sucked lemon look.

'Yes, please, if it's not an inconvenience,' Dylan said. I can also grovel on command!

'Of course,' said Lehmann. 'Remind me to append my Oxford qualification to my signature. Not that anyone around *here* cares about that!'

It was the first time Dylan had heard Lehmann utter a grey thought about the Establishment.

'Much appreciated,' Dylan said, backing off toward the door. 'I probably won't get it, but thanks again just the same.'

He wasn't certain, but Dylan thought he detected a hint of moisture under one of Lehmann's eyes as he backed into the door in his haste to depart.

Dylan had no idea what to expect from the plane taking him from Edmonton to the wilds of British Columbia, but he was pleasantly surprised to find it was a jet rather than a bush prop plane. It had a hundred seats or more, but it was less than half full, obviously not one of Air Canada's[34] premier routes. The First Class section had only one occupant, a suited woman conspicuously sipping her welcome bubbly drink as she stared out onto the tarmac through her equally first class sunglasses.

He'd chosen a window seat, and the passenger in the aisle seat was a young woman with amazingly long blonde hair, a multi-coloured Indian print dress, and a heavy douse of perfume that reminded him of vanilla extract. From the instant she settled into her seat, she immersed herself in a graphic novel that seemed to be populated with superheroes, so that excused Dylan from having to make casual conversation.

After the plane cleared the runway without incident, Dylan was feeling optimistic enough to lash out on a Johnny Walker on the rocks. He realised his interview was that very afternoon but a single scotch surely couldn't do any harm. The woman next to him ordered an orange juice in what Dylan regarded as a judgemental tone.

'Good morning, ladies and gentlemen,' came a voice over the sound system. 'This is your captain. Our flight time to Penticton this morning will be two hours and ten minutes, and we'll have you at the gate at 10:39. We're expecting a bit of turbulence over the mountains, so please keep your seat belts on whenever you're seated.'

Dylan was grateful for his scotch. A Prairie boy, he'd never flown over the Rockies before. He wasn't disappointed. Craggy peaks, some with remnants of last winter's snowfall, zigzagged thousands of metres below them. He nearly elbowed the woman next to him, so that she wouldn't miss the view but her vanilla intensity as she read her novel put him off.

---

[34] http://bit.ly/2BIWj9D

Later, Dylan was mostly through his tasteless chicken sandwich when there was a sudden drop in altitude followed by sustained waves of turbulence.

Without looking up, the woman next to him had dug her nails into his arm. Dylan was sure she'd drawn blood.

'Sorry about that,' the voice came on again, breaking up a little. 'It's going to be a bit bumpy on our approach, so please ensure your seat belts are *firmly* fastened for landing.'

They had to enter a thick layer of clouds on their way down, which only made the bumpiness more bumpy and the wings were having trouble staying level. The woman's grip on his arm tightened even more to the point where Dylan finally had to pat her hand reassuringly.

'S-sorry!' she said, pulling her hand away, pressing it between her legs and turning to the next page.

Dylan stared at the four red welts on his arm and supposed this was the stuff of which statues were made. 'No problem,' he said, resisting the temptation to rub them better.

All at once they were through the clouds, and Dylan could see nothing but water beneath them. Dylan had done his research and knew it had to be either Lake Skaha or Lake Penticton. Almost there!

It was an eagle's one-point landing[35], with the wheel on one side of the plane touching down first, quickly followed by the nose wheel and then the straggling left one.

As they stood up, the woman at the aisle turned to him with puffy eyes. 'I'm a terrible flyer,' she whispered. 'I absolutely loath it!'

'If we were meant to fly…' Dylan started, then abandoned the punch line.

A man in a Mounty's uniform came up behind him as they were filing out. His face was distinctly pale.

'First time I've ever been scared!' he grunted.

As they entered the arrivals lounge, Dylan noticed a

---

[35] http://bit.ly/2BNrQaF

piece of cardboard with a scrawl of his name and that of another person's on it. It was being held up by a tall man with slicked-back dark hair and a goatee.

He and the woman in the aisle seat converged on the man with the sign.

'Welcome to Penticton...' the man said, glancing at the sign, 'Dylan and Melissa! I'm Niall Campbell.'

Any strangers passing at that instant would have concluded that Dylan and Melissa were a couple, or at least related, but Dylan had already deduced that he and Melissa would be competing for that precious teaching job.

'Forgive us for not providing you with separate arrival persons, given the circumstances,' said Niall. 'But I suppose you would meet outside the interview room before or after anyway.'

Dylan resisted the temptation to point Niall to the blood under Melissa's fingernails, instead nodding in syncopation with her.

The interview room was actually a classroom with a semi-circle of chairs occupied by the panel opposite one lone chair for the interviewees.

Niall was in the middle, flanked by bearded Roger, who spoke with a thick Scottish accent and Gloria, who had shoulder-length curly black hair and wrinkled clothes that suggested she'd worn them to bed the previous night.

'How are you and grammar?' said Niall, in his opening gambit.

'We get along,' said Dylan, trying to lighten the atmosphere. 'At Christmas time and birthdays, mostly.'

This was met by a blank expression from Niall and a sour one from Gloria. Only Roger emitted the trace of a smile.

'The average Penticton College student has... basic writing skills,' Niall continued.

'Scandalously so,' winked Roger.

'Especially the males,' snapped Gloria.

'Which means that we instructors must lead by example by championing verb-subject agreement and putting dangling modifiers and comma splices on notice.'

'Absolutely,' said Dylan, hoping they wouldn't ask him to exemplify the offenders. 'They would be endangered species in my classroom.'

'We also offer a course in contemporary Canadian authors,' said Gloria, in a tone that would put a skewer to shame. 'Which are your favourite female authors?'

'Alice Munro and Alice Munro,' said Dylan. 'Everything's she's written. Plus Maggie Atwood, for her poetry.'

'What about her fiction?' said Gloria, suspiciously.

'I can understand why poets try to graduate to fiction,' said Dylan. 'Everyone likes to eat, but I found *Surfacing* a bit too didactic.'

'At least you read it,' said Roger. 'I couldn't get past page ten. Ten typos by then.'

'That was the publisher's fault for not proofreading,' snapped Gloria.

'Publishers, eh?' said Dylan. 'Can't do with them or without them!'

Niall shuffled some papers. 'I didn't find a list of publications on your *vitae*. Have you published anything?'

Dylan cleared his throat. 'I have a novel... underway.'

'Bravo,' said Roger. 'What's it about?'

Dylan bit his tongue. 'These two lovers canoe to the middle of a very deep lake in search of a mystical monster.'

'Hmm,' said Roger, extrapolating. 'Cashew. That doesn't strike me as a name with Scottish heritage.'

Dylan shook his head. 'There are lots of monsters besides Lochy!'

It went on like that for quite a while, with Dylan imagining how Melissa would respond to similar questions.

She was waiting on a very lonely chair in the corridor as

he came out.

'How did it go?' she asked, looking him up and mostly down for signs of dejection.

'Not bad,' he said. 'How's your knowledge of feminist novels about Canadian lake monsters?'

He got a bit of a thrill seeing her squirm.

Back at work, Lehmann was quiet and fatalistic. He seemed to come and go to Dylan's office almost invisibly as D. H., leaving only reports to be edited or proofread as his legacy. Dylan wanted to reassure him that he probably hadn't got the job given his hesitation about Maggie Atwood, but then Lehmann was an innocent canvas when it came to Canadian writing, so he wouldn't have made heads or tails of the discussion.

On the fourth morning after he'd returned from Penticton, with still no word on the outcome, Hillary appeared at his office door with a plate covered in foil.

'I smell something sweet,' Dylan said, pointing at the plate with his red pen.

'Besides me?' said Hillary. When he didn't smile, she added, 'Cheer up, Dylan. No news may be good news.'

'Right,' he said, bravely. 'What's under the foil, Maid Marian[36]?'

'Ta da!' she cried, ripping it off. 'Tablet fudge!'

'Which is?' he asked, sniffing.

'A morale booster. A-waiting-for-the victory-phone-call booster. Try some.'

She set down the plate on his desk then cut off a sliver with a knife accompanying the fudge.

'Umm,' he said, relishing it. 'Do I detect something alcoholic?'

'Something very much like scotch,' she smiled. 'The dregs from a well-aged bottle I found at the back of a cupboard.'

---

[36] http://bit.ly/2I7ol8u

'I feel my morale boosting as we speak,' said Dylan reaching for the knife.

At that very moment, the phone rang. Dylan's hand froze in midair.

'Probably just Lehmann,' he said. 'He's been the invisible man since I got back from Penticton.'

'Pick it up, then,' Hillary said after the fourth ring. 'Go on!'

It was a woman's voice. 'Is this Mr Dylan Cashew?'

'Yes.'

'This is Penticton College. One moment, please, while I put you through.'

Hillary read his eyes and crossed both fingers.

Niall came on the line. 'Dylan Cashew?'

'Hi, Niall,' said Dylan trying for the middle ground between a formal and casual tone but just sounding ridiculous to himself.

'Are you still interested in the position?'

Dylan clenched his fist and thrust it into the air for Hillary's benefit. 'Yes, I most certainly am.'

After he got off the phone, Dylan gave Hillary the highlights. The college semester was six weeks away, and he was to report for orientation a week before that. A contract would be in the post tomorrow.

'There's a relocation allowance of $1500,' he added. 'That's more than enough for *my* stuff.'

She hesitated just long enough to make him nervous. 'Down on your knee, then, Mr Cashew. Or I could do it!'

It was his turn to hesitate. 'But I don't have a ring.'

'And you won't have one – until we get to Edmonton. No bloody way I'm having a ring from the only jewellery shop in Frigid Lake!'

In the fading scent of Hillary's fudge, Dylan was spinning more than usual. He would have to give notice to Lehmann as well as to his landlord. Now that he would be leaving the

Establishment he almost felt sorry for hooking his dream.

Back home at the cabin, he walked down to the edge of the lake and gazed off to the horizon.

'Where are you, Minasoo?' he called over the darkening sunset waters. 'If I'm going to draft that manuscript, I need to catch at least a glimpse of you!'

'No, you don't,' came the voice behind him.

'You missed the news, D. H.,' said Dylan, not even bothering to turn.

'I was there the whole time,' said D. H., coming up beside him. 'And I couldn't help torpedoing the hippie's interview.'

'She didn't strike me as a hippie, even though she was scared of turbulence.'

'They come well-disguised these days,' said D. H. 'With or without the wagon[37].'

'How did she go – in the interview, I mean?'

'She rattled off a lot more women authors than you did, and she worships Margaret Atwood, even without knowing that she'll win the Booker eventually and be shortlisted twice for the Orange Award for her later *novels*.'

'Don't rub it in,' said Dylan. 'I think I nearly blew it with Gloria on that one.'

'You did blow it, as you call it, but the hippie blew it even worse by trying to flirt with the chairman, who is, as we used to say, of a different... persuasion.'

Dylan blinked. 'He's married, for Christ's sake!'

'The times they are a'changing,' sang D. H. in a credible tenor voice.

'So even with my High Distinction on my Master's, two published poems in the *Malahat Review* and a short story in *Prism International*, it came down to my prospects as a sex object?' Dylan held back for a few seconds before bursting out with laughter.

'Some imagine it, some write about it, others do it,' D. H. said, compounding Dylan's laughter with his own.

---

[37] http://bit.ly/2lilc4Y

Chapter 5: Voice in an Almost Wilderness

THE TRUTH ABOUT GRAMMAR WAS THAT DYLAN HAD BEEN SCHOOLED DURING THAT LIBERAL PHASE when what you wrote was more important than the conventions you exemplified or flaunted when you wrote it.

He was assigned two classes of "Composition" populated by students who by and large had no interest in being there. Since Dylan was the new kid teacher on the block and had learned how to write by instinct rather than by rote, he ticked off the textbooks already on the reading list for his students and then was aghast by what he saw just a few days out before classes were to begin.

'Of course it's boring,' Hillary said, pushing the grammar text back to him when he showed it to her. 'It was probably carved in stone[38] at a time when people also accepted absolute monarchies and the infallibility of the Pope.'

'Maybe I should have gone to Sunday school,' said Dylan. 'I don't recognise any of this!'

They had barely enough room to sneeze amidst the stacked boxes in the ground floor one bedroom flat they were renting month to month until they could find something more permanent. It was at the intersection of a main street on the outskirts of town where headlights glared in through thin drapes at least until 10pm every weekday night and midnight on the weekend.

'Well, I went to a churchie school,' said Hillary, putting on airs, 'where the nuns rapped you on the knuckles with a ruler once for each punctuation or spelling error and twice for a grammar error. So you're in luck!'

'Maybe I should do your public relations job and you can

[38] http://bit.ly/2zF5AxC

teach my classes.'

'You don't have the wardrobe to do PR, darling. Which is why I'll be picking out your suit for the wedding.'

'I already have a suit.'

'Yes, *a* suit. From your senior prom, isn't it?'

'It was just fine for my Master's graduation!'

'I'm sure it was. But you won't be wearing a gown over it this time.'

'I thought we were just going to the courthouse for a... quiet ceremony?'

She paused. 'We were,' she said. 'Until my dear mother found out.'

Dylan may have been dyslexic about grammar but he had an instinct for family relations that comes with being an only child of parents who were themselves only children before departing this vale of tears[39] all too soon, too soon.

'They're coming all the way over from Scotland for the wedding?' said Dylan.

'Even better than that. They've offered to pay for the whole shebang – on one condition.'

'Which is?'

'That they get to choose the venue and we spend our honeymoon in Scotland.'

'That's *two* conditions. Three, if we count them vetoing the courthouse. Plus we've just started our jobs. How can we honeymoon in Scotland?'

'Scots can be very patient when they have to be. Otherwise how could they have put up with the English monarchy for so long? Anyway, we can do it next summer, or the one after that. They'll probably book us in for the Edinburgh Tattoo as insurance. After that, we can decide where to go.'

'I'm allergic to tattoos.'

And so it was that they alternated grammar lessons with wedding plans to the point of being bi-lingual on both

---

[39] http://bit.ly/2CfhEJ2

narratives. When put on the spot by a student for an example of a dangling modifier, Dylan might reply with *Having chosen her bridesmaids, the groom booked a suite for her parents.*

'But that makes perfect sense,' a male student might say.

'You're an idiot,' a female student might interject. '*Grooms* don't pick out the bridesmaids!'

'Maybe he's a control freak – like my dad,' the first could reply.

'It's not all about you,' the female might say – and checkmate!

After a while, grammar invaded Dylan's dreams. He was a ship at night straying ever closer to jagged boulders of verb/noun disagreements and the whirlpools of comma splices. Their sexton textbook of scotch had been swept overboard.

Only a few weeks into the semester, Niall summoned Dylan to his office for a 'midterm consultation'. As a junior administrator, Niall was entitled to a slightly larger office than normal instructors, plus, in addition to the requisite desk, two extra chairs and a modest coffee table, and he took full advantage of these perks by seating himself at one of the chairs and motioning Dylan to assume occupancy of the spare.

'So how's it going?' he asked.

'Fine,' said Dylan. 'More than half of my students can now tell the difference between a noun and a verb more than thirty percent of the time.'

'Remarkable,' said Niall.

Dylan sensed a hidden agenda. 'Adjectives and adverbs are still a bit of a black hole, but we're working on it.'

'You mean *them*,' said Niall. 'Subject-verb agreement? Gotcha!'

Dylan couldn't resist. 'Collective nouns take a singular *object*.' It seemed he had the drop on Niall on two fronts, thanks to Hillary.

Niall cleared his throat. 'Quite so. But is that any reason to start a student magazine?'

Niall had the drop on him. 'I was planning to discuss that with you.'

'There's no time like the present.'

'OK. Well, each class will---'

'You mean "would". That is conditional future tense we're discussing here.'

'...be responsible for one issue,' said Dylan, glossing over the part of speech he'd never heard of, 'and each student will either write, edit or produce the issue. There's a lot to organise.'

'There's nothing in your syllabus about this.'

'I didn't write the syllabus.'

Niall nodded. 'That was your predecessor, wherever he might be.'

'And where would *that* be?'

Niall crossed himself, but with a flippant tone. 'The most convenient place in the Okanagan Valley, I suspect, for those who have fallen off the wagon[40].'

'And did he write the syllabus before or after he fell off?'

'Nice try, Dylan. But I as Chair have to approve all syllabuses, not to mention special initiatives like a proposed student magazine.'

Dylan sensed thin ice ahead. 'The students are keen, Niall. So keen they've agreed to do whatever it takes in addition to their normal work.'

'I'll take that under advisement – when you submit your proposal to me.'

'Excuse me, but in the interview didn't you say a teacher's classroom is his kingdom?'

'I may have. But kingdoms at Penticton College are quite porous.'

---

[40] http://bbcom.me/2E4Yjuu

'And subject to veto by the higher kingdom?'

Niall winked. 'I knew we made the right decision in hiring you!'

Hillary was busy with wedding plans that evening, as she seemed to be every evening and every spare moment in fact when she wasn't at work at the Bald Mountain Resort trying to entice big spenders[41] to book their holidays there, so she was just a bit preoccupied when Dylan started his rant about the Higher Kingdom Veto.

When he wouldn't give it a rest, she finally looked up from her wedding planner, raised her hand like a maestro about to conduct the Okanagan Pops Orchestra, and intoned:

> *For he who fights and runs away*
> *May live to fight another day;*
> *But he who is in battle slain*
> *Can never rise and fight again.*

'Robbie Burns?' Dylan asked.

She shook her head. 'Robbie was never one for going quietly. It was Oliver Goldsmith, *The Art of Poetry on a New Plan*, but, like all good Irish playwrights, he stole it from the Greeks, in this case Menander. Do you want the full reference?'

'No, thanks,' said Dylan. 'You're saying I should knuckle under and forget the student mag?'

'Yes,' she smiled. 'You've only been here five minutes and already you're locking horns with a junior administrator who's dreaming of higher things?'

Dylan's jaw dropped. 'You've only met the man once, but you feel comfortable in profiling him?'

She came over to him and gave him a lingering hug. 'On my way through the Glass Ceiling, darling, I've profiled so many men like him. Small dicks, even smaller minds. The

---

[41] http://bit.ly/2Chyx5T

only way you'll get him to approve of your plan is if he gets the credit – or, better yet, can be convinced that it was his idea in the first place. Now, what pieces would you like the quartet to perform before, during and after the ceremony?'

It took a few seconds for Dylan to register that she was back on the wedding plans. 'Do they know anything by Queen?'

'Very funny. The quartet I've hired is a classical group. But you knew that, didn't you?'

'Haven't you heard of *A Night at the Opera?*'

'Of course. And your point is?'

'Maybe they could play an excerpt from "Bohemian Rhapsody" while I try to get the ring on your finger?'

She played along with it. 'If that is your wish, lord and master, it shall be requested. In the meantime, have you come up with your best man?'

'I told you, I don't have any friends. At least none that I would trust with a ring worth two months of my salary.'

'I paid for it,' she reminded him. 'I couldn't wait that long.'

Dylan was not the type of man to be embarrassed by the fact that his partner was now earning nearly twice as much as he was, but he did prefer to cost things by a unit of comparison that made sense in his world.

'The best man,' he mumbled. 'Yes, I suppose that's a higher priority than finding a way to ambush Niall. All right, I'll just take the dog for a walk and have a think about best men.'

'But we don't have a dog, Dylan.'

'I was speaking metaphorically. Or would you prefer me to come up with best men in the midst of a drunken stupor?'

She pointed to the front door. 'The leash is over there. I'll just get back to the seating plan, shall I?'

Dylan knew he was in a bind, and so, apparently, did D. H., who appeared at his side with a leash and a small dog at the end of it seconds after Dylan shut the door behind him.

'I don't suppose you could be my best man?' he asked D. H.

'Aren't you going to ask me where I got the dog?' said D. H., bending down to give it a scratch behind the ears.

'I don't know much about dogs,' said Dylan, 'and even less about organising a best man. Can't you help?'

'I don't know much about dogs, either,' said D. H., 'but I suspect you'll end up with one, as most married people do before they produce offspring. This is a Pomeranian. Yappy little thing. I got the idea from my old friend Chekhov, though I could never identify with his Gurov, the adulterous banker.'

'But you never met Chekhov.'

'Partly right,' corrected D. H. 'That is, not until recently. My Russian was much worse than his English.'

'So you won't be my best man?' said Dylan, picking up the dog and sticking his tongue out at it, until the dog made a half-hearted lunge at the tongue.

'I would if I could,' said D. H. 'But the get out of heaven free card I get from the other side has its… restrictions, you see. No public appearances allowed.'

Dylan had a crooked smile at the thought. 'So this is like boarding school? They give you a pass out for summer holidays. But not for weddings?'

'What about the Mormon?'

Dylan tried to duck the curve ball. 'The Mormon?'

'The one you share an office with at the college.'

'Oh, you mean Joe Pratt. Nice enough guy, but he doesn't drink. How can I have a best man who won't touch alcohol?'

'He teaches the Romantics – that's a start. And Mormons do get married – in multiples of two. They should know all the best man lines off by heart.'

Dylan picked up the scent of wee coming from the direction of the dog, so he put him back down on the ground.

The Mormon? Well, he had to start somewhere.

Joseph Pratt *was* very Mormon. So tall he had to slightly duck to get into the office. Softly spoken. Bushy black beard. Only one wife at this stage, as far as Dylan knew. And only two children – a boy and a girl. From the portrait Joseph kept on his desk they seemed genetic opposites of the parents, with the girl, Sarah, looking like a younger version of him, while the boy, Abraham, was a match for the mother, Esther.

Dylan had no idea how to raise the subject of best man, so he went for a dip-and-weave.

'I suppose you go to weddings all the time,' he said, sitting at his desk with his back to Joseph.

Joseph looked at him, which is to say, at his back. 'Not all of the time,' he said. 'And I have lots of marking between weddings.'

'And when you're not marking,' Dylan said, wheeling around cautiously. 'I suppose you have heaps of best man speeches to practice?'

Joseph grinned. 'You're the one getting married, Dylan. Someone else has to be your best man, and he usually will write his own speech.'

"So you *do* know how it works?'

'There's nothing to be nervous about. The best man will roast you over lightly on both sides before inviting your guests to raise a glass in toast to you and Hillary.'

'Mormons believe in toasts?'

'Some do. Others take *1 Thessalonians 5: 22*[42] quite literally. But we had plenty of sparkling cider toasts when Esther and I were married.'

This was sounding promising. 'And what if some of the guests aren't Mormon. Are they allowed to toast with alcohol – bring their own, so to speak?'

Joseph hesitated. 'What does this have to do with you and Hillary, Dylan?'

---

[42] http://bit.ly/2Iari8t

'Well, it's just… You see… I had two or three possible best man candidates in mind, but they all live back East, and they can't make it to the wedding.'

'I'm still confused. You said I was the first Mormon you'd ever met, so how is this discussion relevant?'

It quickly became the *Groom Stripped Bare*[43] from that point on.

Finally, Joseph clapped him on the shoulder. 'You're asking me to be your best man?'

'I'll *completely* understand if you think it's at all inappropriate.'

'I would be deeply honoured to be your best man, Dylan – on one condition.'

'Name your price,' said Dylan. 'Anything short of surrendering my breeding rights!'

'The Faculty Association is having its annual general meeting next week, and they need someone to nominate for president.'

Dylan looked at him. 'I thought you were president.'

'Was. Am. Soon to be past tense.'

'What does that have to do with me?' said Dylan, before the penny dropped. 'Not a chance. Politics aren't me.'

'There's really nothing to it, Dylan. You rubber stamp a few memos from admin on behalf of the staff, then chair the annual general meeting.'

'*Robert's Rules of Order* is Dutch to me. And if there's really nothing to it why don't you nominate again?'

'Because I've been diagnosed with prostate cancer and have less than three months to live.' He let that sink in before smiling. 'No, only kidding. I'm just tired of being president. It's someone else's turn.'

Dylan thought of his last conversation with Hillary. 'But I've only been here for five minutes.'

Joseph cocked his head. 'Well, do we have a deal or not?'

---

[43] http://bit.ly/2ChDbkg

It was just as well that the annual general meeting came before the marriage. Even so Dylan thought he might succumb to a minor variant of D. H.'s pneumonia. Hillary caught him before he headed out the door and insisted that he change his shirt to something a bit less wrinkled as well as buffing his shoes with a damp tea towel.

'Hardly anyone knows me,' Dylan said. 'With any luck my nomination won't even be seconded.'

'If you know that much about *Robert's Rules of Order*,' Hillary said, 'you'll be a shoo-in!'

She unbuttoned the second top button of his shirt.

'I'm not in the mood,' he said. 'Besides, I have to leave in five minutes.'

'Don't be silly,' she smiled. 'This is for the women at the meeting. No one wants an accountant look in their president.'

'Maybe I'll need an engagement ring – to fend them off?'

'Get elected first,' she said, patting him on the bum and pointing him to the door. 'Then we'll worry about the spoils of high office.'

He arrived fashionably late[44] for the meeting, or so he thought. There were plenty of seats at the front and at the back. Everyone seemed to be talking to someone else about someone else. He was about to sit in the last row when Joseph, already on stage, caught his eye and motioned abruptly for him to come forward. As he headed towards the front, his briefcase caught on the back of a chair, landing with a conspicuous crash in the aisle whereupon papers to be marked spilled out.

Before he could bend down, two women were at his feet almost fighting to rescue the essays.

'Sorry,' he said, opening the briefcase so they could stuff in their prizes as they grinned up at him awkwardly.

One of them winked. Then the other one winked. He had no idea what either wink meant.

---

[44] http://bit.ly/2liumOY

The first one was about his age: short, with dark, gleaming hair and pale blue eyes that glanced away as soon as he tried to make contact. The other was middle-aged, with obviously dyed blond hair, provocatively untamed as if she'd just got out of bed, and a top that was at least one size too tight. Their choice of perfume conflicted in his nostrils.

He resisted the temptation to do up his shirt button.

'You're the new English prof, aren't you?' the short one said, extending a regal hand as though she was a Queen surrogate. 'I'm Anne, your seconder!'

As soon as he took the hand, she drew him into her row and sat him down next to her.

'And I'm Chantelle,' said the middle-aged one, sliding in to the seat on the other side. 'Your designated nominator.'

'Chemistry,' Anne said, pointing at herself.

'Physics,' Chantelle added, squeezing his knee to regain his attention.

'My worst subjects at school,' said Dylan, hoping to discourage them. 'In that order.'

'Opposites attract[45],' said Anne.

'I don't know about that,' said Dylan. 'When was the last time we had a poet as Prime Minister, or even a Prime Minister who could recite a poem?'

'Aren't you the ambitious type!' said Anne, squeezing his other knee a bit more invitingly. 'He's not even Faculty Association President yet and already he's thinking of running for PM!'

Dylan was saved by the sound of the gavel as Joseph called the meeting to order.

He ran through various bits of trivial business with the patience of a taxi driver, slowing down only slightly to highlight what he described lightheartedly as the Association's substantial 'war chest'.

'Point of order, Mr Chairman,' came a voice from the back

---

[45] http://bit.ly/2CbLnVz

corner that Dylan recognised as Niall. 'If we never spend from our war chest, why do we need one?'

'That's not a proper point of order, Niall,' Joseph replied. 'But I'll take it as a comment.'

'We could book at Big White over Christmas,' added another member, referring to the nearby ski resort.

'*Some* of us can't or won't ski,' Chantelle piped in.

'Who said anything about skiing?' the other member retorted. 'I meant *après* skiing, of course!'

Joseph held up his hands as if to freeze a stampede of muskoxen. 'Might I suggest that you give notice for discussion by the new executive? And, speaking of which, the next item on the agenda is the election of officers. I declare the floor open for nominations, starting with Association President. Do we have any nominations?'

Anne and Chantelle held up their hands in competitive unison.

'Yes, Ms McIntyre?' said Joseph, nodding at Anne.

'It gives me great pleasure to nominate... Mr Dylan Catstew,' she said.

Joseph bit his lower lip. 'I think you meant Mr *Cashew*, Ms McIntyre?'

Anne's face went progressively from light to dark purple. 'Forgive me, Mr Chairman,' she said. 'As many of you may know, my precious pussy passed away yesterday after a prolonged battle with a thyroid tumour... So I'm a bit prone to *double entendres*[46].'

'Noted,' said Joseph. 'Seconder?'

'I second the nomination of Mr Cashew!' said Chantelle. As a second thought, she seized Dylan's hand and held it up for all to see. 'In case any of you haven't shared the pleasure I've had of meeting him, here's to an injection of new blood.'

A collective "oo" arose in surround sound from all sides of the room, especially from the female members.

---

[46] http://bit.ly/2E4mLwb

'Further nominations?' asked Joseph.

Dylan mentally crossed his fingers in hopes a rival would surface.

'Second, and last call for nominations,' said Joseph.

'Well, I nominate *you*, Mr Chairman,' said Niall, without putting up his hand.

'Declined,' snapped Joseph. 'As you well knew I would.'

Niall shrugged. 'Well, it wouldn't hurt to have an election for a change. As opposed to a consensus of the unaligned and unwilling.'

He emitted a snorting laugh in appreciation of his stab at political philosophy, but there was only a few shrugs and mild groans from the audience.

'Hearing no further nominations,' said Joseph, after a considered silence. 'I declare Mr Dylan Cashew our new president!'

Anne and Chantelle shot to their feet, lifting Dylan by the hands as though he was some latter day Churchill, to scattered applause, which was sustained long enough to embarrass Dylan.

'Please, come forward,' Joseph urged, waving him up to the stage, and offering him his chair.

'Speech,' Niall called after him. 'SPEECH!'

It hadn't occurred to Dylan that he needed to prepare an acceptance speech. He'd never run for office of any kind before, so he was at a loss for words, even clichés. Where was D. H. when he really needed him? Then again, what office had D. H. ever run for? No wonder he was keeping a low profile of late.

He stood there next to Joseph for what seemed an eternity, opening his mouth now and then in the hope that some words would seep through the levee of his mind, but none did.

Then he saw the smirk on Niall's face, telltale enjoyment of his discomfort, and he knew he would have to break the silence.

'I… thank you for this vote of confidence[47],' he began. 'Especially since I am the new kid on the block. I will do my level best to uphold and defend the values of this Association.'

Whatever the hell they are, he thought. Will I be the next George Washington?

'I hope we can do better on the contract front now,' said a rather rotund fellow off to one side. 'No offence, Joseph, but we haven't had a raise in three years.'

'Do I have to do that, too?' Dylan muttered to Joseph. 'I've never done any contract negotiations.'

'You won't have to,' replied Joseph, pointing down the list of positions to be elected. 'The question comes from Lance Porter, who's nominated for Chief Contract Negotiator, unopposed.'

'If what you say is true, Mr Porter,' said Dylan. 'We'll have a strong case next time around.'

'*Doctor*,' replied Lance. 'I'm a PhD!'

'Sorry, Dr Lance,' said Dylan, bowing slightly in spite of himself.

'And you're not?' Lance pressed. 'A PhD, that is?'

'I'm… working on it,' Dylan said.

'Not that it's so necessary for colleagues in the arts,' Lance sniped.

'Can we just get on with the nominations, please?' said Chantelle, whose name was up for Vice President.

In a matter of seconds there were three nominations for VP, all of them women, each of them regarding Dylan with warm eyes as they rose to give a speech in support of their candidature. Chantelle was last to speak, and she came up to the podium with a stack of note cards.

'If you do me the honour of electing me as your Vice President,' she began, 'I will put the interests of this

---

47 http://bit.ly/2BJBuLf

Association first, and make each and every one of you as my top priority, second only to my teaching responsibilities. If asked to serve, I would even give away my bridge night to ensure I have the time to fulfil these weighty responsibilities.'

'Weighty?' Dylan said, leaning over to Joseph. 'I thought you said even the President has very little to do!'

'That's true enough,' Joseph whispered back. 'But some people manage to expand the demand to fit their image of the position.'

'And each of them is flirting with me,' Dylan said, even more softly. 'Don't they know I'm *engaged*?'

'Never under-estimate the optimism or tenacity of an unmarried woman,' Joseph said. 'Where there's time to spare, it's possible to alter the Earth's orbit[48].'

Chantelle won by the narrowest of margins and had the pleasure of standing between Dylan and Joseph, vaulting their hands into the air to accept the token applause. Since they stood together behind the podium, no one but Dylan noticed her knee rubbing ever so slightly against the back of his thigh.

Dylan made a mental note to be sure they were chaperoned from that point on.

---

[48] https://go.nasa.gov/2CgyLKm

Chapter 6: Get Me to Your Church on Time

AT FIRST GLANCE IT SEEMED THAT DYLAN HAD NO ONE HE COULD INVITE TO THE WEDDING. His father had vanished into the ether when he was just a boy as a protest against not being shortlisted as the first Canadian astronaut to be accepted for NASA training. One of the women who *had* been shortlisted was suspected to have enticed him out of the marital cocoon by suggesting she knew a way to put him on an invisible waiting list in case any of the successful candidates developed terminal motion sickness during training or otherwise met with foul play. If only *Canada's Got Talent* had existed then, Dylan's mother would have entered to be discovered by Stephen Moccio for her excellent mezzo-soprano voice and under-appreciated bosom and then immediately signed for solo work by the Red Deer Light Opera while she waited for more celebrity-charged offers. As it was, she handed over the keys to their Calgary flat to Dylan as he drove her to the airport for what was supposed to be a two-week exploratory trip in New York with a confirmed appointment at the Met, and sent him one postcard from the Statue of Liberty before assuming radio silence. The subsequent FBI investigation found that she was not listed on any flights entering New York that day, including the one on her itinerary that had flown there with a brief layover in Chicago.

As he explained all this to Hillary, her grip on his hands tightened.

'Why didn't you tell me this when we were still at the Establishment?' she asked. 'I'm sure someone there has contacts who could track one or both of them down.'

Dylan shrugged. 'And I'm sure that if they wanted to be found they would have been in touch by now. Besides, if I ever write about it, it will be easier if it's an unresolved mystery.'

She dug in her nails. 'Not everything has to be reduced to fiction.'

'It was no accident that she sent me that postcard,' he said. 'The only mystery was how she managed it.'

The plane that did arrive came from Glasgow via Vancouver. Hillary's family had booked a block of seats on the Air Canada flight on which they reportedly exhausted the supplies of scotch, at least for the adult members of the contingent, as verified by Hillary's father, Peter.

He was tall and lanky, and his cheeks had a reddish afterglow that came from being on intimate terms with Glenfiddich IPA, a duty-free case of which he had in tow as they came through the Arrivals gate. They being Hillary's mother Maria, three sisters, two brothers, as well as a flurry of aunts, uncles, and a mixed bag of cousins.

To Dylan's relief, none of them wore kilts[49].

'So this is your lad!' Peter declared, with a crushing handshake. 'Welcome to the clan!'

He was the first in line for the contingent offering less intimidating handshakes or blushing left and right cheeks to kiss as they ambled along to the baggage area.

He and Hillary made sure they were all safely aboard the hotel airport van before they trailed along to the hotel, where they'd booked accommodation, as well as the venue for the reception after the ceremony at St Ann's Church, which neither of them had set foot inside until the day of the wedding rehearsal – the day before her family touched down.

'You're sure you don't mind us being married in a Catholic church?' Hillary asked on the way.

---

[49] http://bit.ly/2C22iun

'The closest synagogue is in Calgary,' said Dylan. 'And I haven't set foot in it since my Bar Mitzvah, so there's no point in acting the purist now.'

She squeezed his knee. 'You looked so religious in that photo. I feel like I'm luring you onto the dark side.'

'Some of my best friends are fallen Catholics,' he smiled.

There were two clear days until the wedding, which gave the tourists plenty of time to transform the immediate vicinity into a credible facsimile of Scotland. Strategically, Peter and Maria had brought a genuine MacEwan tartan[50] for not only Dylan but also Joseph to wear at the ceremony.

Hillary unwrapped his and then held it up to Dylan's waist, taking the opportunity to give his bum a surreptitious pat at which he blushed, seeing Maria's nod of appreciation.

'A perfect fit!' Hillary declared. 'You won't need to wear anything under it – only joking.'

'And my favourite colours, too,' Dylan said. 'Blue and green, with just a suggestion of red and yellow, with ample space to show off my knees. But will we have a piper to lead us in?'

'Of course!' Peter bellowed. 'William MacEwan arrives tonight from Vancouver. He can trace his line right back to the clan who settled in British Columbia in the early nineteenth century.'

Dylan was getting into the swing of things. A kilt would be the perfect disguise for a not-so-good Jewish boy in Catholic surrounds. And he could hardly wait to see Joseph's face when he was told that this was to be his outfit as well. I wonder, he thought, if any Mormon missionaries have made it as far north as the Hebrides?

'And will you be wearing a kilt, too... my darling?' he said to Hillary, with a romantic swirl mostly for Maria's benefit.

'No,' she said. 'That's never done.'

---

[50] http://bit.ly/2lakqrl

'I've brought her Nanna's wedding dress,' Maria announced. 'I'm sure it'll be a perfect fit, but, just in case, I packed in my sewing kit.'

'And I brought the Quaich we had for our wedding,' said Peter, giving her cheek a fond rub.

'Quaich?' asked Dylan.

'Better known as the loving cup,' Hillary said. 'Dad will fill it with scotch to be passed around to the wedding guests after we sign the register.'

'Hmm,' smiled Dylan. 'What a quaint tradition!'

The next day went by in a semi-blur, and not just because Peter kept them lubricated with shots of scotch between rehearsals for the wedding running order. He and Maria also had to agree on a suitable colour for the Audi that would spirit them away to their Big White chalet after the reception, and ensure the wedding cake's icing complimented the floral arrangements organised for the church.

Joseph took his kilt in stride, after confessing to Dylan that he'd invited the Faculty Association executive to the event, along with members of the English Department and assorted other faculty members who he was sure would add good value to the wedding present table.

'Besides,' he said. 'There isn't a whole lot going on in Penticton this weekend, and you need to have at least a few friends on your side of the aisle!'

The weather gods were determined to be unfriendly. Even before he got out of bed, Dylan could hear wind buffeting the hotel window. It was worse than it sounded. Drawing the drapes open he could see rain pelting down on the street below, and traffic dragging along with headlights on.

He thought of ringing Hillary, who was staying with her sisters who were to act as bridesmaids, and Connie Brewster, the maid of honour she'd partied with throughout her university days, but then he remembered the prohibition of the groom making contact with the bride until she came up the aisle at church, which Peter, a stickler on tradition, had reminded him about at the stag party.

He looked for a washable wool label in his kilt but found nothing.

He wondered how Nan's wedding dress would fare in gale force winds between the hotel entry and the limousine and then into the church.

Even more strangely, he found himself humming *I'm getting married in the morning...* as he brushed his teeth, as if that would chase away the clouds.

'Look on the bright side,' he said aloud. 'Some people have boring wedding days and have to skip that chapter in their memoir.'

Joseph met him at the hotel front door with a huge blue and white umbrella emblazoned with Penticton College.

'Sorry about that,' he said, motioning Dylan toward the waiting car. 'This was the only umbrella I could find at short notice. It hardly ever rains here at this time of year.'

'Is that a bad omen?' Dylan asked, feeling cold rain on his bare legs as they made a dash for the car.

'Only if you're superstitious,' said Joseph. 'Which, apparently, most Scots are.'

They were halfway to the church when the raindrops seemed to metabolise into fluffy snowflakes.

'Now this is more like it,' said Joseph, leaving ample room between them and the car in front.

'More like what?' asked Dylan.

'October sleet. But at least it'll be proper snow by the time you get to Big White.'

'I can see the headlines now,' said Dylan. 'Pale blue Audi Wedding Limo Skids Off Mountain Road On The Way To Honeymoon. Venue Retains Deposit.'

'Well, at least the bride's family is paying for the honeymoon,' said Joseph, playing along.

'No, they aren't,' said Dylan. 'That's one part of the tradition they were happy to skip. Apparently none of them are skiers so they couldn't understand why we'd want to honeymoon at the top of a mountain.'

Joseph skidded only slightly on the drive up to the church where several of the Scottish clan stood in a nervous phalanx of umbrellas.

'You get out here while I find a park,' said Joseph, checking his watch. 'The bride won't be here for at least ten minutes.'

The Clan had gone beyond the call of duty in transforming the inside of the church into a Scottish heath. A team of seemingly invisible elves had suspended sprigs of heather in various shades of mauve, pink and red below the stained glass windows, and on either side of the altar bristled generous bunches of lilies.

Father Martine, the parish priest, unapologetically Scottish by heritage and accent, waited by the altar with fingers folded in devout determination. He didn't notice D. H. behind him, tickling the lilies.

'Speaking of eloping,' D. H. called out when Dylan was only halfway up the aisle.

'You took your time,' Dylan mouthed in reply, as he nodded to acknowledge the smiles of the guests standing in the pews along the way. 'And, no, we weren't talking about eloping,' he added, stopping at his appointed place.

'Just as well,' said Father Martin, giving him an odd look as though he'd just stolen the holy water.

'Can he see you?' Dylan asked D. H., meaning Father Martine.

'He can see everyone – especially you,' smiled Father Martine.

D. H. rolled his eyes. '*Listen*, Dylan, don't speak. Or the congregation might think you have a wire loose. I meant, about the eloping, and all that confusion about mountains, that reminded me of those heady first days with Frieda after she left her husband and kids for me, when we ended up in Germany where they accused me of being a spy just because I kept to myself, and we had to slog through the snow over the Alps to Italy – no Audis back then!'

'True romance,' Dylan muttered. 'So why are you *here*?'

'I thought you might like me to inspire you with a few lines from Byron:

She walks in beauty, like the night
Of cloudless climes and starry skies…

You know the poem?'

'*A heart whose love is innocent*… yes, I have it right here,' Dylan said, holding up his note card. 'I might have known you would be looking over my shoulder.'

A bit soppy,' D. H. said, 'but appropriate enough, I suppose, for a formal occasion.'

'Like your "Wedding at the Marsh"?'

'I was far better writing about it than living it,' smiled D. H.

Father Martine had opened his mouth, doubtlessly to remark on Dylan's flippant tongue when the organ sprang to life. Joseph was hop-skipping down the aisle, while Hillary, arm in arm with her father, dawdled awkwardly at the back, just behind her sisterly bridesmaids, who seemed to be waiting for a freshened signal after the organ's opening chords.

'Sorry,' Joseph said, all red-faced. 'I was all set at the entry when I remembered I'd left the ring in the glove box and had to go back. Then I slipped on the way back and had to… tidy up somewhat.'

Glancing over his shoulder, Dylan could see that Joseph's bum was still a bit wet. 'Are you sure you didn't drop the ring when you fell?'

Dylan could see the look of slight panic in Joseph's eyes as he patted his pocket for reassurance.

'Actually, he did,' said D. H., looking even more translucent than usual. 'But I tucked the box back in before it could get wet. Well, it looks like as though it's show time, so I'll scout ahead for black ice on the road up to Big White. See you at the reception!'

'Do we have a choice?' said Dylan.

'Why are you talking to the lilies?' Joseph whispered, as the organist returned to bar one. 'Never mind: everyone gets cold feet when it comes to saying *I do.*'

First down the aisle came the bridesmaids in their silky dresses, youngest to oldest, then Hillary's friend Connie in a gown that was perhaps just a bit too revealing, but Dylan thought she might be making a bid for catching the bridal bouquet[51]. And then, after a suitably dramatic pause, Hillary appeared with her father, doing her best to keep their steps in time with the music. Her hand-me-down dress and veil were of embroidered antique white silk, which, even up close, looked so new that they could have been unwrapped that very morning from a dress shop.

As the procession reached the altar, Dylan could see a welling of tears not only on Maria's face, but, on the other side, among a clutch of women from the Social Sciences Faculty at the College who he'd met only in passing, but who Joseph would later classify as 'career singles' and possibly more tearful over a prospective catch lost than surrendering to emotions of the moment.

'And who giveth this woman…?' Father Martine began in an even thicker accent than Dylan could remember from the rehearsals.

'That would be me,' Peter piped in. 'Laird of our Clan.'

Hillary noticeably gulped. After a few glasses of champagne, she would let slip to Dylan that that was the first she'd heard that Peter had been so anointed.

Dylan was braced for mishap, but he and Hillary recited

---

[51] http://bit.ly/2BMr5hU

their vows without a hitch, Joseph extracted the ring from his pocket without dropping it to the floor where it might have rolled out of sight under one of the pews, and, only after Father Martine had declared them 'man and wife' to a slight bristle from Hillary, who'd only given into tradition for the sake of avoiding a spat with her father, and whispered the word 'husband' to Dylan as he lifted her veil for the congratulatory and lingering kiss could Dylan relax with the tickle of her tongue in his mouth, but only briefly before the piper let loose at the back of the church signalling the formalities were over.

Outside, more than a skiff of snow had fallen and accumulated, and once they had run the dry shower of rice to the waiting, steamy Audi they were farewelled with a pelting of ad hoc snowballs as the car idled its way out of the driveway, following the piper.

'Never mind *The Rainbow*,' Dylan said, settling into the back seat, after easing the folds of Hillary's dress out from under his bum. 'We'll invent a better chapter!'

'The Rainbow?' Hillary asked.

'It's a colourful story,' Dylan said.

As they drove north through Summerland, Peachland and then took the turn-off in Kelowna to Big White, the snow angered to the point of a blizzard. There were just the two vehicles on the road now – the Audi following the hire bus packed with guests.

Only a few metres after the turn-off, the driver pulled over to the side of the road as the bus disappeared around the bend ahead.

'Chains,' he grunted, popping open the truck. 'Should have put 'em on before. Better late than at the bottom of a ravine!'

A whoosh of snow blew in as he slammed the door after him.

Hillary gave Dylan's arm a nervous squeeze. 'Darling,' she said, putting on a spotty American accent. 'If you'd told me you'd brought chains for our honeymoon, I'd have packed in my whips!'

She kept a straight face long enough that Dylan had to respond in kind. 'No need,' he said, as seriously as he could manage. 'They say that *Crescendo* caters to every taste – forgotten whips as well as toothbrushes!'

'Well, then,' she smiled. 'Let's hope the reception doesn't drag on too long!'

By the time he'd finished with the chains, the driver was nearly a snowman and had to stamp the ground vigorously before getting back in.

'All set, then… what did you say your name is?' asked Dylan.

'Matt,' said the driver, backing the car out carefully.

'An are ya from these parts?' asked Hillary, still polishing her American accent.

'Yes, Ma'am,' said Matt, slowly accelerating. 'My people are the Sylix.'

'Ah,' said Hillary. 'First Peoples. Are they… a big tribe?'

'Not all that many, Ma'am,' said Matt, smiling at her in the mirror. 'Unless you count our Okanagan cousins from south of the border. We got stranded after the Washington Territory was made a State.'

The car skidded a bit just then, but Matt quickly righted it.

'Yes,' Matt added. 'It makes treaty negotiations awkward when the United Nations has to get involved.'

'Really?' said Dylan. 'I've never heard---'

'Only joking,' said Matt. 'I try that line out with all the tourists.'

'But we *live* here now,' said Dylan.

'Which makes you almost locales,' said Matt. 'So no more cheap jokes on you!'

They caught up with the bus just before the turn-off to the Crescendo, which glowed only faintly through the storm as they eased in to what looked like a parking area. Alcohol must have been flowing freely in the bus because the passengers launched into a snowball fight seconds after alighting.

'Follow me, Ma'am and Sir,' Matt urged, trying to open an umbrella for them, but it was immediately caught up by a gust and blown from his hands to land like a spear only centimetres away from the closest snowball combatants.

Dylan hummed "Good King Wenceslas" as arm in arm they stumbled in Matt's footsteps along the entryway.

Off to one side, steam was rising from what appeared to be an outdoor pool, masking the glass frontage of the resort even more.

The reception area was a layered universe – tropical, a whiff of Mozart in the air, resort staff in shirtsleeves. The receptionist did her best to ignore their snow-swept appearance.

'Welcome to Crescendo,' she said. 'I trust you'll find your stay more... hospitable than the current weather.'

At that very moment, the front door blew open again, and Peter and Maria staggered in, with other guests hastening behind.

'Where's the bar, Lass?' he cried, pushing Maria in front of him like a medieval shield[52]. 'My wife needs a drink!'

The receptionist managed a brave smile. 'Your bar will be open in the events room shortly – after you've had a chance to... freshen up.'

Peter paused at the front desk long enough to give the receptionist a wink. 'Dress code, eh? This is my kind of place!'

Crescendo had gone all out to mask the weather outside with their indoor decorations, which included sprigs of

---

[52] http://bit.ly/2CdIIM6

heather and a flourish of fragrant rose petals on every crisp tablecloth in the reception room. There were waiters and waitresses positioned strategically behind each table, ready to refill wine glasses, or, in the case of purists like Peter and most of the tourist male guests, the scotch glasses.

After their choice of a first course of deconstructed mackerel tartlet with red pepper compote, pink peppercorns & squid ink dressing, *or* specially imported Loch Duart smoked salmon with citrus fruits, seasonal leaves and a wholegrain mustard dressing, *or* plum tomato & mozzarella salad with rocket leaves, basil oil & balsamic pearls, guests had their choice of baked fillet of salmon served with parsley mash, blanched greens & a lemon butter sauce, *or* roast loin of venison [supposedly sourced from local farmed stock rather than from impromptu hunting expeditions] served with skirlie potatoes, honey glazed root vegetables and a port & redcurrant jus venison. While more than a few people seemed to be slowing down after the second course, there appeared to be renewed enthusiasm when the dessert menu appeared offering whisky & orange bread & butter pudding served warm with glayva custard, *or* raspberry crème brulee served with homemade shortbread, *or* vanilla pannacotta with raspberry compote.

Not surprisingly, the Chef de Cuisine[53] and Sous-Chef were thanked with a standing ovation and raised scotch glasses as they eased out from the kitchen just before the plates were cleared.

Peter remained standing at the head table as the others reclaimed their seats and then intoned:

> O my Luve's like a red, red rose,
> That's newly sprung in June:
> O my Luve's like the melodie,
> That's sweetly play'd in tune...

Et cetera, et cetera!'

---

[53] http://bit.ly/2lkWSzw

'That's the only poem he knows!' laughed Maria, jerking on the back of his suit jacket as if to get him to resume his seat. 'Don't ask him for the second stanza!'

Clearly, everyone was well-lubricated by then and would not, even if they could have seen him, have noticed D. H. rising like his phoenix[54] just behind Dylan as the champagne glasses were being filled for the wedding toast.

'I must say,' he whispered in Dylan's ear, 'that our Peter is playing the laird very well indeed.'

'Behave yourself,' Dylan said, slurring slightly, under his breath. 'It won't do for me to be chastising a ghost from the head table!'

'Oh, I will,' said D. H. 'Behave myself, that is. I've just come along in case Joseph there needs any note cards for his speech.'

Dylan went all red. 'What speech?'

It was as if Peter had read D. H.'s mind. 'And now, please be upstanding for the Best Man!'

Dylan tried to get up, but was tugged back down by Hillary.

'No, not us, silly!'

Joseph's face had turned the colour of the raspberry compote he hadn't quite managed to finish.

'Here!' D. H. said, slapping some actual note cards to Dylan's chest. 'As a college lecturer, he should at least be able to read, even if he didn't know enough to prepare a toast speech. Give him these!'

Dylan did as he was told, invisibly as possible.

Joseph's complexion lightened somewhat as he managed to find his feet. Flipping through the cards quickly, he gradually calmed down.

'Thanks to all of you for coming today, especially those of you who have come nearly halfway around the world to celebrate this glad occasion.'

---

[54] http://bit.ly/2IlzWAj

He proceeded to run through all the key guests and their relation to Hillary, stumbling over only a couple with Gaelic spellings.

'How do you know all these names?' Dylan said to D. H.

'Shhh,' whispered Hillary. 'Now's not a good time to be talking to yourself.'

'I concur,' said D. H. 'Besides, it doesn't take a genius – which admittedly I am – to copy names off the hotel register!'

'For those of you who are meeting Dylan for the first time,' Joseph was continuing, after flipping to the second note card, 'let me assure you that his character is without tarnish. After all, the Canadian Government does not grant Top Secret Clearance to people who even remotely could pose a security risk.' Smiling, he added, 'And this surely must apply as well to the sacred state of marriage.'

'Here, here!' shouted Peter, winking at Maria. 'I think I remember the next verse of the Burns now. Should I---'

'Heavens, no,' said Maria, elbowing him. 'You've said your piece.'

'And a silly quote it was,' muttered D. H. 'If only he knew what a rake Robbie was to his supposedly beloved Jean, he might have gone for Byron instead.'

'But...' Dylan started.

'Only joking,' D. H. added.

As a dancer, Dylan made a slightly better editor, but the tradition of having the first waltz with his bride could not be avoided, and he managed it quite well with D. H. at his back sounding out the beat. Once they had been joined on the floor by several other couples, Dylan and Hillary decided to take a break, but Peter waved them over to his table.

'Would you care to dance with the mother of the bride[55]?' he said. It wasn't a question.

'Well, I...' Dylan began, exaggerating his breathless state.

---

[55] http://bit.ly/2pJXOmh

'Better hop to it,' said D. H., 'or I'll have to step in. And it would certainly look odd to have the mother of the bride dancing on her own!'

And so it was that Dylan led Maria onto the floor to the softening eyes of Peter's stare and a stifled giggle from Hillary. Of course it was a slow number, and of course Maria pulled him in a bit closer than he had been even with Hillary.

'I… like you,' Maria said, her eyes fixed right on him. 'And I know you are the right man for our Hillary. I must admit that Peter had his doubts, but I never did.'

'Thanks… Mother,' Dylan said, forcing the last word.

'Don't be silly,' Maria said, squeezing his hand. 'Call me Maria. I know that's what you'd feel more comfortable with. *Mother* is so formal, and it makes me feel so… ancient!'

Dylan sensed it was going to be a long song.

'So you teach writing?' Maria said.

'And literature. Actually, mostly literature.'

'But are you an *author*?' she said with hopeful eyes.

'Yes,' he admitted.

'And have you been published?'

'Several few times,' he lied.

'How nice for you!' she said. 'And you being so young. Will there be a novel some time soon?'

'After I finish my dissertation, perhaps.'

'A dissertation!' she exclaimed. 'Yet another publication. Oh, how lovely. And what will it be on?'

'Well,' he said, glancing around for you-know-who. 'I started one on prose styles of D. H. Lawrence, but I had to defer it when my first job offer came up.'

'D. H. Lawrence? He's one of my *favourite* authors. All that steamy stuff between gardeners and sex-deprived lasses[56]. At least it was back then, in Victorian times. It shows how far we've come, doesn't it?'

---

[56] http://bit.ly/2C3lUOQ

Dylan was definitely getting worried about the twinkle in her eyes. 'Y-yes,' he said, looking longingly at the band, which seemed to be in no hurry to finish the song.

'I'm something of an *auteur* myself, you know.'

'Oh, really?'

She paused. 'Well, aren't you going to ask me what I write about? It's rather impolite to leave it at such an open-ended question!'

'Sorry,' he said, half stepping on her foot. 'Sorry!' he said again, meaning his heavy footing.

'No need to apologise,' she said, breathing the next phrase into his ear. 'I write romances. Under a pseudonym, of course. Mary Tyler. That's very universal, don't you think?'

'Yes,' he said. 'Easy to remember.'

'So why haven't I been published?'

'Oh, I thought you had been – published, that is. I mean, why bother with a pseudonym?'

She dug her nails slightly into his leading hand. 'Peter has offered to pull a few strings with the London crowd, but I've said, no, I must make it on my own. An author must believe in her work to make it contagious, so I do. The work must shout out to the publishers: publish me or be damned[57]. But so far it has fallen on deaf ears.'

'You mean deaf eyes?' he quipped.

'Oh, how clever you are… with words. Now that you're one of the family, I must send you my latest manuscript, so you can cast your clever eyes over it.'

'I'm not that kind of… serious editor,' he said. 'I just look over student work – the kind of stories and poems they'll disown once they know better.'

'Ah,' she said. 'So it's high time you set your sights onto to a more… professional plane. My manuscript will be waiting for you after the honeymoon. Don't disappoint me!'

---

[57] https://ind.pn/2BMVZqf

Chapter 7: Grafting a Thickened Skin

MAYBE IT WAS THE SECRET WHISPER OF THE DUCTED HEATING SYSTEM, or the slippery touch of silky sheets, or even the unpredictable blasts of blizzard gale against the draped picture window, but it was more likely the thought of Maria's manuscript waiting for him upon their return home that made it hard for Dylan to, as it were, maintain his… interest in the narrative at hand.

'That's OK,' Hillary murmured, snuggling into him like a cued teddy bear. 'It's not like we have anything to prove on our wedding night that we haven't already rehearsed.'

'It's your mother,' he confessed.

She stiffened. 'You're having fantasies about my *mother*? Wow, I thought she was past trying to seduce my boyfriends! Now that you mention it, you do have a ruffled Dustin Hoffman look.'

He slapped her on the bottom.

'Coo, coo, ca-choo, Benjamin,' she giggled, slapping him teasingly. 'Slap me again like that, and you might be back on message!'

He did.

And they did – with a Simon and Garfunkel refrain.

Afterwards he thought he'd better come clean about her mother. 'She mistakes me for someone interested in publishing,' he said, adding, 'her book.'

She renewed their glasses with champagne. 'Some people boast about having a personal trainer. My mother wants a publisher at her fingertips so those of her friends who don't know any better will be impressed. Anyway, who's to say – you might go into publishing one day!'

'No chance,' he said. 'Teaching's as close as I want to come to Nirvana.'

'Not so fast,' D. H. interjected as his opacity increased over a bedside chair. 'First there was Ford Maddox Ford, then Edward Garnett who live-wired me into writing *Sons and Lovers*. After that, the thought of teaching was just a lonely guitar in a symphony orchestra---'

'What?' Dylan said, rolling his eyes. 'You're really stressing that metaphor.'

'Dylan,' Hillary said, slightly fearful. 'Who are you talking to?'

Dylan pulled her into his chest and covered her ears. 'She's going to think I'm nuts, D. H.,' he whispered, 'if we keep... meeting like this.'

'I suppose now that you've tied the noose[58],' said D. H. 'It would be inconvenient not to include her in my materialisations.'

Hillary pushed herself away. 'Mr Cashew, I demand an answer!'

D. H. produced a 3D dial that he spun to increase his opacity even more. 'I wish I *had* been born yesterday,' he said. 'So many funny gadgets to distract one from writing!'

Dylan gestured over at him, Hillary saw, and, in a gasping reflex, covered herself with the closest pillow. 'W-who is this? And how long has he been perving on us?'

'Allow me to introduce myself,' D. H. said, with a slight bow. 'David Herbert Lawrence. Novelist, painter and sometime poet.'

'Is this some kind of joke?' said Hillary. 'Where's the stripper and the silly balloons?'

If D. H. understood, he chose to ignore the question, instead bowing even steeper. '*Not* at your service in present circumstances, if you get my meaning.'

'I would hope so,' said Hillary, clutching the pillow to herself all the more tightly. 'You've been dead for ages!'

---

[58] http://bit.ly/2C2SjFn

'Dear Lady,' D. H. said calmly. 'Be assured that I mean no harm by my presence, which I provide most economically in the circumstances so that you will not doubt the sanity of the very worthy man you have chosen as your husband.'

Hillary clenched her eyes closed for several seconds, opened them, then clenched them again. 'What was in that champagne besides alcohol?'

'D. H.,' said Dylan. 'Tone it down – you sound like a walking corpse. You're not helping.'

'How morbid,' said D. H. 'I always did have problems with word choice when the scent of sexual intercourse – in this case, pillow dialogue[59] – still lingered in the air.'

'This can't be happening.' Hillary said. 'Unless you are someone's idea of a sick Strip-O-Gram. Or a variation on Elvis. Did one of my brothers---'

'Dear Lady,' said D. H. 'I'm afraid I'm not familiar with current ideograms like that. Sick-O---'

'You see?' Dylan said to Hillary. 'He really is – or at least was – who he claims to be.'

'Well, tell her about the thesis you promised me,' D. H. said. 'Otherwise I wouldn't have bothered hanging around Limbo for this long.'

Hillary reinforced her covering with a sheet. 'This better be good, Dylan.'

'To make a long story short,' Dylan began, like Benjamin trying to explain his connection with Mrs Robinson to her daughter. 'You remember that PhD I told you I started – on prose styles of D. H. Lawrence?'

'Not that again,' she said. 'Which you had the sense to drop when you got a real job. So what you're saying is that… D. H. here has come back to haunt you for not finishing it?'

She leaned forward and made a tentative jab at him, but of course her finger only displaced the adjacent air, yet she pulled it back as if she'd been stung.

---

[59] http://bit.ly/2ljakE8

D. H. winced. '*Haunt* is such a… pedestrian word. I prefer business mentor, in the current jargon.' He winked at Dylan. 'I've been reading up in my spare time.'

Hillary wheeled on Dylan. 'And you didn't think it was pertinent to let me know you were hearing or seeing… voices? And that I'd now be sharing this with you?'

'It could be worse,' D. H. sniffed. 'He could be of… the *other* persuasion… Which was never grounds for divorce in the UK – much to the displeasure of many wives who found out the hard way how the law defines adultery.'

'This is unhelpful, D. H.,' said Dylan, turning back to her. 'I was going to tell you, but I thought you might think I was mad or something. I mean, would you have believed me if I said I was having the odd chat with my literary hero – without clear evidence to back it up?'

'Flattery will get you everywhere,' said D. H. 'All the more reason to get back to that dissertation!'

Hillary hesitated. 'You're right. I probably would have thought you were on something, if not nuts.' She reached for the almost empty bottle of champagne and examined the label closely before sniffing the contents. 'Maybe it *has* been spiked. I wouldn't put it past brother Ben. Now there's someone who really *is* mental!'

'So you believe me – us?' said Dylan.

'We said for better or worse,' said Hillary, still regarding D. H. through narrowed eyes. 'But no more secrets, OK? And I'm not into threesomes – at least not yet, or probably ever – so could we agree that our bedroom is off-limits to Lady Chatterley Man?'

'Fine by me,' Dylan said, glancing at D. H.

'Of course, Dear Lady,' said D. H. 'Henceforth, I won't intrude on anything more intimate than a High Tea without a white flag. But I'll need you to give me one of those special winks that women are so good at *before* turning on your bedroom eyes[60].'

'Wait a minute,' said Dylan. 'What if it's my idea?'

'Men are so less subtle about their animal instincts,' said D. H., staring at Dylan's groin with a perfectly straight face.

'Maybe he does know women after all!' said Hillary, stifling a laugh.

Back at Penticton College, his wedding ring was noted by several pairs of eyes in Dylan's very first class, and Vanessa, a mature age student who Dylan had guessed was a bit older than he, but who wore very tight skirts to enhance her posture in the front row, couldn't resist as class ended. She came up to the lectern and leaned one elbow on it.

'Yes?' said Dylan. 'Are you still confused about *Leaves of Grass*?'

'Not at all,' she said, eyes glinting. 'Though I wonder what he's on about in the line *I do not hurt you any more than is necessary for you.* Was Whitman into rough sex?'

Dylan bit his lower lip. 'Out of that very long poem, you've picked that line – why?'

She paused a fraction of a second. 'I couldn't help but notice your wedding ring.'

He tilted his head. 'Which is supposed to make me an expert on Whitmanesque sex?'

'You tell me,' she teased. 'All I know is that there are a few disappointed girls in this class. You were the only single teacher in the Department up for grabs.'

Dylan smiled as distantly as he could manage. 'Then you can let the others know that I'm also not one for *rough marking* – so long as they write a good essay.'

She picked up his hand and rubbed her cheek against it. 'Such a waste,' she said, slowly backing away. 'But I'll do my very best for you, Dr Cashew, on the assignment – and during office hours, if you ever have a spare appointment time.'

---

[60] http://bit.ly/2BOeOcZ

'I-I don't have a PhD, Vanessa,' he said. 'As yet.'

She tilted her head. 'If you were my husband, I'd make sure you got onto that. Without one, you're just, well... an ordinary *Mr* Cashew.'

'Thanks, Vanessa,' he said, hastily stuffing notes back into his briefcase. 'I'll keep that in mind.'

He kept his eyes averted from her as she walked from class.

A bad feeling welled up in Dylan's chest two days later when Niall Campbell summoned him for a 'chat'.

Dylan hadn't mentioned anything to Hillary about his encounter with Vanessa. It was water under a dangerous bridge[61]. Anyway, what was there to confess?

As he walked to Campbell's office, he wondered if he should make a preemptive strike, in Establishment lingo, just to cover himself, before things got any more complicated. Vanessa was bright, and probably quite capable of "A" work, but what if her major essay came in at "B" level or even worse? Would she try to blackmail him by concocting some story about him trying to seduce her with a "lay-for-an-A" come-on?

But then maybe she was a harmless flirt, aware that he was married and safely out of bounds. He didn't pretend to understand women; maybe the whole thing was a trick of the mind.

Campbell was at his desk marking essays when Dylan knocked at the door. 'Come in, Cashew,' he grunted, eyes still cast down. 'Take a seat.'

Dylan scooted up a chair and sat down. 'You wanted to see me?'

'Yes,' said Campbell, finally looking up with a squint as though the sun was at Dylan's back. 'Just thought I'd check how you were getting on – with classes, and the like.'

Dylan thought he detected some special significance in the phrase *and the like*, but he was determined to play

---

[61] http://bit.ly/2C13zlf

innocent.

'I think it's still going well,' he said.

'Even with that American Lit survey?' Campbell said. 'It's a pretty demanding course, for any of us Canadians, I mean. *Leaves of Grass*, and all that over-written Romantic Yankee crap?'

'It grows on you,' said Dylan. 'I could never have lived at Walden Pond[62], but I enjoyed looking over Thoreau's shoulders.'

Campbell remained unimpressed. 'You're young. Hardly older than most of your students.'

Here we go, thought Dylan. 'I see that as an advantage,' he said, clearing his throat. 'I remember how I felt in my first literature class, studying the classics, wondering why we bothered – until it all made sense. And more than that, when they spoke to us in retirement village lingo.'

'Very good,' said Campbell, relaxing a bit. 'So long as we keep the... felt emotions on an impeccable plane.'

There were suddenly hot coals underfoot. 'Excuse me, Niall. Are you suggesting that I haven't been doing that?'

Campbell looked confused. 'Doing what?'

'Maintaining proper distance – in the classroom?'

'Not at all. I'm sure that things will be fine – now that you're visibly married.'

'So you think they weren't fine, before that?'

'Chill out, Dylan. I'm only saying that Penticton is a small town, and the College is an even smaller community. Gossip has a way of being blown out of proportion – speaking in general terms – if we give it oxygen[63].'

'Are we talking about Vanessa?'

'Vanessa?'

'You called me in here for something. Could we please cut the crap and get on with it?'

---

[62] http://bit.ly/2DoFFwC
[63] http://bit.ly/2E2aZSV

'All right, then. We can come back to Vanessa, or whatever her name is, later, if your conscience is bothering you. I actually called you in to say that your proposal for a student magazine has been approved, admittedly with minimal funding at this point, but, if all goes to plan, we might be able to improve on that if sponsors can be found.'

Dylan took a deep breath. 'Oh,' was all he could manage.

'A *thank you* wouldn't go astray at this point,' Campbell added, humming something like, 'an administrator's job is not a happy one. My take on Gilbert and Sullivan?'

'Sorry, Niall. If that's what it was about, I do certainly appreciate your efforts.'

'It *was* about Vanessa, too,' he said, returning his gaze to his papers.

'There's absolutely nothing to the gossip you've heard.'

'How can you say that until I tell you what I've heard?'

'OK, out with it – I'm listening.'

Niall leaned over the desk. 'I'm sure there's nothing to it.'

'How long are you planning to go around in circles with this?'

'Let's just say the feedback has come from a source other than Vanessa, concerned that she might be getting special treatment.'

'In exchange for…?'

'I'm sure there's nothing to it.'

'You keep saying that!'

'You *are* a happily married man, right?'

'Very much so!'

Campbell waved it away like a pesky fly. 'Then there's probably no substance to the chit-chat.'

'There *is* no substance to it!' said Dylan. 'OK, she's an attractive woman, and she knows it. She sits in the front row with her skin-tight, short skirts and flirts with me now and then. Maybe the others pick up on that. But I don't encourage her. Satisfied?'

Campbell managed a crooked smile. 'I believe you. It's an occupational hazard for us, this sort of thing. And it helps to be aware of the warning signs. That's all this is about – just to be sure you're on guard. Before a... situation develops.'

At the liquor store on his way home, Dylan found himself with a bottle of Hillary's favourite shiraz in each hand.

'No,' he said aloud. 'One bottle's romantic, two are apologetic.'

An attractive woman slipped between him and the shelf just as he put the second bottle back. 'Oh, dear,' she said, 'has someone been a *bad* boy lately?'

Dylan brandished his ring finger like a cross over a sleeping vampire. 'Till death do us part!'

'Pity,' the woman said over her shoulder. 'Vanessa is already disappointed!'

Dylan nearly dropped the orphan bottle. Either Niall Campbell was right about small town Penticton, or Vanessa had hired someone to stalk him.

'Excuse me...' he called out. But the woman had already disappeared around the aisle and out of the store.

He made sure the wine was properly aired and that his pumpkin risotto[64] was well and truly under way before Hillary arrived home.

'Mid-week?' she said, pointing at the wine bottle less than a minute inside the house. 'What have you done?'

'We've only been married for five minutes,' he said. 'I think that allows me a few excuses for romance.'

She tossed her bag onto the couch, gave him a big hug, followed by a playful slap on the bum. 'Mid-week shiraz plus risotto still smells a bit like guilt... darling!'

He freed himself from her grasp long enough to pour the wine and signal for her to stir the risotto.

'Cheers,' she said, with an expectant aftertaste in her kiss.

[64] http://bit.ly/2Ce9uTu

'All right,' he said. 'My Head of Department thinks I'm being chased by a horny woman. Satisfied?'

She didn't miss a beat. 'Just a student, then?'

'Why do you say that?'

'Well, with all due respect to your colleagues, I've sussed them out, and all of them are either too old to be bothered for the third or fourth time, – or batting for the other team.'

'Point One taken, Point Two, I hadn't really noticed.'

'What's her name, then?'

'Vanessa.'

'It's probably just hormones. This too will pass.'

'Niall suspects it's more than that.'

'Oh, dear. You're not up on charges, are you?'

He noticed the twinkle in her eyes. 'It may be perfectly innocent, but Niall points to gossip in the ranks.'

'Oh, to be eighteen, pimply and unrealistic again,' she laughed. 'Maybe you do need to go into publishing.'

Dylan decided not to correct her on Vanessa's age. 'How would that help?'

'A small firm,' she said, licking her finger and testing the air. 'With a finite and fairly stable supply of post-menopausal freelancers to make the slush pile tolerable.'

'And you'd be the head of PR?'

'Off and on. Mostly off, but on often enough to head off any harems forming under my watch!'

From the instant Niall confirmed that the student magazine was a goer, Dylan began to wonder if it was a good idea. He tried to make the appeal in the department newsletter for student assistants as bland as possible:

Announcing a new quarterly literary publication, *Daedalus' Wings*. Seeking dedicated student volunteers to assist with editorial and marketing work. No pay. Class credit may however be negotiated. Submit expressions of interest to Mr Cashew by next Friday.

D. H. was waiting for him back in his office after he delivered the notice to the departmental secretary for distribution.

'You'll be swamped,' D. H. said. 'Everyone wants to be published. Few are worthy.'

'So you're not omnipotent after all,' said Dylan. 'I specifically did not say that applicants could contribute to the magazine.'

'But you didn't specifically rule it out, either.'

Dylan hesitated. 'Surely they would understand –'

'Hope burns eternal[65],' said D. H., wagging a finger at him. 'Dreams can be as soft-boned as a mouse in the cracked wall of opportunity.'

'I really wish you'd stop trying to be poetic. I don't know where to begin in unmixing those metaphor[66].'

'They'll tempt you with secret fiction, unless you put a stop to it. Now.'

Dylan opened his mouth to protest but thought better of it. D. H. clearly had future powers as well as past vision.

'Just to make you happy,' he said, already one foot out the door.

By the time he reached the secretary's office it was too late. There was a pile of photocopied notices on her desk, and she and her assistant were busily stuffing envelopes.

'Almost finished, Mr Cashew,' the secretary smiled. 'Is there anything else we can do for you?'

Dylan might have just imagined a hint of flirtation in her tone.

'Uh, no,' he said, striking a casual pose in the doorway. 'Let me thank you for all your help – and efficiency.'

'That's quite all right,' said the secretary. 'In thanks, we wouldn't mind a drink after work one day – or better still the Association's support in our pay dispute with the College.'

[65] http://bit.ly/2CgkPCC
[66] http://bit.ly/2mVctGP

Dylan didn't have a clue what she was on about, at least on the latter point, but made a mental note that, as newly confirmed President of the Faculty Association, he'd better form a view on that.

'Of course,' he said. 'Can you send me a backgrounder on that for our next meeting?'

The secretary lowered her voice. 'They'll be plenty of time for that – if we have to go out on strike!'

Dylan had never been a joiner, least of all a union member, so he didn't have much of a clue about what going out on strike meant. He recalled a few whispers in the corridors about how negotiations between the College administration and the support staff union had been strained for months, but he assumed it was bluff on both sides and that the parties would settle before it came to anything so dramatic as a walk out. In any case, what could that possibly have to do with the Faculty Association?

He thought he'd better check with his Vice President, Chantelle, just in case.

As it happened, when he arrived at her office, there were three other faculty members already cramped inside, including Joseph.

'Dylan!' cried Chantelle, as the others turned to look at him. 'I was just about… to ring you.'

Something in her tone made Dylan doubt that, but he decided to go with the flow[67]. 'Oh, what about?'

Chantelle hesitated. 'Come in, and shut the door.'

It all seemed a bit cloak-and-daggery, but Dylan did as he was told.

'We've got a bit of a… situation developing,' said Nadine, who Dylan recognised as the head of the Nursing faculty.

'Yes, a situation,' coughed Joel, the head of Chemistry.

'OK, what's up?' asked Dylan.

---

[67] http://bit.ly/2BKn2CB

Chantelle, who was chewing a nail, reminded herself not to do it. 'We have it, on reliable advice, that the support staff will be going on strike tomorrow.'

'I thought she was kidding,' said Dylan.

'Who?' asked Joseph.

'Our department secretary,' said Dylan.

'Marilyn,' Chantelle said. 'As Faculty Association President, Dylan, you really need to remember the names of key support staff, especially their Shop Steward.'

'Sorry,' said Dylan. 'I'm not very good with names... Chantelle.'

'Thanks for remembering mine,' said Chantelle. 'Anyway, I think you need to call a special meeting of the Association.'

'Why?' said Dylan. 'We're not the ones going on strike.'

'No,' said Joseph. 'But there will be a picket line.'

Dylan knew just enough about unions to know about picket lines. 'So are you worried that our members won't cross, or that they will?'

Joel stiffened in his chair. 'The admin will expect us to cross, and the support staff will expect us to respect the line. We could end up meat in someone else's sandwich.'

Dylan shook his head. 'Isn't up to them to work it out?'

Chantelle took a deep breath. 'Look, there will be pregnant women on the picket line. There will be workers at or near retirement age. And there's a cold snap forecasted for the rest of the week.'

'Bad timing,' said Dylan. 'They should have waited till Spring.'

'You've only been here five minutes,' said Joel. 'These so-called negotiations have been going on for over a year.'

'Wait a minute,' Dylan said, waving his arms. 'We're an association, not a union. So we're not entitled to respect picket lines. Wouldn't that be illegal?'

'Quite right,' said Chantelle. 'And many of our members will take that as an excuse to do nothing. But others will say we have a moral obligation to respect the rights of other workers, especially when we depend on them to get things done. If those people refuse to cross the picket line without the support of the Association, the College could fire them.'

'Surely it would never come to that!' said Dylan.

'Like I said,' Joel said, wringing his hands, 'You've been here five minutes!'

Dylan turned to Joseph. 'Yeah, and *someone* convinced me that becoming President would be a cakewalk[68]!'

It was too late in the day to organise a special meeting of the Association, but they agreed to come in early the next morning to get out the word as quickly as possible. Chantelle rang Marilyn to explain the situation, then, after what seemed like a tense conversation, hung up the phone.

'She's not happy,' said Chantelle. 'But she's agreed to instruct her members not to make a scene if faculty cross the line tomorrow – at least until we have our meeting.'

'Have they ever gone on strike before?' asked Dylan.

'No,' said Chantelle.

'Then maybe the admin will see they're serious, and settle.'

'And maybe they won't,' said Joel. 'If they save heaps of money for every day the strike goes on, where's their incentive?'

What have I gotten myself into? Dylan thought, in yet another déjà vu moment.

It was well below freezing when Dylan left the building for home. His car spluttered a few times with each turn of the key but then finally roared to life. As he backed out, D. H. appeared in the passenger seat.

'Minus ten degrees, to be precise,' said D. H. 'It'll be worse before dawn when the pickets set up their line.'

Dylan skidded slightly on a patch of ice before edging the car forward. 'I've never had to cross a picket line before,

[68] http://bit.ly/2C29KWo

D. H.'

D. H.'s head sagged back against the seat. 'They're a terrible thing – strikes. It's not just workers against owners. They can set village against village, even members of a family against each other. My father was one of those who defied the union and gave up the strike in Nottinghamshire. They called him a scab, but what choice did they have? It's all about the balance of power, and, if the workers don't have it, they starve or freeze.'

'You fictionalised it, didn't you?'

'Yes, in *Lady Chatterley*. I made her pathetic husband a mine owner. With all the controversy that book faced abroad for its sex scenes, at home they just hated it for the way I portrayed the characters, which they thought were real, which they weren't – and yet they were.'

Large flakes of snow were drifting down on the windscreen. Dylan switched on the wipers.

'Do you reckon books make any difference?' Dylan asked.

'Yes,' said D. H. 'They give writers something to do instead of crossing a picket line!'

Chapter 8: Colder Inside Than Out

NEXT MORNING, DYLAN WOULD HAVE WELCOMED THE EXCUSE OF HAVING SOMETHING TO WRITE, or even publish, rather than having to go into campus.

Hillary saw it in his eyes. 'I don't suppose you could call in sick?'

'I'm President of the Faculty Association – how would that look?'

'Not good,' she conceded. 'Even worse than not good.'

'I wonder if they would accept a medical certificate signed by a public relations consultant?'

'I doubt it,' she laughed. 'My handwriting is too legible!'

'D. H. reckons I should respect the line.'

'Does he now?' she smirked. 'He's still granting you private audiences, then? And where is our peeping tom[69] this morning?'

He shrugged. 'Where the action is. Said he hasn't witnessed a good strike since management tried to starve out the coal miners back in the Midlands.'

'Ah, yes, the good old days. Someone should write about it.'

'Not this boy. I just want to keep my head down, teaching notes in order, and just think of where we'll take our summer holidays – in Scotland, of course.'

'Do you get paid if the college shuts down?'

'Who said anything about the college shutting down?'

She smiled. 'Naiveté is one of your endearing traits, darling. If the picket line holds, there'll be no teaching, and if there are no teachers to teach, admin may try to cut their losses.'

69 http://bit.ly/2BM6cDF

'OR they could settle the dispute by putting a bit more money on the table.'

'Which would be a sign of weakness, especially with contract negotiations coming up soon with the Faculty Association, right? And every other major employer in Penticton will be watching for signs of weakness that could affect negotiations with *their* support staff.'

Dylan nodded. 'The old snowball effect, eh?'

'Speaking of which, the college admin might reckon they have the weather on their side, and hold out until the cold has frozen a few toes. No, this won't be over in a day or two.'

'In which case, the faculty will need a plan.'

'Yes, they will,' she said, wrapping her arms around him. 'That's where you come in, Mr President!'

'I... have papers to mark!'

A light snow was falling in the darkness, glistening in the headlights as Dylan drove into the campus. He was hoping to see a few scattered pickets, huddling with placards around some fiery drums to keep warm. What he found was worse – far worse – than that.

There was a line of several cars in the entrance drive, and they were going nowhere. There was a picket line all right, but it comprised dozens of burly men shouting at the passengers and even pounding on the windows and the front of the cars. Clouds of steam drifted above the shouting men, vanishing into the darkness. There were only a few faces that Dylan recognised from the support staff, including Marilyn, the shop steward, who spotted him before he saw her.

He rolled down his window as she reached his car. 'Morning, Marilyn,' he ventured.

'Hey, Dylan,' she grimaced. 'We have a... situation here, which has the potential to turn ugly – unless you get off your butt. Follow me!'

It was not a request.

Dylan left his engine running and followed her over to a clutch of men who turned to meet their approach. He didn't know a single one of them – except of course for D. H., who was lingering on the fringes rubbing his hands. The introductions were brief and to the point, and Dylan just as quickly forgot their names as he stamped his feet to keep warm.

D. H. came up to stand invisibly next to him. 'You don't want to mess with these blokes,' he said. 'They represent some of the toughest unions in the Province. Simon there is one of the top guns from the BCFL.'

'BCFL?'

'BC Federation of Labor. And not just the Okanagan Branch. He's from head office.'

As if to confirm D. H.'s espionage, Simon thrust his hand in Dylan's direction. 'My name's Simon, Simon Gallagher, and I'm from the---'

'BC Federation of Labor?' said Dylan.

'No credit necessary,' smirked D. H., as if in anticipation of Dylan turning to him.

'I'm impressed, comrade,' said Simon. 'You've done your homework!'

'Thanks,' said Dylan. 'I guess you haven't come all the way from Vancouver for the cross-country skiing.'

Simon cleared his throat. 'Too right. We have a picket line here. It consists of workers at the very lowest of pay scales in the Province who are seeking justice, equity in the workplace. Loyal trade unionists, every last one of them. Are you a card carrier, Mr Cashew?'

'Call me Dylan,' said Dylan, stamping his feet again to bring the fading sensation back into his toes. 'My father was, and his father before him.'

Simon sighed. 'Cutting to the chase, then, you're *not* a union member, right?'

'Well, there's some ambiguity on that point,' Dylan replied. 'Our Faculty Association's constitution refers to us as a union, so---'

'Oops,' winced D. H. 'You should have seen this coming!'

'What?' muttered Dylan.

'From where I stand,' Simon went on, taking note of Dylan muttering seemingly to himself. 'Your so-called union, which doesn't even have the guts to call itself one, is piss-weak. Made up of latte-sipping[70] jokers who would cross a comrade's picket line if they could get away with it.' With that he leaned down, nose to nose with Dylan. 'But surely that doesn't include you, Mr Cashew, as President of this piss-weak *Association*?'

Dylan stood his ground. 'You know we don't have the right to strike.'

Simon laughed. 'Like I said, piss-weak. You don't have the *legal* right to strike. Let me tell you… comrade, if unions in this country always did what was legal, we'd still be working in sweatshops.'

'OK,' said Dylan, trying to avoid a latte tone. 'Your union is taking legal action here, and however much my Association members might sympathise, we would be breaking the law if we honoured your picket line.'

'It's us or them, comrade,' said D. H. with a wry grin. 'Non-fiction writers or novelists: pick your side.'

Marilyn elbowed in. 'We know you're caught between a rock and a hard place,' she said. 'But I think Simon and I have worked out a temporary fix that might just work for you – and us.'

'I'm listening,' said Dylan, not wanting to mention that he'd now lost all sensation in his fingers, despite his rabbit fur-lined gloves.

It took a while, but eventually all the faculty got the message that teaching was off for the day, and they were to

[70] http://bit.ly/2C0TpkJ

assemble in the cafeteria for a briefing on the situation. The smell of vending machine instant coffee was thick in the air as they congregated in little groups to gossip.

Dylan finally had to rap a spoon sharply on his table to get their attention.

'Thank you all for coming at such short notice,' he began. 'I think we certainly have a quorum today.'

'Who called this meeting?' someone called from the back. 'My students are having snowball fights rather than attending my captivating lectures.'

'The only thing captivating about them, Bob,' the woman next to him replied even louder, 'is the *captive* audience!'

Begrudging scattered laughter followed to which Dylan held up his hand. 'We all want to get back to our classrooms, but we can't ignore what's going on out there.'

'Yes, we can,' said one of the business instructors. 'This is between the College and support staff, not us.'

'*Our* support staff,' Dylan corrected him. These are people we see every day, shovelling snow, fixing our computers, brewing *decent* coffee.' He held up his paper coffee cup and wrinkled his nose in disdain.

'There's a lot more at stake here than barista coffee[71],' one of the business instructor's colleagues piped in. 'Like our jobs?'

Joseph, who was sitting next to Dylan at the head table, elbowed him. 'You need to call the meeting to order,' he muttered, 'before things get completely out of control.'

'Point taken,' said Dylan, rapping the table with his spoon again as if everyone had heard Joseph. 'This special meeting of the Association is hereby called to order. If you want to be heard, you must first be recognised by the Chair.' He impressed himself with his decisiveness.

A hand shot up from one of the young nursing instructors in the front row.

---

[71] http://bit.ly/2DoPR8g

'Yes, Belinda?' said Dylan. 'Do you have a contrary opinion?'

'No,' she said, 'a positive one. There's a moral issue here. Most of us in this room regard ourselves as professionals, somehow better than those people out there, but we're all workers, and if the College has their way with the strikers, we could be next.'

Dylan let it go on for a bit like that until it was clear that opinion was divided. 'OK,' he said. 'Everyone's put in their two cents. Now you need to know what will happen if we don't respect the picket line. I was told that the Labor Feds see this as a cause cèlebré. They've brought in their heavies to enforce the picket line. It could well get serious. Really serious.'

'Or they could be bluffing.' someone called out.

'True,' said Dylan. 'And then again they might not be. They gave us a free pass today to debate the issue. Tomorrow could be a different story.'

There was an uncomfortable shifting of bums on seats. Dylan sensed the time was right to spill the beans about the interim compromise he'd reached with the Labor rep. The cafeteria would be regarded as neutral ground, and the Association members could cross the picket line to debate the issue – until they reached a final decision about whether or not to support the strike.

'They don't expect us to strike,' Dylan added. 'Just to stop work until the College agrees to negotiate in good faith.'

'That could take ages!' the same business instructor said. 'And what about our students? Where's the neutral ground for *them* if they cross?'

'First things first,' said Dylan. 'We need a motion to debate.'

Joseph put up his hand. 'I move that we serve notice to the College that we are stopping work effective immediately until an agreement is reached between the College and the support staff union.'

'That's blackmail!' the business instructor said.

'I prefer to call it a pressure tactic[72],' Marilyn said, with the faintest trace of a smile. 'Right now they have the weather on their side. This would just even things up a bit.'

After much discussion and wringing of hands, the motion was passed by a surprisingly large majority, but only after Dylan pledged to let the College admin know about the Association's plan, and then, pulling a final rabbit out of his hat, guaranteed that a settlement would follow in no more than a week after they pulled the plug.

'You're the one mixing metaphors now,' the invisible voice of D. H. whispered in his ear, 'but I like it!'

Dylan knew that simple words wouldn't win the day with admin, so he typed up a press release on Association letterhead and had it at the ready for his meeting with Frank Browbait, the College's President.

Dr Browbait was halfway through his mid-morning scotch, the glass of which he had hidden in the top drawer of his desk just as Dylan and Joseph were shown in by his secretary.

'Nasty out there,' Browbait said, gesturing at the window behind him.

'The snow or the strike?' Joseph said.

'Another rhetorical question from the Association's ex-president?' Browbait smirked, looking straight at Dylan.

'A bit of both,' Dylan said, handing him the press release. 'But mostly the strike.'

'What have we here?' said the President, skimming it. 'A wildcat strike? You must be kidding me.'

'The phrase I use is "job action".'

'Same difference,' grumbled Browbait. 'You've only been president for the blink of a sow's eye. I can't expect you to understand what a wimpy group of members you have. They'll never go out as one.'

---

[72] http://bit.ly/2BNwF3s

'This isn't a bluff,' said Joseph. 'The motion was unanimous.'

Browbait yawned. 'Faculty have never gone out on strike in British Columbia. And they won't start here.'

'There's a first time for everything,' said Dylan.

'You've read your contract, Mr President?' said Browbait. 'Including the clause in the *Higher Education Act* where it deems your work as an essential service, forbidding strike action?'

'Yes,' said Dylan. 'I've also read the *Labor Relations Act* clause where it claims to take precedence over other legislation seeking to curb union rights.'

The smirk dissolved from Browbait's face. 'That amendment has never been tested in the courts,' he coughed.

'There's always a first time,' Dylan said, pressing his advantage.

'You *are* bluffing,' Browbait said. 'And the media won't be interested in your little press release, with its literary turn of phrase.'

'They will,' said Joseph, rising from his chair, and pointing out the window at the snow, which was coming down all the heavier, virtually obscuring the distant picket line, 'if you don't agree to go back and bargain in good faith with the support staff.'

'Bluffing,' insisted Browbait. '*Bluffing!*'

And so it was that Dylan and Joseph returned to the cafeteria empty handed, but defiant, answering a barrage of questions from those who had lost the vote on job action and who feared the College would come down hard on them for choosing sides in the dispute.

Morning droned on into afternoon, and the staff brought out their lunches to chew on thoughtfully, dreadingly. Some even attempted to mark assignments. Snow continued to fall as the afternoon thickened into a funereal grey, obscuring the picketers until quitting time when Dylan had to inch his car along behind the motorcade, trying to strike a pose between serious and affirmative as he formed eye contact with the probing stares of the immobile strike leaders.

It reminded him too much of the last lines of that story by Joyce that he'd almost memorised about the snow falling, falling incessantly on the graves of the dead and the soon-to-be-dead.

Hillary was busily sautéing onions and didn't detect the wine until Dylan had set both bottles of red down on the countertop and popped the first cork.

'*Two* bottles now, and at *mid-week*?' she said. 'I'll make a Scot out of you yet.'

Without a word, he fetched three wine glasses from the cupboard.

'Company?' she said. 'You might have rung.'

'No,' he said. 'I thought D. H. might join us.'

She added some meat to the pan, and a pleasant aroma almost circulated through the kitchen.

'What have you done?' she said, stirring in some curry sauce. 'Or what's been done to you?'

'More the latter,' he confessed, 'but a generous dollop of the former, too.'

'You'd have been proud of him,' said D. H., lifting the open bottle to pour the first glass of wine.

Hillary's jaw dropped but no words came out.

'How'd you do that?' said Dylan.

'A guest always offers to pour,' said D. H., not spilling a drop.

'But you're a---' stammered Hillary.

'A presence, not a ghost,' said D. H., offering her the glass, 'There's an important difference, Dear Lady!'

'We're waiting,' said Dylan.

'Of course eating and drinking in the physical sense is

only pretend. But I was allowed to retain a certain affinity to wine, especially when it's offered.'

'You knew he could do this?' Hillary said to Dylan. 'We agreed – no more secrets, right?'

'I didn't know,' Dylan protested. 'It was more of a symbolic gesture, like the Jews do at Passover, filling the extra glass of wine for Elijah[73].'

'I've drained a few glasses at the appointed time, before the father could secretly drink them,' said D. H. 'Always happy to be of help at a sacred time.'

'Enough of this,' Hillary said, gesturing at the second glass, which D. H. had filled just as precisely as the first. 'Get that down you and then tell me exactly what happened today.'

Dylan was slurring his words before he knew it.

'You'd have been proud of him,' D. H. said, staying a half a glass ahead of them.

'Not that you were of much help,' Dylan accused, 'especially with that toad of a college president.'

'I was *busy*,' D. H. claimed.

'Excuse me, was there a snowball fight I missed?' Dylan said.

'Ingratitude, thy name is Dylan,' said D. H. 'I was in Vancouver, pouring oil into the ear of the Minister of Labor.'

'The Minister of Labour?' said Dylan. 'Wouldn't it have made more sense in the ear of the Minister of Education?'

'You still have a lot to learn about politics,' said D. H. 'I could write a book on it. Might still do it – through a ghost ghost writer, of course.'

It didn't happen overnight. In fact, it didn't happen after the second night. But on Day 3, after the assembled lecturers were working their way through their tasteless sandwiches, the call came.

[73] http://bit.ly/2laOCmi

A small crowd gathered around Dylan as he listened to the distant voices. There was a string of nods and the occasional 'yes' but no one other than Dylan knew what was going on.

At long last he set the phone down and rejoined the head table. He gazed at his half-eaten sandwich thoughtfully then looked up.

'Well?' asked one of the lecturers. 'What gives?'

'Apparently the story is all over the CBC News, with a big spread this morning in the *Vancouver Sun*. The Minister of Labor has summoned both sides to Vancouver by government jet. They're meeting right now.'

'The Minister of Labor?' asked one of the business instructors. 'Shouldn't that be the Minister of Education?'

Dylan shot him a patronising stare. 'Don't you know anything about politics?'

The rest of the day passed slowly, and then they were into the next day. The instructors' bank of assignments already marked, spontaneous games of poker and bridge were brought out. Coins and then bills began to appear on the table, and Dylan noticed furtive sips from flasks concealed in backpacks and briefcases. Petty bickering[74] ensued. Facial stubble prospered.

Then, in a Disney moment, the snow stopped. Seconds later the clouds parted enough to free slender rays of sunshine from detention. As Dylan kept staring at the phone like a love-deprived teenager.

Finally, it rang.

Dylan suppressed the impulse to dash for it, knowing he would more than likely trip over the obstacle course of briefcases and make a fool of himself.

It was Simon, the Fed of Labor rep.

'Greetings, Dylan,' he said, his tone not giving anything away.

---

[74] http://bit.ly/2I8ETx2

On his way back to the head table, Dylan enjoyed the sight of the crowd of anxious instructors parting like the Red Sea before matzoh balls. Reaching the front table, he motioned for them to resume their seats, but no one did. They wanted the Word, and they wanted it Now. So he did something he'd never done before. He pulled out a chair and climbed onto the head table to address them. Only then did he see a clutch of TV cameras and microphones at the back of the room.

It was an historic moment. He could almost taste the headlines:

Rookie Faculty President Pulls Off Coup

He heard cameras clicking. Cameras whirling. He felt like Thoreau arriving back in Concord after his extended camping trip.

'I have good news and better news...' he began.

The air was electric. Micro-shafts of lightning burning over their heads.

'Start with the better news!' someone shouted off to one side.

'No,' Dylan laughed. 'The good news is that at precisely 4:02pm Pacific Time, the College signed a contract with our support staff union.'

The ensuing clapping was the overdue thunder from the mini lightning bolts.

'What's the *better* news?' someone else ventured.

'The parties actually reached an agreement mid-morning,' Dylan went on, 'but the College told the arbitrator that they intended to sue the Association and especially its executive members for breach of contract.

Cameras began to flash again, and a hush broke out over the room.

'But the union negotiators refuse to sign the agreement until the College guaranteed no action would be taken against you and your executive. The College refused to budge for more than four hours. It took a walkout by the union negotiators to settle it. In the words of the union's chief negotiator, "When he finally signed, it looked like President Browbait had just come out of a hernia operation[75] without anaesthetic!"'

The joy in the room was thicker than strawberry cheesecake, and someone even broke into "Solidarity forever", tripping over the words, before being stared down. They may have taken action, but they weren't a union – yet.

The nearby pub had never seen so many patrons from the College at one time.

Hillary steered him out of there some hours later. He had a grateful glaze in his eyes.

'It was on every news report since 5pm,' she said. 'I especially liked the hook that said, and I quote, "Freshman Penticton faculty president leads wildcat strike – and gets away *Scot*-free."'

'A baptism of fire, all right,' Dylan acknowledged. 'But it wasn't a wildcat, and they didn't even get my nationality right. Who the bloody hell told them I was an American?'

'Where to from here, my hero?' said Hillary, backing out the car across the crunchy snow. 'State politics? Federal politics? Maybe even the United Nations?'

'I don't know,' said Dylan, suddenly far away. 'Now that I've pulled this off, they'll expect Spiderman every day. Maybe I should quit while I'm ahead.'

'You're joking. You look good in a limelight suit.'

But, as Hillary was soon to learn, limelight wasn't his colour.

---

[75] http://bit.ly/2pK0laY

PART 2: GENESIS

In the Beginning there were no books, no toll-free numbers to Heaven, and even the Snake could not take trees for granted.

Chapter 9: From Germ to an Idea

FLASH FORWARD TEN YEARS, SHORT ONE DAY. WHY? Isn't there more to explore in the journey of Dylan the wildcat president, and then Dylan the chief contract negotiator, even more despised by the College administration, and then Dylan the candidate for Provincial Member of Parliament, who only lost by a cat's whisker becoming Minister for Tourism when the party president spooked the Catholics by threatening not to lower but rather not to increase funding for their schools. Of course there is. But once again you remind me that you were expecting a story about publishing not politicking, and you now know far more than you need to about this reluctant president, reluctant negotiator, reluctant potential MP, so it's high time we see what made Dylan into the publisher he never expected to become.

If the true fiction be known, the more Dylan worked for other people the less he liked it. Nine years and three hundred and sixty-four days on, Dylan was unanimously elected to be English Department Chair, partly because he had now resigned from his Association work, but mostly because the other department members didn't want to do it, and Joseph had sworn to retreat to a seminary if they elected him again. Dylan didn't want to do it either, but 364 days on, he didn't want to do it less than other members on the day didn't want to do it more, and so, predictably, he was elected, cornered.

He had a day in hand before he would be officially appointed to the post and so that evening, well into a bottle of scotch, Hillary cut to the chase.

'So why don't you want to be department chair?' she asked, contemplating the last slice of spicy pizza left in the box.

'I just don't,' he said.

'You didn't want to be Association President, either,' she went on, waving the slice in mid-air in triumph, 'but you accepted. You didn't want to be chief negotiator, but you took it on. You didn't want to run for Parliament but let yourself be pushed into it. So why not this?'

'I'd hate it,' said Dylan, making a half-hearted lunge at the slice before she chomped on it.

'Then why did you accept the nomination?'

'There wasn't anyone else.'

'There wasn't anyone else either for president or chief negotiator, but you accepted those posts. There was hardly anyone else for party candidate nominee but you let yourself be drafted to run---'

'That was different. Max Framer was a two-timer loser and a drunk. I couldn't vote for him any more, so yes I agreed to run against him on principle.'

'Don't get me wrong,' Hillary went on, licking her fingers. 'I didn't mind the sessions until two o'clock in the morning marking your students' essays, or even when that twice-divorced party strategist took it upon herself to restock your wardrobe with "more acceptable" outfits, straighten your tie in front of the cameras, and practically pinch your nipples off-camera, but I was just amazed that you didn't realise how close you came to be foisted into that poor excuse for an adult childcare centre they call a Parliament!'

The longer her sentences went on, the more slurred her words became, but Dylan hardly noticed since he was processing only every other word at best.

'A chance is as good as a holiday,' Dylan reminded her.

'Don't you mean a *change*?'

'Whatever. In any case, that's water through the culvert,' winked Dylan.

Hillary thought about that expression then rolled back her eyes. 'So, if they won't let you be a president or a chief negotiator anymore, and you don't want to be a chair, or a two-time loser as candidate, what do you want to do?'

'Starting tomorrow?'

'You can't accept the position and then just resign.'

'I could.'

'Think on the bright side: with your reduced teaching load, you'd have half the marking.'

'And twice the number of migraines.'

'You've never had a migraine.'

'I would, starting tomorrow!'

With the foot closest to him, she crushed the innocent lid of the empty pizza box on the coffee table. 'Don't change the subject. What do you want to be when you grow up?'

'A poet.'

'Don't be silly – you've never written a poem.'

'I have,' he insisted.

'How, what, where, when, why?' she blurted.

'There was that girl in my first year of university whose father owned a toy shop that I fell in love with---'

'The girl or the toy shop?' she smirked. 'Another misplaced modifier. Nah, nah, nah, nah, nah!'

'I would never write an ode to a toy shop[76],' he said, pretending deflation.

'Prove it,' she dared. 'Show me the poems.'

'You're jealous!'

'No, I just want proof. So go lift up the floorboards, or wherever you've hidden them, and show me.'

'I… burnt them.'

'No!'

'She dumped me, for an English exchange student called Orange, so I burnt them.'

'What a load of crap – even for you. Burnt Orange, indeed!'

---

[76] http://bit.ly/2BLuTA3

He sniffed. 'There was something lost in the ashes of those poems that I want to rekindle...'

She paused. 'I think you're more pissed than I am, and that's saying something.'

'Only joking,' he said. 'They *were* crap, and rightly torched. But now I want to give it a go again.'

'And how will you support yourself?' she said, surprisingly sober. 'Remember our deal?'

'Of course. I fully intend to pay my own way.'

'With poetry? Dream on!'

'No, as a *publisher*.' he said, as if it had just occurred to him.

Her lower jaw dropped to unprecedented depths. 'You know even less about publishing than you do about poetry.'

'True,' he said. 'If it's a double learning curve, I'll never be bored.'

Dylan woke up the next morning resolved. He would do the right thing and serve notice to the College until the end of the semester, which was only three weeks away. That would give the department plenty of time to find a replacement chair, maybe even hire an off-balance new staff member with prior experience and kill two birds with red pen.

Hillary, brewing coffee, noticed that his lower lip was firmer[77] than usual.

'You don't have to go through with this, you know,' she said, 'We could write it off to an autonomous bottle of scotch.'

'Lately, I do my best thinking under the influence,' he countered. 'That's how I'll draft my first poetry book. Before editing it in a somewhat more sober state, of course.'

'Be serious for a change,' she said. 'Last night could be our secret, consigned to the archives of mistakes we almost made.'

'So you think this would be a mistake? I thought that Scots were an adventurous breed.'

---

[77] http://bit.ly/2C1Lsvx

'We're more practical than adventurous. I don't want you getting frustrated by staring at the proverbial blank page for days on end, waiting for the poetry muse to wink at you.'

D. H. materialised wearing a mortarboard. 'Stick by your guns, Dylan. If you fail at poetry and publishing, there's always the academy to retreat to.'

Dylan took his appearance in stride, as if he was on cue. 'If I get stuck, you can be my muse.'

'I wasn't much of a cross-dresser, though,' said D. H., adopting an awkward pose he must have thought resembled a transvestite.

'Do what you want,' said Hillary, smiling at D. H.'s antics as she poured the coffee. 'I might even support you more than usual if it doesn't work out – for a while.'

'Or better yet,' said D. H., 'take the long view, finish your book on me, and hop on the academic circuit. I can give you insights that will make you a leading Lawrence scholar.'

'Not the *leading* Lawrence scholar?' Dylan said.

'I can give you an advantage but no guarantee,' said D. H. 'The Einstein of Lawrence may already be on the scene.'

Dylan snatched his lunchbox from the fridge. 'There's no reason I can't work on the thesis in between publishing *and* writing poetry. I'm off.'

'That's the spirit!' said D. H., opening the door for him. 'Publishers and poets may come and go, but the Classics live forever!'

President Browbait was grumpier than usual that morning. The College budget had been knocked back by the State Treasurer, and he had a short deadline by which he had to resubmit it. Or rather, his bursar had the deadline since Browbait had a hatred for columns and rows of figures only exceeded by his dislike for unionists or their next of kin, Association officers.

The instant his receptionist Miss Frumpley notified him by intercom that Dylan was outside, Browbait assumed a strike position[78].

'See him in,' he replied, flicking his tongue.

As he slipped in the room, Dylan seemed somewhat smaller than Browbait remembered from his nightmare years as president and chief negotiator.

'Good morning, Cashew,' he said, grudgingly. 'Congratulations on your election as Chair. I look forward to working with you in a somewhat less confrontational role for a change.'

'That's what I'm here about,' said Dylan. 'I intend to resign as Chair as soon as possible.'

'Impossible!' Browbait blurted. 'I haven't accepted your appointment as yet.'

'I've got a Get Out Of Admin free card,' said Dylan. 'And I'm sure you'll be happy to see the back of me after our harsh words over the years.'

'Not at all,' said Browbait. 'I've enjoyed all those hours of strain and strife. Not to mention the medication I've been on to treat my bleeding ulcers. The College will be a dull place without you deconstructing the cogs of sound administration.'

'I'll take it, then, that you have no objection to my serving notice?'

'Notice?' said Browbait. 'You can leave today if you want to.' He caught himself. 'Then again, we wouldn't want your colleagues, or the media, to draw the wrong conclusion.'

'And what would that be?'

'That I had somehow induced you to leave – with a golden handshake, perhaps.'

'Or a sharpened hatchet?'

Browbait paused. 'And be an extra[79] in some murder mystery? Too messy.' He adopted an almost friendly tone.

---

[78] http://bit.ly/2pKXLa7
[79] http://bit.ly/2lmPhk6

'So what will you do, out in the real world. Start your own political party?'

'I want to write a book of poetry.'

'You could have done that here – if you hadn't been so determined to meddle in other people's affairs.'

Dylan leaned over Browbait's desk and stared him right in the left eye. 'You don't get it. I didn't want any of that.'

'You *stood* for Association president. You seemed to relish your role as contract negotiator. You *ran* for political office. Sure smacks of ambition to me.'

'I was adrift in a sea of indifference. Last penguin standing.'

'Good luck to you, then,' said Browbait, withering slightly with forced sincerity. 'Poetry? I'll wager you'll be back in six months, red pen at the ready.'

'Marking's the worst part,' Dylan said, feeling like he had to repay the president's slip with something. 'It drains you of every ounce of originality.'

'Really? You should try administration.' Browbait smiled in spite of himself. 'Second thought---'

Dylan felt a twang of empathy for the president then, but he got over it just as quickly. He was in training for becoming a publisher, and publishers couldn't afford to be empathetic.

His colleagues in the department were ten-pin-bowled by the news, to say the least. They fell into two camps – those who were openly critical of Dylan, calling him self-centred and irresponsible, and those, like Joseph, who were silently envious of him taking a leap from the hammock of employment to venture into the shark-infested waters of irregular pay cheques, or worse. By the end of the meeting, though, most of them wished him well, and even expressed interest in his new publishing venture.

Joseph stayed behind after the others had left. Dylan thought he saw a bit of moisture in the corner of his eyes and couldn't put it down to dust in the air.

'Ten years,' Joseph remarked. 'It's been more than that since we interviewed you for the job.'

'Call me Sylvia Plath,' said Dylan. 'Time to take my head out of the oven.'

Joseph nodded. 'Some of your colleagues see it as quite the opposite.'

'And you?'

'I've got a wife and three children and a mortgage that won't go away. You have a wife and no children and a month by month flat. You can afford to take risks.'

'Just as well our stove is electric,' said Dylan. 'Although, one day, I hope to cook with gas[80].'

In the days that followed, Dylan had no trouble keeping himself busy during the day setting up his writing space and musing on shortcuts to becoming a publishing executive. When the words wouldn't come, as they mostly didn't in the first few weeks, and he tired of D. H. staring over his shoulder at his attempts to draft out romantic poems about their camping trips in Saskatchewan[81], he spent hours poring through issues of magazines like *Publisher's Weekly*, as well as searching on the Internet for advice on independent publishing.

It was in the former that he noticed the ad:

Applications for the Radcliffe College Publishing Course are open now. In this intensive, highly acclaimed six weeks course, you'll get the inside story from industry experts. Apply now!

'Do you believe in fate?' he asked Hillary that evening as they finished dinner.

'Did Lady Macbeth wear glass slippers?'

'I'm serious!'

'And I'm Scottish,' she said, tossing some salt from the grinder over her left shoulder. 'Of course I believe in it. Why?'

---

[80] http://bit.ly/2Cflxxt
[81] http://bit.ly/2DmCaGY

He pulled out the ad, which he'd excised from the magazine before gingerly replacing it on the library shelf. 'Then this might be a sign.'

She skimmed it. 'Yes, a mega-dollar sign. With four zeros behind it. Isn't Radcliffe that women's college at Harvard?'

'Is it?'

'Yes, pure Ivy League. I'd say they're fishing for students with deep pockets – or with rich parents. Neither of which describe you.'

'You've got to spend money to make money. And when I get in, I'll get the latest tips on the industry, make some useful contacts, and then be able to hit the ground running.'

'*If* you get in,' said Hillary.

'Why wouldn't I? I have a Master's degree in English, editing experience, ten years---'

'Yes, yes. But they're probably looking for sweet young things who get off at the thought of refilling coffee cups for grumpy editors trolling for the next Stephen King.'

'I could apply as a sweet young thing[82]. It might be good practice for my character development.'

She leaned across the table in an interrogating pose. 'Fictional, or real?'

He stuck out his lower lip. 'If I can qualify to write a dissertation on D. H., I should certainly be OK for this!'

'You have $263.96 in your bank account,' she said. 'Just how do you plan to pay for this fantasy?'

'Ah, ha,' he said. 'My termination payout, remember?'

'You really expect Browbait to deliver on that?'

Dylan leapt from his chair to produce the letter from his briefcase. 'Remittance advices, unlike college presidents, don't lie. He didn't have any choice.'

'Umm,' she said, as if she'd just sampled a boutique dark chocolate. 'But this would cover a month in Tuscany plus a case or two of decent Italian reds.'

---

[82] http://bit.ly/2IaBvl7

'Mine, all mine,' he said.

'I'll remember that when you file for bankruptcy,' she smiled, notching it up.

And so it was that Dylan applied to the Radcliffe Publishing Course – as himself rather than a sweet young thing, just in case he was admitted. A month later, he was.

D. H. took full credit for it, of course.

'It's true, you had something of an inside track, being Canadian and a "mature" candidate,' he said, reading the acceptance over Dylan's shoulder. 'But that might not have been enough, given the field of straight-A private school co-eds whose daddies and/or mommies are Harvard alumni. Fortunately, New England is rife with presences like yours truly, several of whom served as Ivy League presidents, so I called in a few favours, and…'

Dylan nearly wrenched his neck in turning back on him. 'And here I thought we were alone in the universe.'

D. H. narrowed his gaze. 'Did you think this is the only one?'

'Does it matter what I think?'

'Dust to dust, ashes to ashes, etc., etc. What a waste of great thoughts those tepid outcomes would be!'

'And so you can just flit off to New England, or wherever, for cocktails with them?'

'Mostly wherever,' said D. H. 'You've heard of conference calls. Well, we can meet in space lounges without the clutter of bodies, remembered or holographic.'

'That I'd like to see.'

'Sorry,' said D. H. 'You don't have nearly enough galactic status credits. You'd need to work up to Platinum, which is reserved for only the best in their field, such as eminent Lawrence scholars. Or at least be knighted by the Queen. And then of course we'd have to arrange your death, preferably in tragic circumstances, even by self-inflicted methods, or a convenient stroke of Nature.'

'I'll take a rain-cheque,' Dylan shrugged, suddenly feeling happy to be *very* ordinary.

Even Hillary was surprised by Dylan's burst of creativity over the following weeks as his departure day for Boston drew closer. He had a poem almost every day to show her after work, and, in her words, some of them weren't 'half bad'. More than one drop of wine was spilt on her favourite, "Firefly", to wit:

> To love you like that —
> pulse of light at nightfall.
> And your rainforest:
> death adders random as dice
> to keep intimacy on edge
> your amber eyes inciting
> afternoon's purple thunder.
> You sealed me in a drizzle
> of discontent that wet season.
> Suspicious of daybreak
> you knew that undergrowth
> sunlight would miss until
> storms could leaden my wings.
> Back then I had to be grateful
> for any intuition of feral grass
> beneath the perforated lid.
> Charcoal dreams were all I knew
> in those countertenor nights
> before the pubic surge.

'You're sure D. H. didn't help you with that?' she asked, the first time she read it.

'No,' he said. 'When it comes to poetry, he's worse than a bridge player in an old folks' home. Absolutely no kibitzing[83]!'

'Just as well that you weren't writing about me,' she said. 'Your 'drizzle / of discontent' is so last century!'

---

[83] http://bit.ly/2E6BmqO

By the time Dylan reached Cambridge, Massachusetts and checked into his room on campus, it was dusk. There was an envelope waiting for him on the bed, lightly scented with lavender, and addressed to Mr Dylan Cashew, M.A., Group 6:

> Dear Mr Cashew,
>
> You are cordially invited to the Course Opening Reception at 6:45pm for 7:00pm.
> Formal end time: 8:30pm.
>
> Your attendance is anticipated and would be welcomed.
>
> Dress: Smart Casual

Dylan whispered a silent thanks to Hillary, who'd packed in one of the sport coats and two pairs of slacks left over from his run for Parliament. The morning after his narrow defeat, she's rescued them from the car before he could drop them off at the Goodwill Centre.

'No way I'll ever run again,' he'd protested. 'What possessed me?'

'Thank goodness,' she'd winked. 'But you might need them for a funeral – or maybe even a wedding!'

He had to concede, glancing at the mirror and then at his watch, that he looked decently smart casual, not to mention anticipated.

He was met at the door to the reception room by a very smartly dressed woman of Indian descent behind a desk with nametags. 'Good evening, sir. Your invitation, please?'

Dylan felt a twinge of panic. 'I...I'm afraid I left it in my room.'

The woman seemed mildly surprised. 'Your last name, then?'

'Cashew,' Dylan said. 'With a "C". He pointed to his nametag. 'That's me, there.'

Not content with his assurance, the woman produced a list, scanned it. 'Ah, yes, our esteemed Canadian candidate.'

She offered him his nametag with two hands, then gestured to the door behind her. 'You're very welcome, Mr Cashew, please, right through here.'

The reception room was brimming with "candidates" brandishing flutes of champagne. Almost all were young women dressed to impress, and well beyond Dylan's benchmark of smart casual[84]. In amongst them were a few stiff collars who Dylan guessed were either course conveners or industry types.

Hillary's advice at the departure gate, resurfaced: 'Network, network. Put your faith in that!'

He made a move toward the first stiff collar, only to be intercepted by a young waitress with drinks.

'Champagne?' she offered, in a tone that Dylan thought was mildly flirtatious. 'Or we have wine or even Guinness. What can I get you?'

Dylan hated champagne and, thanks to Hillary, had formed more than a casual association with Guinness, but he smiled with a thin gesture to protocol and took the champagne. Best to keep his wits about him, at least for the first night. He took a sip of the champagne so as not to appear ungrateful and then was pleasantly surprised by the taste. Obviously the quality was at least one grade higher than the Canadian vintage that he'd tasted in the last New Year's party.

He joined the largest circle of people he could find and was noticed straight away by one of the stiff collars. 'Greetings,' the grey-haired man said, squinting at his nametag. 'Are you magazine or book?'

The woman next to him, slightly shorter but definitely older than the encircled candidates, leaned slightly toward him to whisper. 'He means *industry* – mags or books? That's Max, from Bantam Dell.'

'Well, books,' said Dylan, straining for choice.

---

[84] http://bit.ly/2laMo6i

'I thought so,' said Max. 'I can always pick out a Knopf type, even in disguise.'

'Actually, I---'

Fortunately, or unfortunately, Dylan's reply was interrupted by a male waiter with an array of skewers that suggested diced chicken. The others in the circle deferred to seniority, allowing Max to take one and then a second, dipping them in turn in a satay sauce, which dribbled unnoticed to the floor. By his second satay stick, Max had forgotten about Dylan.

'You're from Canada, aren't you?' said the woman next to him, holding out her hand. 'I'm Irena, your Program Manager. I handle all the applications that make it through the second cut.'

Dylan was distracted by her impossibly large gold earrings that he guessed were the real thing. They shimmied with every word.

'Which means I only had to go through 200 applications,' Irina added.

'How many were there in total?'

'Over a thousand,' Irina gestured, as if outlining the perimeter of a planet. 'Praise the Lord for support staff – and overtime.'

'Yes, praise Him,' said Dylan, remembering his accidental reading of *The Handmaiden's Tale*. 'Where would we be without support staff?'

'So you're a fan of Margaret Atwood, too?'

'Uh, yes. But I didn't mean---'

'Finish your drink, Dylan. I'm buying the next round. And we'd better make it a Guinness this time? You don't strike me as a champagne sort of guy.'

'T-thanks,' said Dylan, warily.

She motioned over a waitress and made no secret of the special order.

'I was delighted to see your application,' Irina went on.

'Surprisingly, we don't get many applicants from Canada. And you came highly recommended by some notable VIPs.'

Dylan didn't have the nerve to ask.

The next day, it was down to work – or at least listening. The opening address was by none other than Max, CEO of Bantam Dell. If he was hung-over at all, given the frighteningly early morning session, it didn't show. Dylan admired his stamina.

He gave himself some recovery time mid-course with a self-playing video that extolled the virtues of the Bantam Dell empire, with clips of their many Pulitzer Prize and National Book Award winners, and bird's-eye views of their renovated headquarters, with dizzying close-ups of smiling editors, production staff and even their cued-in mailroom staff.

Despite the glitz, Max seemed somewhat bored by it all, as if he'd seen it a million and one times since 'The Frankfurt' [read Frankfurt Book Fair] nearly a year ago where it had its 'premiere'.

'From Frankfurt to Hollywood,' Dylan mused, a bit too loudly, earning an exasperated stare from two students in the row in front of him.

With rapid-fire clicks from his remote, Max flipped through slides of imprints that made up Bantam Dell as well as competing publishers and then the international conglomerates like Bertelsmann SE & Co. that had swallowed up so many of them for few reasons other than expanding their profit base.

'I'm showing you this to scare you,' Max said, freezing the screen on a tentacled montage of Bertelsmann SE & Co. logos.

Looking around, Dylan saw voracious scribblings by members of the audience; whereas his notepad remained blank. Still, he was keen to hear why he should fear a company he'd never heard of.

'Once upon a time,' Max continued, 'publishing houses were founded by men of ideals, who would mortgage their houses if necessary to bring literature and art to a hungry populace. These were people without degrees, people with the intuition to recognise a prospective bestseller, who would hire the best talent their scarce resources could afford to discover, nurture, develop, polish, produce, promote and distribute the best books possible. This was a world in which the most deserving rose to the top[85] purely due to the quality of expression rather than the *sexiness* of the author and her subject matter.'

Max seemed to enjoy the muffled gasp from the best-dressed pockets of the audience at his emphasis on the word "sexiness".

'If I can leave you with just one thought from this course, let it be that there's very little room for sentiment in the publishing industry. It is a business, and only the strongest minnows make it into adulthood. Most will be eaten by sharks, idealistic bones and all.

'The other point to remember is that editorial is not the only division in a publishing company. It's the role that 95% of grads aim for, but fewer and fewer editing jobs are up for grabs. Think pre-production. Think admin. Dare I say *think marketing and sales.*'

As if anticipating a collective groan from the gallery, he forged on. 'No, the future belongs to the bean counters, the adept and ruthless marketers. When I first entered the industry, we made decisions about prospective authors on an educated hunch, and recorded everything on paper. Editors were regarded as philosopher-kings[86], second only in power to the publisher himself. In editorial board meetings, soliciting editors presented their list, senior editors devised plans and then dispensed tasks like Moses on the Mount. Now, increasingly, it's all about computers, apps, ads,

---

[85] http://bit.ly/2zF2lX3
[86] http://bit.ly/2CiB0gp

spreadsheets, projections, outcomes. A pitch to an editorial board that might have taken a week to formulate can be erased with the ease of a backspace.'

This guy's a survivor, all right, thought Dylan. He'd outwit a pack of wolves in a blizzard. He wrote down a single word on his blank sheet: *survival*.

In rapid-fire, Max put up slides of young women who could have been cover art on *Vogue* – except for their telltale briefcases and calculators.

'Meet the decision makers of the future,' said Max. 'On one side of the editorial board table we'll have the brow-beaten editors, doing their best to make a case for their literary novels, while on the other side could be people like you, feeding data into your laptops and then saying *not for us* or *tell me more, much more*. It's your choice.'

He went on like that for a while, before, having sensed the deflated mood of the room, concluding with, 'but don't let me discourage you from applying for editorial jobs – just be aware that the odds are stacked against you. Any questions?'

The room went stone silent.

'Don't be shy,' Max dared. 'The student with the best question gets a guaranteed interview at the end of the course!'

Dylan was the only one to hold up his hand, even then.

'Ah, *Mr Knopf*,' said Max. 'Keen to jump your sinking ship?'

Dylan was so focused on his question that he'd missed Max's previous offer. 'What about independent publishers – is there any hope for those of us aiming to work there?'

'Thanks for that question, Mr Knopf,' said Max. 'There is indeed hope for the independently minded of you. For those with a start-up mindset. Very slim, but existent. Many CEOs broke in that way, not by serving coffee or emptying dustbins, but with an idea, a commitment, and the energy and resources to see it through. Some, like your statuesque

Alfred, immortalised themselves with a company name, preserved to this day if not as an independent, but, as in your case, a respected imprint in a global enterprise, publishing marginally commercial but culturally important titles. Poetry, even. Where would the Günter Grasses, the Ken Keyses, the Alice Munros be without them? Not to mention the Nobel laureates from other language communities!'

Max was getting so pumped up that Dylan worried he might have a stroke. 'Thank you, sir,' he said, still standing. 'But I actually don't work for Knopf or any other publisher. I'm here to learn how to start my own publishing company – and make a success of it.'

Max nodded, and broke out in the first smile they had seen from him all session. 'Of course you don't,' he said. 'Yet – see me later.' He checked his watch. 'Finally a bit of advice to the wannabes among you: sign on, take notes, absorb what you need, *then* break out on your own.'

Irina appeared on stage out of nowhere. 'Mr Max will be back later in the course, but he has a flight to catch now, so please join me in thanking him for his keynote address with its keen insights into the book publishing industry!'

'Hey, *Mr Knopf,*' said the young woman next to him in a decidedly Southern accent as the applause finally died down. 'Congratulations on getting an interview for a company you already work for.'

'He was kidding about interviews, wasn't he?' said Dylan, leaning over.

'Not at all,' she said, smiling warmly, with her pale blue eyes. 'It's on the program. Didn't you see?'

Dylan shrugged. 'I was taking it one name-drop[87] at a time.'

'Here,' she said, hyped, snatching his program and turning it over. 'You complete the expression of interest and hand it in to Irina. If you get invited, you travel on down to

---

[87] http://bit.ly/2CgsLUs

New York for your interviews. It's optional, but they say at least 75% of candidates who get an interview come away with at least one job offer, so, if I get any, believe me, I'm a-going! How 'bout you?'

She had the drop on him. 'I'm from Canada, you see. I don't think I could afford to live in New York.'

'Oh, You've got to start *somewhere*. And it's too easy to find a share apartment. Think Seinfeld Adventure. I just love Jerry and that Kramer[88] guy. I can so see myself as an Elaine stand-in!'

'I thought you wanted to go into publishing.'

'Weren't you listening to Max? We've got to keep our options open!'

Dylan suddenly realised that they were the only ones left in the auditorium. Time to transition to the next scene. 'I think it's coffee break time,' he said.

'Hopefully with Tim Hortons,' she said, leading the way. 'I so need a sugar hit.'

She's already auditioning, Dylan thought, keeping a respectful distance behind the wake of her perfume.

---

[88] http://bit.ly/2Cf22aJ

Chapter 10: Criss-crosses and Crossroads

IT TURNED OUT THAT HIS ELAINE STAND-IN REALLY WAS AN ELAINE IN REAL LIFE, and she managed to slip in next to him in every plenary, every focus group, even as the book sessions gave way to the days on magazines. Dylan's favourite was the keynote that focused on *Esquire*.

Billing it as 'Not Just a Men's Mag', Mr Arnold launched into an impressive slideshow of the magazine's achievements since its inception in the early '30s when it notched up stories from literary stars like Hemingway, F. Scott Fitzgerald, André Gide and Raymond Carver.

'If book publishers seek to embed cultural icons[89], magazine publishers must anticipate them,' said Mr Arnold, 'criss-crossing and curating the fashions of the day. They seize on the best hooks of the print and broadcast media and expand on them to entice their readers to reflect on consequences and deeper implications. While newspapers, radio and television hacks live by the day, or even the hour, magazine staff live by the week or month, but the demands on them are no less frenetic.'

This guy needs to write a book, thought Dylan. He's frying my brain!

'Great magazine editors go beyond merely featuring authors of note,' Arnold went on. 'They inspire or even extend their talents. For instance, take J. D. Salinger, the celebrated recluse. Or, should I say, an author whose greatness was intensified if not exaggerated by his aversion to the glare of public exposure. Gordon Lish, our fiction editor at the time, frustrated by Salinger's creative inertia, published an unattributed story with character names from "For Esme –

---

[89] http://bit.ly/2lgkxBO

with Love and Squalor", leaving it to our readers to draw their own conclusions as to its authorship. Meanwhile, backstage, Lish was prone to edit Raymond Carver's prose down by half or more into a silky minimalism that even Hemingway would have applauded.'

Dylan could feel electricity in the air. They were being seduced from book to magazine publishing by an arch demon – and, everywhere he glanced, it was working. Except for him. It was one thing to hitch a ride on a magazine with more than two centuries of history behind it, built on the shoulders of celebrity authors and thinkers, quite another to start one from scratch, hours from Vancouver, which in itself was hardly the centre of the universe.

The last day of the course was allotted to the dreaded "Simulation Competition". In the morning, students were assigned to groups with briefs to either prepare a pitch for a novel tentatively entitled "From Darkest Matter" that they, as genre editor, wanted to have published under a so-called Wattage House imprint. Others were in marketing/promotions groups who were to play devil's advocate, opposing publication on whatever grounds they could muster. Both groups were given data sheets on the fictitious author and her creative background as well as two reader's reports that were unanimous in recommending the manuscript be published.

Over lunch and through most of the afternoon, the groups were to debate the manuscript's fate. Irina told them there was no right or wrong answer or outcome – their report would be judged by a panel of three esteemed publishers from the major publishing houses lecturing in the course, in an *X-Factor* format. The winning groups would have their expenses paid to New York and guaranteed interviews with three publishers of their choice.

As chance would have it, Dylan and Elaine were assigned to the same group, but on opposing sides. Elaine was on the editorial team, Dylan with the bean counters.

I think I'm going to enjoy this, Dylan mused. In fact, I'm *sure* I am!

The data sheet on the author was somewhat revealing:

- **Lisa Everton**

- B.A. [Magna Cum Laude], Bennington College, Liberal Arts, 20xx-20xx

- MFA, Yale University, Music Performance [Contemporary Voice], expected completion year 20xx

- Silver Medalist, Breast Stroke, World Championships, 20xx

- Personal Assistant to CFO, Citibank, Providence, RI [part-time], 20xx -

- 'My Life as a Harp', poetry chapbook [self-published, 20xx]

- Résumé presented on hand-pressed parchment, neatly calligraphed, in triplicate

'An uncut gem', the first appraiser concluded. 'Don't let this one get away!'

'Narrative control and sumptuous craft rarely seen in a debut horror author,' crowed the second. 'An Agatha protégée?'

Mildly impressed, Dylan turned to the author's synopsis.

> With wife Felicity and psychic son Johnny in tow, frustrated writer Frank Lawrence takes a job as the winter caretaker at the opulently ominous, mountain-locked Ventnor Hotel so that he can write in peace. Before the hotel is vacated for the Lawrences, the manager informs Frank

that a previous caretaker went crazy and slaughtered his family. Frank laughs it off. Settling into their routine, Johnny cruises through the empty corridors and plays with Felicity, while Frank sets up a study in the cavernous lounge with strict orders not to be disturbed. But Danny is plagued by blood-soaked nightmares of the past, and a blocked Frank starts slipping into the hotel bar for a few visions of his own. Frightened by her husband's behavior and Johnny's visit to the forbidden attic, Felicity soon discovers what Frank has really been up to in his study all day, and what the hotel has done to him.

'Not bad,' Dylan said, sufficiently out loud that his other group members looked up.

'Not bad?' said William, a lanky chap with the cleanest hair parting that Dylan had ever seen. 'It's *terrific* – I want to read the whole thing!' He paused. 'Sorry, your name is?'

Dylan could tell he was William from his nametag, which everyone in the group, except Dylan, had remembered to put on that morning. 'Dylan,' Dylan said.

'I agree with Will,' pitched in Rachael, encouraging murmurs of support from other group members. 'I wish I had written that. Why don't you like it, Dylan?'

For an instant, Dylan felt like he was the target of stones[90] in a reenactment of "The Lottery". 'I'm not saying I didn't like it, just that I'd like to read the sample before I whip out my wallet – that is, our publisher's wallet.'

Pimply Stan – not that the adjective was on his nametag, but some of his inflammations were so large that Dylan felt the urge to pop them in Rachael's direction – shifted uncomfortably in his seat.

'Do you have an opinion?' Dylan asked.

'Who appointed you group leader?' Will sniped.

Dylan knew he was on dangerous ground. Had Will detected that he was an ex-academic? Once an academic…

[90] http://bit.ly/2C8HXUb

'I-I do,' ventured Stan. 'Aren't we supposed to be business skeptics here? We won't win if we just let the editorial team romp over us.'

'That's right,' said Dylan. 'If we don't play devil's advocate, you can kiss Manhattan good-bye.'

'Let's not fight among ourselves,' Rachael said. 'Why don't we have a silent reading of the sample and then try to reach consensus?'

Instinctively, everyone raised their hand, with Dylan only a microsecond behind the others.

> Dawn brought back a stack of blueprints and slapped them down on the manager's glossy redwood desk. Frank looked over his shoulder, very much aware of the scent of Richman's cologne. *All my men wear English Leather or nothing at all came into her mind,* and she had to clamp her tongue to stifle a bray of laughter. Beyond the wall, faintly, came the sounds of the Ventnor Hotel's kitchen staff, clearing up from lunch.
>
> 'Top floor,' Richman pointed, briskly. 'The attic. Absolutely nothing up there now but crap. The Ventnor has changed hands several times since World War II and it seems that each successive manager has stuck everything they don't want up there. I want rattraps and poison put out. Some of the top-floor chambermaids have reported rustling noises. I don't believe them, not for a moment, but there mustn't be even the slightest chance that a single rat lurks in the Ventnor Hotel.'
>
> Dawn, who suspected that every hotel in the world had a rat or two, held her tongue.
>
> 'Of course you wouldn't allow your daughter up in the attic under any circumstances.'
>
> 'No,' Dawn said, flashing her best PR smile again. Humiliating situation. Did this officious little prick actually think she would allow her kid, if she had one, to goof around in a rattrap attic full of junk furniture and only God knows what else?
>
> Richmond consigned the attic floor plan to the bottom

of the pile.

'The Ventnor has one hundred and ten guest rooms,'
he proclaimed. 'Thirty of them, all suites, are here on the
third floor. Ten in the west wing [including the Presidential],
ten in the center, ten more in the east wing. All of them
command our best views.'

Could you at least spare the sales talk? she thought.

But Dawn kept quiet. She needed the job.

Dylan waited until everyone had looked up from the page. 'Well, what do we think?'

'Can't fault it,' said Will. 'Well-written, concise, good differentiation of characters...'

The others nodded, and then looked at him, stones at the ready.

'Hmm,' he said. 'I agree that it's well written and all that, but how does the sample fulfill the promise of the synopsis? None of the main characters are even mentioned, and where's the horror in it?'

'We're at set-up stage,' remarked Will, patronisingly. 'You could view it as almost Shakespearean where the interaction between secondary characters anticipates the entrance of the main characters.'

'And the rustling in the attic could be a hint of some alien force up there,' added Rachael. 'Dawn has an inkling when she thinks "God knew what else?"'

These kids are sharp, thought Dylan. Well beyond my third-years – forgetting for an instant that he was now a card-carrying ex-academic. At least they haven't picked up on my non-directive lecturing strategy!

'OK,' he conceded. 'But is it all strong enough for us to agree to offer a five-figure advance?'

'Dylan's right,' said Stan, more assertively. 'It's fine that we're anticipating the editors' rationale, but we also have to pick holes in it to justify rejecting their recommendation.'

'From my notes,' said Gloria, her blonde hair tied back in a severe accountant's bun, 'I see that we can object on the editorial grounds of lack of originality, derivative nature of the contents, authorial arrogance, or, from a marketing perspective, a poorly defined or overly specialised audience, a work that duplicates something already out in the marketplace, especially works that we have already published, and... I can't read my writing here---'

'Why don't we begin with the author's personality?' Rachael interrupted. 'She does seem to be a bit all over the place, enrolled in a music degree, working part-time as a personal assistant to a senior bank executive... how did she get there? Mommy and/or Daddy must be really well connected.'

'Our opponents will simply counter that by saying she's shown initiative,' Will said.

'And who's ever heard of submitting a résumé on parchment, for Christ's sake?' Rachael continued, ignoring him.

'Are you sure you're not just a *teeny* bit jealous?' Will said.

'Now children...' Dylan began, catching himself before he adopted too much of a lecturer's tone. 'Let's assume she is all that she claims to be, and that she got that job honestly. As Rachael says, we could still question her focus, whether or not she'd have the time available to properly promote her book as most publishers, even major ones like our house, must expect of first-time authors.'

Murmurs of support around the group.

'OK, I've got that down as my first dot point objection,' said Gloria. 'What else have we got?'

'I agree with Dylan,' said Stan. 'Even if she was fond of Shakespeare's method, why would she offer up this particular passage to an editor as representative of her best writing?'

Suddenly, he was aware of a presence behind him. Oh,

no, he thought. Not here! Sure enough, D. H. leaned over to whisper in his ear. 'Call for a time out,' he urged. 'What I have to show you will take your full concentration.'

Dylan checked his watch. 'Irina said we're supposed to take a break once an hour. Coffee, anyone?'

He trailed behind the others out to the morning tea table, spotted D. H. off to one side but was cut off at the pass by Elaine, who was already halfway through a mug and had a saucer stacked with cookies.

'These are great,' she said, pointing at them. 'Almost homemade. Want one?'

Dylan glanced at D. H., who merely shrugged, then accepted one.

'So,' she said. 'How's it going? I don't envy you guys. Our author's got it all: good looks, brains, and no run-on sentences. Are you ready to throw in your erasures?'

'Not a chance,' said Dylan. 'The object of the exercise is for us to veto what you've recommended.'

'Aw, c'mon, it could be a trick. What if the editors and bean counters are supposed to agree for a change? This gal's a sure thing. Citibank alone will probably order in ten thousand copies to give away as staff Christmas presents. What's not to like about her?'

Dylan nearly swallowed his cookie whole. 'We're not supposed to talk about it until we're in front of the judges. He pointed at the ceiling and leaned over to her. 'Concealed cameras[91] – we could be disqualified.'

She stuck out her lower lip. 'No! You really think they're watching?'

'*1984* wasn't just a work of fiction.'

She interrogated his face with those piercing blue eyes, then nodded. 'OK. But I still think I'm right.'

'The drinks will be on me if you are,' Dylan said, as if he were in a dare with a colleague back at Penticton College.

---

[91] http://bit.ly/2Cmbl6x

'You're on, dude,' she said, giving him a look that made him worry that she'd taken it the wrong way.

'I didn't mean---'

'Shhh,' she said, backing away as if from a hissing snake. 'They're watching!'

D. H. was still waiting for him over in the corner. He pointed to a dog-eared book at the very end off the trestle table, well away from the refreshments. 'Not that I want to give your group an unfair advantage,' he said, as Dylan picked up the book, 'but you'd better read this.'

The author's name was Stephen King, and there was a glowing holographic bookmark, a few pages into the book, which materialised as soon as Dylan touched it.

Dylan's team was up last for judging of the Simulation Competition, which was bad and good. Bad because they heard the other editorial and bean counters debate points already on their list, often quite eloquently, but good because, being off-stage, they could observe the judges' reactions to the earlier contenders.

The judges were Max, Arnold and Irina. Dylan focused on Irina, since she was the least poker-faced of the three. Max was a consistent sourpuss throughout, while Arnold seemed to fixate on some of the boys with a faraway thin smile. Irina, on the other hand, couldn't resist nodding her encouragement when the speakers were on the right track, or sitting stock still when they weren't.

It was sweaty palms all around, including for Dylan, when it was time for them to take their seats on the stage. Elaine, who'd been appointed senior editor by her group, was designated speaker and advanced to the lectern.

"Distinguished members of the publishers' panel, I am pleased to recommend "From Darkest Matter" by Lisa Everton for publication. In Ms Everton, we have a hitherto undiscovered talent, who comes to us without an agent, which means, if we act promptly, we will avoid the inevitable expense of an auction with our publisher rivals. She is well educated, articulate, sublimely aware of the demands of her craft, and undeniably photogenic. Properly managed by our PR team, she will mesmerise book club interviewers at the major networks.'

As Elaine spoke, Irina was captivated, Max mellowed ever so slightly, and even Arnold seemed to drift down from Cloud Nine. Dylan shifted a bit uncomfortably in the hard-backed chair, but he was still quietly confident that the tip D. H. had shared with him would win the day.

'Of course,' Elaine continued, 'Though we know a book may be judged by its cover, and, even more so by the charisma of its author, its ultimate fate rests with the critics. While we had only a brief sample of Ms Everton's writing to go on, we saw it had a sense of uncertainty bound to captivate the reader, calculated foreshadowing that some in our group found reminiscent of Shakespeare, as well as a fine-tuned economy of expression that will certainly vault her to the forefront of practitioners of the horror genre. In conclusion, we have no reservation in recommending "From Darkest Matter" be offered a contract as soon as possible, and have every confidence in its prospects for commercial success.'

Scattered polite applause was heard back-stage and behind the judges as Dylan exchanged places with her and made sure he was the last person to stop clapping before speaking.

After the usual deference to the judges, his team members and the opposition, he continued. 'With all due respect to my editorial colleagues, and the arguments already mounted by the other marketing teams, which I won't bore you with by repeating, there's one reason this submission must be rejected. The sample we were given, and, I suspect, the entire ms has been *plagiarised* from a work by...' Here, he paused for effect, before going on, 'Stephen King's work

The Shining.' He took pleasure in the gasps from all except the judges. 'I'm probably one of the few people in the world who hasn't read at least one novel by Mr King, but I'm a big fan of Jack Nicholson, and some of the lines from Ms Everton simply rang a bell. I can do a comparison if you like.'

'Excuse me,' said Max, glancing at the other judges. 'If, as you say, you haven't read any Stephen King, how did you come by a copy of *The Shining*?'

Dylan's mother, God rest her soul, had always said, when you're caught on the verge of a lie, always latch onto the closest truth. 'I... found it on a table, at morning tea.'

'Let me be clear on this,' Max pursued. 'You just happened to find that book and just happened by chance to skim to the key passages?'

'That's right,' said Dylan. 'It's near the beginning. Everton actually improved on the style and changed the character names, but it's pretty much verbatim other than that. Do you want me to prove it?'

Arnold was shaking his head back and forth so vigorously that Dylan thought it might turn 180 degrees, but Irina was looking profoundly red-faced. Max shot up from his chair.

'Did you – ?' he accused.

'Well...' she replied, almost inaudibly. 'I *thought* it was in my bag the whole time. I checked before morning tea, but then later I found that it was missing. So I ran back to the refreshments room and found it there, at the far end of the trestle table.' With trembling hands, she drew the copy from her bag and held it up in the air. 'I assumed that none of the students would have seen it, but---'

'You obviously assumed wrongly!' Arnold roared. 'This whole exercise has been compromised. How ridiculous!'

'Hang on,' said Max. 'There are just too many coincidences here. This... *import* from Canada claims to recognise lines from a book that may or may not have been used in a film script, and then just *happens* to find the crucial text on a table at morning tea. Smacks of an inside job[92] to me!'

Since Max was glaring straight at Dylan the whole time, it took a few seconds for Irina to realise she was being implicated. She sprang up, finger shaking at Max. 'How dare you! I *swear* I had nothing to do with this.'

All eyes shifted to Dylan. The other team members drifted onto the stage from the wings to have a closer look. The silence was thicker than gouda cheese.

'Cross my heart with a maple leaf,' Dylan said. 'No one in this room, including Irina, gave me that book. It was just there, and when I saw the title, the memory just clicked. I thumbed through the pages, and there it was – our sample.'

'Game over,' declared Arnold. 'The means by which Mr Cashew came upon the source book is irrelevant. The fact is that his team has been given an unfair advantage.' His chair scrapped backwards like fingernails on a chalkboard. 'Now, if you don't mind, I have a plane to catch.'

Irina's delicately drawn mascara slewed down her face.

Elaine and Dylan retreated to a café-bar in Cambridge. No one had won the bet, so he thought the decent thing to do was to shout her a Manhattan to match his well-aged scotch. They exchanged small-talk stares.

'What happens to New York now?' she said, playing with her swizzle stick.

'Nothing,' he said. 'New York is forever.'

'Damn,' she said. 'You really screwed things up, didn't you?'

'I did what every editor worth his salt should do – rule out plagiarism. Imagine the cost if we *had* published such a book.'

'It was all *pretend*, Dylan,' she reminded him. 'We were in Fantasyland – we were never going to publish anything.'

They finished their drinks in a heat.

'My shout,' she said, reaching for his glass.

---

[92] http://bit.ly/2zJkFOR

Something told Dylan he needed to apply the brakes. 'Maybe we should get something to eat first?'

Still standing, she leaned across the table to stare at him with those penetrating blue eyes. 'Actually, what I need right now is a good f---'

He put a finger across her lips. 'I'm married, you know.'

She was letting her perfume do the work. 'I've heard about those literary conferences, and what goes on, married or not.'

'Have you really?'

'And I'm keen to get my money's worth[93]!'

---

[93] http://bit.ly/2leXoQm

Chapter 11: Ruby in the Rough

HILLARY HEADED STRAIGHT FOR THEIR FAVOURITE PUB AS SOON AS SHE PICKED HIM UP FROM THE AIRPORT.

'Not as fancy as your Cambridge bars, I'll wager,' she said, 'but your next stop better be Glasgow – with moi.'

'It's a date,' he said, squeezing her hand.

'Did you miss me?'

'You asked me that at the airport.'

'Your answer seemed slightly non-committal.'

'I was distracted. My bag was the last to come out on the turnstile, and I thought I'd lost your Hershey's chocolate.'

'Liar,' she grinned. 'I've heard what clichés[94] happen at those literary conferences – especially with all those dewy-eyed graduates and their disruptive hormones.'

He found a smile. 'What makes you think they were dewy-eyed? Most are from Ivy-league private schools, with war-paint for makeup.'

'I was like that once, before you seduced me.'

'I've never understood that nonsense. Someone always has to seduce someone else. Why can't lightning strike two people at once?'

'Because, on average, we're shorter than men – and more agile. So we let the lightning strike you first.'

'I need another drink,' he sighed.

'You're only halfway with that one.'

'Watch me disappear.'

Three scotches in, and he began to lay out his plan. 'Joseph rang me in Cambridge. He's finished his second book of verse and wants it to be the guinea pig for Black Books.'

---

[94] http://bit.ly/2BQrtfo

'Whoa, horsey,' she said. 'You were at the College for ten years, and he never said anything about a poetry book.'

'It was his deep, dark secret. He wrote two poems a month on the same day each month for three years, let his former high school English teacher edit them down to the best forty-eight, then gave them away at his twentieth reunion. After he found one just a few months later at a used bookshop, he didn't know whether to be insulted or flattered since he never intended to sell them. That was six years ago.'

'When did he start writing again?'

Dylan cocked his head. 'An hour after I left the College for good.'

She cocked her head back at him. 'I think he misses you.'

'Of course he does. Maybe I'm his Hector.'

'I meant in the *right* way. And why call it Black Books?'

'We took a side trip up to Salem after the course, while the dewy-eyed sirens headed for New York and their job interviews.'

'Who's *we*?' she said, seizing on it.

'I meant the editorial we,' he said. 'That is me, myself and I.'

'Go on,' she said through slit-eyes.

'And they've got all these neat witchcraft places crammed with curious tourists mad about everything black, so I thought *Black Books Publishing*: that's got to be a winner.'

She considered it. 'OK. I'll admit it's different. I think I can work with Black Books as a brand.'

'*You* can work with it?'

'As I said ages ago, we're talking fractions here. An hour here and there. In the evenings. And the odd weekend. Maybe.'

First things first. What is a publisher without a letterhead, one that fits the 'brand' as Hillary called it? Dylan was determined to come up with one before he responded to Joseph's query, which of course he had decided to accept, pretty much sight unseen, because what is a publisher without a list? His own draft, demurely entitled Arctic Secrets was still poems away from completion, and, besides, it would not do to have his own book be first off the mark.

He played with fonts on his shiny new Black Books iMac for more than an hour before he was satisfied with:

```
Black Books Publishing P/L
Penticton Mail Centre
PO Box 3xxx
Penticton, BC
Canada V2A 1E4
```

Glancing through other letterheads in the latest *Publishers Weekly* he realised he was missing one primary element: a logo. He spent the rest of the day sketching out ideas. Piles of scrunched up sheets later, he finally came up with a figure in profile that reminded him of a cross between Benjamin Franklin [to attract American readers] and Alfred Hitchcock, with his cult following. The shadowy figure would have a ring on his finger with a large glinting ruby.

'There,' he said aloud. 'Let see what Hillary thinks of that!'

'That's awful,' she said that evening, barely holding back tears of laughter. 'Stick to your day job. I'll get our graphic designer to come up with something. You want a logo that will stand out not only in large format but when it's thumbnail size on the spine or back cover of your books.'

'Fine,' he said, swallowing his pride. 'How about the font I chose for the text?'

'Hmm,' she said, glancing at the screen. 'American Typewriter would be fine if you were a junk mail distributor, but, as a publisher, you want something clean and simple. Try this...'

```
Black Books Publishing P/L
Penticton Mail Centre
PO Box 3xxx
Penticton, BC
Canada V2A 1E4
```

'Avenir Light is so this century.'

'I like it,' he conceded. 'And this graphic artist of yours. Does he charge by the hour?'

'*She,*' she corrected. 'And she's a whiz kid. I think she's working on a novel in the evenings, so if I mention that I'll slip it under your nose once it's ready she might do it for nothing.'

'I like the ruby ring,' he said, limply. Can she somehow work in the ring?'

'As in *Lord of the*…?' She patted his hand. 'We'll see.'

The whiz kid did her damage in record time. Two days later, there it was, *sans* Ben Franklin, *sans* Hitchcock, and sadly, *sans* ring:

He stared at it, speechless.

'Mia kept all of your essential elements,' she said. 'The inner ring won't be ruby when you print your internals in black and white, but it'll still stand out in grey, and sort of have the effect of an inner drop-shadow to the outer ring. I think it's great.'

He took a very deep breath. 'If her writing style is as minimalistic as her art, Hemingway would write a blurb for her.'

'Hemingway's dead.'

'So's D. H.,' he reminded her.

'Departed, more accurately,' D. H. said, peeking at the screen between their shoulders. 'I like it – the logo, that is. Don't be ungrateful, Dylan. I see that your logo artist has got a juicy romance novel underway. Properly mentored, this Mia could turn out to be your first breakout author. And if she can design her cover, so much the better for your pre-production costs.'

'You're volunteering to mentor her?'

'Televerbally, perhaps,' winked D. H. 'Through your lips.'

And so it was that Dylan keyed out his first acceptance letter on letterhead for a manuscript he'd accepted sight unseen, a habit he was determined not to perpetuate. He emailed it off to Joseph's home address, and, just to be safe, posted him a copy. When he returned from the post box, an email reply was already waiting for him.

> Dear Publisher [I mean Dylan ;]]
>
> Thank you for your quick response to a manuscript I have yet to submit to you. Please find it attached. I trust it will meet your expectations; however, if it should somehow fall short, I will understand it if you withdraw the contract you have yet to send me.
>
> Yours faithfully,
>
> Joseph Pratt, B.A. [Hons.], M.A. [Tor.]

So much for "gentlemen's agreements"[95] Dylan thought. Yes, contracts. Fortunately, he had kept the handout from the Radcliffe course. It had only been included to alert the students about the key pitfalls of contracting work with authors without the assistance of legal eagles. But as an ex-chief negotiator, Dylan thought he had enough knowledge of legalese to be less than dangerous, so he set about adapting a template intended for a mass market romance novel to one that would serve for a [very] limited market poetry book.

Just as he had printed it out, ready for Joseph to sign and have witnessed, an email came in from Hillary at work, with the subject line, Canadian Centre for Arts Law, and the warning 'Don't sign anything before clearing it with them!'

It seemed as good a time as any to actually read the work he was going to publish, so he found Joseph's attachment,

---

[95] http://bit.ly/2lmWeBH

poured out the remains of a lonely scotch bottle and clicked through to the title page, A Prairie of the Mind.

It was a memoir in verse, poems of consistent length and regularity of stanza. But absolutely no rhyme scheme, which pleased Dylan to no end. He had an allergy to lines straining for rhyme, as they almost always did in the hands of students, or others who thought all poetry since the Lord Byron and Keats they'd suffered through in high school had to conform to rhyme or be consigned to the trash heap of genre-less chit-chat.

No one believed him, of course, even his students when he'd set them assignments with the strict instruction *not* to rhyme, to pay attention instead to the rhetoric, rhythm and music of the line. He was regarded as the Pretender Incarnate, and his brighter students simply did an end-around with near rhymes[96].

It was a relief, then, to read Joseph's carefully sculpted lines about growing up on the Prairies, each poem inspired from a snippet from his childhood, teen-age years and early adulthood. He soon saw this was no ode to a "wind-swept" landscape but rather a reflection on a family in turmoil, with an alcoholic father and a mother prone to suicide, and seven children powerless to alter the inevitable downward spiral. Joseph, in contrast to his Biblical namesake, had exiled himself into a safe cave of books.

Dylan had known this man for a decade, and yet he'd not known the secret heart of him, until now.

'I will certainly publish this,' he said to the first cushion that met his line of sight as he finished the manuscript. 'Yes. YES.'

And so it was that, three rounds of editing and proofreading later, Prairie of the Mind was ready for typesetting. It occurred to him that it was high time for him to learn how to use the program InDesign, which had lain

---

[96] http://bit.ly/2CkBl4k

throbbing lightly in his applications folder since the day he installed it along with a suite of other cleverly named applications such as Photoshop, Illustrator, Dreamweaver and Acrobat. He'd heard that these programs were more or less "user-friendly", but a tutorial later convinced him that InDesign at least was less rather than more.

Electrifying his synapses with scotch didn't help.

Mia to the rescue.

Joseph had generously offered to commission her to design the cover art for his book, and since she couldn't do this on company time, she'd agreed to work that weekend, or however long it took, for a modest fee.

She turned up at 8am that Saturday morning when Dylan and Hillary were still in their bathrobes, staring vacantly at twin slices of fruit bread on their plates as their French-press coffee brewed.

'Oops!' she said after Hillary managed to make it to the door. 'I thought when you said "an early start" that---'

She was noticeably taller than Hillary and her hair was populated by amazingly tight brunette curls frosted with an afterthought of red matched to her lipstick.

'It's fine,' said Hillary, shaking off the apology. 'Dylan will pour the coffee while I escort you to his global headquarters.' She pointed in the direction of the Japanese paper screen Dylan had erected to define his premises. Scotch-taped to the sky of the translucent scene was an enlarged BBP logo, the lettering of which Dylan had ensured was perfectly aligned to the floor by means of a spirit level.

Mia stood there in Middle-Earth[97] while Dylan struggled with the French press, dividing the coffee between three assorted mugs, dispensing milk and sugar as required.

It was only as he handed her her mug that he noticed that the tint of her hair perfectly matched the ruby of the logo. Coincidence?

---

[97] http://bit.ly/2GNeixS

She was on a first name basis with Macs, so he left her to it while he and Hillary subjected their fruit bread slices to their lime marmalade fate.

They were only halfway through their second cup when Mia emerged from Dylan's studio. 'It's still a concept, and pretty rough, but see what you think.'

Dylan followed her scent, with Hillary close behind. What he saw amazed him – a prairie scene that reminded Dylan of van Gogh's lighting and just a suggestion of a farming family, granular, melding into a fertile background.

'It's brilliant, Mia,' said Hillary. 'But bring up the title font a bit more. It's not all about you.'

There was a sting in her remark that surprised Dylan and made Mia flinch. Jealousy?

'I did say it was just a draft,' Mia said.

'Never mind,' Hillary said, quickly. 'I only meant---'

'No, you're right,' Mia said. 'Cover art has to be about the book. I'll fix it.'

Minutes later, there it was, in a firm serifed font they could all agree upon, before a print out made it real, though somewhat paler than they could expect from a professional printing job.

'Can't wait to see it in real life!' Mia said, standing up. 'Can I buy a few copies?'

'No,' said Dylan. 'They'll be free for you, and we'll get the author to sign them. I'm sure he'll need the practice before the launch.'

'Thank you!' she cried. 'My first book cover!' She gave him an almost suffocating hug. 'If that's all...'

'Actually,' said Dylan, hoping he wasn't blushing when she finally backed off, 'Could you give me a few pointers about InDesign?'

'Sure,' she said. 'It's pretty intuitive once you get into it.'

'I'll leave you two to it,' Hillary said. 'How does smoked salmon with cream cheese on toasted bagels sound for lunch?'

'Terrific,' said Mia. 'My gran was one quarter Jewish, you know.'

'I'll be off to the shops then. Have fun, you two.'

Dylan noted Hillary's subtle note of caveat.

PART 3: NUMBERS

And the Lord said unto them: 'If they should ever question how it was determined that 10% should be the sacred royalty paid unto authors, remind them that it was so, with each of the seven lambs, one tenth.'

Chapter 12: Calling in Even More Favours

WORD GETS AROUND. OR AT LEAST DYLAN HOPED IT WOULD. His recurring nightmare was to have a book launch, complete with lavish refreshments, attended by no one other than him and the author.

Of course, the book had to be printed first. After the abrasions of his first encounter with InDesign had worn off and he'd printed out a "final" proof, meticulously checked by Hillary, Joseph and the two other English Department faculty who did not still bear a grudge against Dylan, corrections were made, and InDesign itself gave him the go-ahead by displaying a "no errors" green light at the bottom of his screen.

He arrived bright and early the next morning at the local printer's with a CD of the cover art and the text internals. George, the printer, held up the CD to the light as if it were a Rosetta Stone[98], and smiled before sliding it into the drive on a nearby computer.

'Ugh,' he said.

'Ugh?' said Dylan, weak in the knees.

'InDesign for Mac, eh?'

'Yes, is that a problem?'

'Well, no,' said George. 'It's as good a typesetting app as they come. But all you've copied is your reference file – no fonts folder, no images folder.'

Dylan vaguely recalled Mia mentioning something about an InDesign "package" during her greased lightning tutorial, but that was one of several final steps she offered to 'walk him through' when the time came. The time had come and gone, but the crucial step had skipped his mind.

---

[98] http://bit.ly/2F5lbvZ

George scribbled a few points down on the back of a coffee-stained invoice and handed it to him. 'Do this, this, and that, and report back. Or better yet, ftp the file to me.'

'ftp?' Dylan said.

George hesitated. 'Just report back with two InDesign *packages* – one for the cover, one for your internals, and we'll be on our way.'

That night, Hillary was greeted at the front door by the smell of almost hot pizza and a somewhat deflated Dylan who'd run out of time to fix dinner as per their agreed schedule. To make matters worse, the liquor store had been out of their familiar scotch, and, rather than compromise, he had grabbed the last case of Guinness from the refrigerated section.

'Don't tell me,' Hillary said, kissing him on one cheek and rubbing him reassuringly on the other. 'The learning curve doth steepen?'

'Publishing 101,' Dylan mumbled, unscrewing the Guinness bottles. 'I now understand the process for creating an InDesign "package" and the elegant means of transmitting it to my patronising printer via file transfer protocol.'

'You don't seem the happier for such profound discoveries.'

'Knowledge is power. Power enables dominance.'

She reached for her first slice of pizza. 'Maybe you will make a good CEO some day!'

The long-awaited delivery had arrived. The bright red Aurora Print Factory truck backed down the driveway and soon Dylan, Joseph and an impatient driver were hauling book cartons into a corner of the garage. A utility knife slice later, and copies of Joseph's book welcomed the light of day.

'It's... perfect,' Joseph said, bending the cover of his first copy as he gave Dylan a very firm handshake.

Penticton is a small town, and word gets around the college quickly. Before Hillary could think of a venue for the launch, Browbait was ringing her at work, offering the college boardroom and even wine and cheese for the guests.

'That's very generous of you,' she said. 'What's the catch?'

'I haven't always been a college principal,' Browbait said. 'I earned my stripes in PR with BC Hydro.'

'Yes,' said Hillary. 'But you're not all that fond of Dylan. You wanted to have him sacked for leading that work stoppage years ago and then showing backbone as the Association's contract negotiator.'

She could hear a deep sigh at the other end of the line. 'At the end of the day, Dylan earned my respect. And this isn't all about him anyway. It's a launch for the longest serving member of the English Department. I put it to the College Board, and they unanimously voted to support this event.'

Hillary bit her lip. 'OK, I'll ask Dylan about it. He's the publisher and calls the shots.

'Fine,' said Browbait. 'Pass on my... regards.'

Dylan was suspicious. 'He wants something.'

'Of course he does,' she said. 'How often does the college get a press opportunity like this? Or maybe he's up for contract renewal and hasn't yet ticked off his performance indicators[99] for community contact?'

'That's impressive,' said Dylan. 'With jargon like that, you could go for the public service.'

Misgivings aside, Dylan had to admit that a free venue would help keep costs down.

Hillary then went into overdrive to promote the event, calling in favours from the local media, organising catering, distributing posters in the shops, and the town library. She didn't have to do much at the college because, true to his word, Browbait made sure that posters with the college's logo slightly larger than Black Books Publishing were splashed liberally around the campus.

---

[99] http://bit.ly/2pRy3AE

'What if no one shows up?' Dylan asked her, mildly sick in the stomach at the prospect.

'We've got the numbers – you'll see. Go practice your launch speech.'

'I haven't written it yet.'

Browbait sauntered up to the boardroom lectern not unlike a King Penguin returning to his mate after months at sea. He scanned the multitude of faces, most of them relatives of Joseph and staff members at the college, as if he'd never seen them before.

'Friends,' he began. 'On behalf of Penticton College and its Board of Governors, as well as the Penticton Indian Band as they represent the First Nation communities who settled here, let me welcome you to yet another event hosted by our vibrant academic institution.' Glancing at the back cover of the book, he continued, 'I rarely have time to read much fict – *poetry* – these days, but I am so pleased that one of our most distinguished staff members, Mr Joseph Pratt, M.A., has not only found the time to create a sheath of such wonderful poems but also to launch this esteemed publication by new house Black Books Publishing at this centre of excellence, Pentiction College...'

He droned on like that for more than five minutes, despite Hillary's attempts to get his attention to cut it short, which he surely saw. At length, he discovered he had misplaced a sheet of his notes, and then invited Joseph to come up, but Dylan responded to a swift elbowing from Hillary and bounced up to wrest the mic from Browbait, just as the cameras started to flash and the video recorders started to roll. Browbait had no choice but to stifle a cough, introduce Dylan as the publisher, and even hazard a light arm around him, which actually never touched his back.

'Typical,' he muttered to Dylan as he took his seat in the front row.

Dylan savoured the moment, glanced at the pile of notecards in his hand that Hillary had prepared for him, then set them aside on the lectern. 'Thank you, Mr Browbait, for that... generous introduction. It's not every day that a new publishing house is born. These days, in fact, some would regard the act of making a career change into publishing like constructing your own plank to walk into a treacherous sea. I hope I have better balance than most and can do justice to those authors who entrust their work to me.' He paused. 'And I hope that my similes will improve with age.'

And so it was that Joseph's book was ushered into the world and he and Dylan were to bask in the flurry of cheques and notes and coins, and Joseph certainly had "writer's cramp[100]" by the end of the second wave of signings after the stock of passable wine that Browbait had left over from some other unrelated event had been consumed by the attendees.

'A collector's item,' one buyer remarked.

'An historic day for Penticton!' one of the board members added.

'I hate poetry, but I'm sure I'll love your book!' said yet another, clapping Joseph on the back.

Dylan, who was taking the money as Joseph signed the books, recognised the man in front of them as Editor of the *Penticton Herald*. 'Would you like to take an extra copy for your book editor?' he asked. 'Complimentary, of course.'

The man smiled, waving away the copy. 'Obviously, you don't read us very often. We've never done book reviews, but I might just do one myself on this occasion.' He leaned over conspiratorially. 'Especially if there are any juicy lyrics in here about the college!'

Dylan dog-eared the copy he'd offered. 'Here are a couple of choice ones for you,' he winked, handing it back to him.

'Once a rabble-rouser...' the editor smiled, accepting it. 'I'll see what I can do.'

---

[100] http://bit.ly/2C5smEP

It may have been the luck of the Scots[101], good timing, or even the quality of the writing, but *Prairie of the Mind* not only found its way onto the pages of the *Penticton Herald* with finely-veiled references to the checkered past of the college, but also as a short review in the *Vancouver Sun*, and the Victoria *Times Colonist*.

But the book's biggest coup was being shortlisted a few months later for the coveted Dorothy Livesay in the BC Book Awards about which the panel of judges said:

> …is a masterful and carefully depicted exploration of one's
> relationships with oneself, friends, memories, strangers, and
> a not-so-cleverly disguised academic institution. The three
> parts of this collection are variations building on a theme—at
> times lonely, sometimes adoring, but always honest.

There was a brief note a few weeks later in the *Globe & Mail*, which extended the celebration, giving rise to a raft of submissions from all over the country.

Black Books Publishing had arrived.

Black Books Publishing was a force to be reckoned with.

First, Penticton, thought Dylan, next the world – or at least the Lower Mainland.

Unfortunately, even with all the hoopla, and the award shortlisting, *A Prairie of the Mind* just barely broke even when the printing and shipping costs were considered, not to mention the weekend down in Vancouver for the Book Awards ceremony, where Dylan and Hillary chose to stay, eat and drink at the Hilton for good luck ['To become a winner, you have to *look* like a winner,' Hillary had said].

As it turned out, Dylan didn't need the notecard Hillary had prepared for him in case Joseph fainted at the news he had won, because *A Prairie of the Mind* didn't win, and the few words Joseph had prepared to accept the award were easily adapted to a brief few sentences of thanks.

'Never mind,' Dylan said to him, as they toasted him

101 http://bit.ly/2BQOvCM

back at the Hilton bar. 'The judges always pick the known quantity. We know who should have won.'

Joseph nodded. 'The judges looked surprised when you stood up during my speech. Maybe they had thought the book was self-published.'

[Those were the days when author-published books were still in the daydreams of Jeff Bezos, when some competitions wouldn't even consider self-published books, as though they nurtured silverfish in their spines.]

Dylan was happy enough to ignore the MasterCard bill for that month amidst the raft of submissions that arrived in various shapes, envelopes and even by courier. He'd heard of the term slush pile before, reinforced by his sojourn at the Radcliffe Course: the first ring of "assistant editor limbo", Max had called it, but now the full force – and weight – of it came home to him as piles of unopened manuscripts began to compete for space on either side of the wastebasket, a very strategic locale.

'I need help,' he blurted to the iMac screen a few weeks into the torrent.

'You are not the fairest editor of them all,' the iMac answered, in a tone very much like D. H.'s, though D. H. had [in]visibly exempted himself from all of the pre- and post-book launch fervour.

And then Dylan spotted D. H. reflected in the screen. He wheeled around, but there was no D. H.

'I never liked that mirror in *Snow White*,' he said, turning back to the screen. 'I hope you're not planning to infect my only computer – just after my AppleCare expires!'

'I like the feel of cathode rays on my skin,' D. H. replied, growing in profile until he was only a face staring back at Dylan.

'You're just a hologram, D. H. Skin doesn't come into it.'

'eBooks are so much the happening thing, Dylan. If you don't claim your stake in virtual space, someone else will do it for you.'

'Fine. Let them. I have my hands full, as you can see, with the physical ones.'

'"I need help",' D. H. mimicked. 'You rubbed your magic lamp, so I returned.'

'You'll help with these?'

'Of course,' D. H. said, materialising to sit on one of the piles. 'It gets boring always dealing with those self-important souls like Dickens and Eliot, and especially Hemingway, with that unsightly hole in his temple. Everyone knows he suicided for attention, and holograms don't require such distasteful displays of the evidence from a show-off, so---'

'Too much information,' said Dylan, putting his hands over his ears. 'You're giving me tinnitus.'

D. H. stood up, grabbed a handful of manuscripts and began tossing them into three of his own piles. 'Reject, reject, reject…maybe, reject, reject…hmm, lavender scent, better open this one.'

'Hang on,' said Dylan, 'How can you reject or accept on the basis of smell?'

D. H. smiled. 'You've obviously never been assigned to work in a coal mine, let alone on a slush pile, have you?'

Dylan sighed. 'I suppose we have to start somewhere. Let's have a look.'

He tore open the envelope, noted with satisfaction that it included a self-addressed stamped envelope to one Hattie Greerson, with a post office box from a town in Manitoba Dylan didn't recognise. The lavender scent grew stronger as he leafed through the pages.

D. H. seized on one:

> Here lamps are white like snowdrops in the grass;
> The town is like a churchyard, all so still
> And grey now night is here; nor will
> Another torn red sunset come to pass.

'Nice rhythm,' he said. 'Good use of the semi-colon to

reinforce a breath pause and to compensate for the two lost syllables in the third line.'

'It rhymes, D. H., a-b-b-a,' said Dylan, pinching his nose. 'With capitals at the start of each line – what century are we in?'

'Keep an open mind. This poor woman is pouring out her soul to you.'

Dylan snatched it away. 'A maybe-minus,' he said. 'Now, please, no more rhyming manuscripts. This is doing in my head!'

'Precisely,' said D. H., nudging the manuscript over closer to the maybe pile. 'As every good book should.'

Some time later, when Dylan's hair was chaotic as whitecaps in a storm, they came across a pristine envelope sealed with wax at the back.

'My God,' Dylan said. 'As you sure all your friends are dead?'

'No guarantees,' said D. H. 'People have been tinkering with cryogenics[102] since James Dewer caused a stir with his experiments back in 1892. Who knows what goes on behind closed crypts?'

Dylan refreshed his scotch glass. 'Ah, ha,' he declared, still slightly sober. 'A *typed* covering letter. In Times New Roman, yet!'

'Sorry to disappoint,' said D. H., cocking his head at the letter, 'but I think you'll find it's actually Book Antiqua.'

'That figures,' said Dylan. 'From his vocabulary, I'd say he's a contemporary of your father. "Esteemed Sirs"? "Yours Most Faithfully"? Is he writing from the turrets of Windsor Castle?'

D. H. snatched the letter away. 'Never mind the salutation, let's see what he has to say for himself.'

> Having served for some forty-six years as an officer of senior rankings in the Canadian Forces, or whatever the Govern-

---

[102] http://bit.ly/2BOLNO7

ment now calls our army, navy and air force these days, I now find myself in the position to release my memoirs, drafted, redrafted, and then, following critical review by no less than three of your professional colleagues, i.e. editors, polished to a spit-shine for publication. Your publication house came to my attention by referral of a colleague at Aerosystems Canada, who has more than a passing acquaintance with your work, at least on technical documentation. I have therefore decided to offer you this scintillating account of my life. Lame as I may be in body, I trust you will find in me a tireless spiritual agent for my work who will ensure it rises to the heights of bestseller, at least in the Canadian meaning of the word. I hereby commend it to you.

'"Spiritual", eh,' said Dylan. 'Did you write this? Is this Major-General Angus M---, Retired, nothing more than your pen name?'

'Innocent as charged,' said D. H., throwing up his hands. 'He provides a contact phone number. Ring him if you don't believe me.'

Dylan narrowed his eyes. 'I'll need a refill first.'

There was something in Angus' voice that reminded Dylan of something that he couldn't place or dismiss, so he convinced Hillary to go for a drive to Angus M---'s estate in the foothills above Vernon, just a couple of hours away.

'With a name like Angus,' he said, as they hit the highway. 'He must have Scottish roots – so I might need a translator.'

'With a name like Dylan,' she replied, 'you must have Welsh roots, so what happened to you?'

It was a dusty road in from the main highway, with hibernating grapevines defining the way. The house at the end of the road was sturdy, even muscled, with a pair of Doric pillars at either side of the front door.

'Do they get tornadoes around here?' Hillary asked, as they got out of the car.

'Nope,' said Dylan. 'Like I said, he's a military man. I wouldn't be surprised if he has a bomb shelter downstairs.'

Suddenly they were met by barking, and not a light, drop-kick sort of barking, but rather a Marvel menacing kind that made them grip their respective car door handles in a reflex. No less than a dozen dobermans converged on them before a shrill whistle from the house froze them in their tracks, followed by a series of two short whistles that prompted them to retreat from whence they came. Soon after, a heavy figure emerged from the door, motioning to them with a walking stick that glinted in the sun.

'That would be the man,' said Dylan.

Angus had servants, yes, several of them. In a warmer climate, with higher humidity, Dylan could imagine Angus as a plantation master. There was a crisply dressed butler who showed them the way to a table in a ballroom-sized atrium with tropical plants and colourful birds of various species flitting overhead.

'I spent several years in charge of a commando training camp in the Amazon,' Angus explained, a bit chesty from what might have been a chronic lung disorder. 'And I just couldn't get over the bird life there. So I had to bring the memories back with me.'

'Very nice,' Dylan said, wondering what import restrictions on exotics had been waved in Angus' favour. 'I did note a fondness for birds in your manuscript.'

'You actually read it?' said Angus.

'Of course. My first reader insisted that I read it cover to cover.'

Angus apparently missed Hillary rolling her eyes back.

'Thank you,' said Angus. 'You're the first publisher that's shown me that courtesy. Their loss, I say.' He caught sight of a young woman coming up to the table with water glasses on a tray. She was dark-skinned, with waist length hair, and dressed as colourfully as the birds overhead. 'Now, what can Isabelle get you? A Black Russian perhaps, or a Scotch Horse's Neck[103]?'

---

[103] http://bit.ly/2pPTrGF

It was only 11am, but Dylan's exchange of glances with Hillary said what the hell.

'It's been years,' Hillary confessed. 'The latter, please?'

Dylan had no idea what she'd ordered but assumed it had scotch in it, so he held up two fingers to Isabelle, with a smile as a garnish. He was right about the scotch, which was cunningly masked with ginger ale but had an aftertaste of angostura.

Angus looked after Isabelle appreciatively. 'Not something they drink in the Amazon,' he noted, 'but she learns… very quickly.'

Isabelle gave a slight bow and departed.

'What did you think of the chapters on Afghanistan?' Angus asked, poised for Dylan's reply.

Truth be known, Dylan had not read every word of the manuscript. Or even every second word. With the slush pile growing almost exponentially of late, he was more than happy to rely on Hillary's advice, or even D. H.'s on his irregular visits.

'Oh, those,' said Dylan. 'Very… readable. Couldn't put them down.'

Angus brightened. 'You don't think I'm being too harsh on the Government?'

'About?' Dylan glanced at Hillary for a clue.

'I think Angus means those parts where he takes the Government to task for glossing over the remediation of returning veterans with PTSD.'

'Oh, those,' Dylan said. 'Yes, *very* serious problem. Much in need of… remediation.' It seemed like the best word to use at the time, even if he was repeating Hillary's choice.

'Between you and me, and the foxholes[104] that no longer exist,' said Angus, smiling at Hillary as if she was calling the shots, 'I have a lawyer's advice that it's so contentious,

---

[104] http://bit.ly/2Ds2lfk

months out from an election, that the Government might try to quash the book with a court order.'

'So much the better for *us*,' said Hillary.

Dylan felt a mild chord – no, a chorus of – panic. 'Court order?' he managed. 'Lawyers, and all that?'

Angus' eyes narrowed. 'The other publishers got twitchy, too, at the thought. And they have lawyers on staff.'

'Of course it's a risk,' said Hillary, 'but think of the *publicity* – the interviews with Angus, the exposés!'

Dylan saw dollar signs fading more quickly than D. H. on his way to a shady cocktail party.

Speaking of which, Isabelle returned with theirs, complete with bright red swizzle sticks and a brigade of maraschino cherries impaled on sword-length toothpicks. Before Dylan knew it, the spirited conversation was so spirited that he was half finished with his drink and nodding at everything that was being said, mostly by Hillary and Angus. Somehow, Isabelle had disappeared and reappeared with fresh drinks. He was about to tell her he was fine with his drink when he noticed the glass was drained.

'Book sales,' he slurred, at various levels of intensity. 'Media coverage. Reprints. New s-staff…needed.'

The next thing he knew, he was waking up to an annoying ray of morning sunlight in a bed that was definitely not their own. A shower in a bathroom also not their own was steaming away, hopefully with Hillary in it, and there were thankfully no traces of Isabelle to match his swirling dream.

'Drat you… sunlight,' was all that Dylan could manage at that instant of cranial ache. He fended off the glare with a pillow unmistakably scented with lavender.

Angus clearly had done his homework on this prospective publisher.

Hillary emerged just then, wearing nothing but the towel she was using to dry her hair. 'Well-done, you,' she declared, peeping under a corner of the pillow at his tightly closed eyes. 'You set an all-time speed record for mixed drinks and still managed to have passable sex.'

'Ouch,' said Dylan, as she ripped the pillow out of his hands. 'I hope it was with you – the sex, I mean.'

She laughed. 'I had the sneaking suspicion that someone was watching us, even filming your adorable acrobatics, but it wouldn't have been the lovely Isabelle. I suspect that she has a boyfriend with brass knuckles[105] tucked away in a strategic place.'

Dylan groaned, distancing himself as far away as possible from the intrusive sun. 'You don't think that she and…?'

'Angus? Don't be ridiculous. The man can barely walk. Nevertheless, money can buy attention, and he certainly has plenty of dosh.'

Dylan managed a 90^0 angle, barely. 'My kingdom for an aspirin! Several, in fact.'

'Poor dear. I recommend massage pulse setting numero uno on the showerhead. Or perhaps you'd like to kick start with a refreshing bidet?'

He rubbed his head. 'I thought those were for the genitals.'

'Mind, body, genitalia: they're all interconnected, love.'

'I'd prefer a coffee-maker.'

'Over there,' said Hillary, pointing at the kitchenette. 'Arabica, Kona, or Black Blood of the Earth?'

'There's coffee called Black Blood of the Earth?'

'Yes, and I'm going to fix some now.'

'Whatever,' said Dylan, heading for the bathroom.

He emerged only after the supply of hot water had gone cold. She had his cup of freshly brewed Black Blood of the Earth ready.

He took a tentative sip before gulping down the rest. 'Christ, this is strong!'

Hillary was reading the packet. 'It says here that it's 30-40

---

[105] http://bit.ly/2pU0kqu

times as strong as regular coffee. And that they recommend that you drink no more than 3.5 ounces per day.'

He looked at the cup. 'How much is 3.5 ounces in metrics?'

She smiled. 'About half of what you've already drunk, boy!'

It was touch and go who should drive home after they'd both consumed twice their daily ration of Black Blood. Mostly go, go, go.

'I'm not sure anymore,' Dylan said, with his brain not sure whether it was in spinning or just throbbing mode.

'About?'

'Angus' book. He may have a lawyer on retainer, but we have *pues nada* as Hemingway would say, nothing is with us in terms of legal backup.'

She sniffed. 'Maybe so. But legalities are always more bluff than bite[106], and publishing is probably no different. If the Government applies for an injunction against the book, then Angus' brief can handle that because his interests are our interests, and vice-versa.'

'Yes,' said Dylan, slowing the car down from fifteen kilometres over the speed limit. 'But let's just say they decide to sue him for breach of the *Official Secrets Act*, or whatever they call it. We could be drawn into that.'

'You're ducking at shadows, Mr Publisher. Think of the press coverage you'd get. Independent Press Cited for Treason by Government. Canadian remix of *The Pentagon Papers*?'

Dylan addressed the window screen wiper. 'Hmm, what would Max do?'

There was a message waiting for them on the BBP answering machine. It was from Angus. 'Thanks for taking the time to visit me and hear me out about the book. As it happens, one of the majors I had given up on months ago has

---

[106] http://bit.ly/2lewbxg

responded with a six-figure advance. Care for an auction? If so, ring this number…'

'What the f---?' said Dylan.

Hillary shook her head. 'You should have signed him after that third Horse's Neck. Bloody hell!'

Chapter 13: Kings and Versifiers

AND SO IT WAS THAT BLACK BOOKS PUBLISHING REMAINED MOSTLY A POETRY AND LITERARY FICTION PUBLISHER for the next few years. Their list included a series of loosely related odes to native flora and fauna dusted off from the drawer of the Arts & Entertainment editor of the *Kamloops Daily News*, who had a premonition that the newspaper would cease operations soon and that he would then be free to grow his hair into dreadlocks and then express his creativity without reproach by the newspaper's publisher, who considered any poetry written since Keats to be presumptuous.

It turned out that this editor-come-poet was very well connected with scores of people who had absolutely no interest in and even less understanding of poetry, so his book launch at the prehistoric Kamloops Centre for the Arts set BBP records for the best attended and least number of books sold per attendee of any event up to that time. On the plus side, he managed to corner the Minister for Arts & Tourism into giving a launch speech by threatening [if he declined the invitation] to expose him as a closet poet of many yellowed sheaths himself.

The drinks and finger food were well in motion before an exceptionally tall suited woman Dylan didn't recognise appeared at the entrance door. She was at least the hundredth person there that Dylan didn't recognise, so he took no notice of her arrival, until, glancing down at her phone, she took notice of him and elbowed her way through the crowd, stopping only briefly to accept a flute of champagne, which she drained before making it to Dylan.

'This is dreadful,' she said of the empty glass. 'Whatever

prompted the Okanagan vintners to venture into champagne – or whatever they're permitted to call it – now?'

'No idea,' said Dylan. 'We supplied the snacks, but the author was in charge of the drinks. And you are?'

'Candice Blunt,' she said, handing him the flute. 'Private Secretary to Minister de la Hunt.'

He caught the flute with his free hand seconds before it would have otherwise crashed to the floor. 'Charmed,' said Dylan. 'And the Minister is… where?'

Candice glanced back at the entryway. 'Out in the car I suspect trying to find an excuse to exempt himself from this tawdry event. Not that we have anything against *literature*,' she added, holding a copy of the book at viper's length, 'but it is increasingly hard to find these days and, from the blaringly tedious pages I was subjected to by your author to prepare his launch speech, which the Minister may or may not have to deliver, that esoteric delight is not to be found in this book. Nice cover design, though.'

Dylan relaxed his dropped jaw. 'Thanks,' he said. 'I did that.' [He hadn't, but this seemed an opportune time to deflect the discussion away from the bristling text inside the cover.]

'Oh, God,' she said. 'He's here. OK, you've got five minutes from now to remix this… gathering into lecture mode because we have to be out of here in no less than seven minutes, give or take ten seconds, to make it to his next event.' She pointed at the flute. 'Oh, please say you have some nice French, or even Californian, on reserve in your fridge?'

Dylan shrugged. *'Pues nada.'*

'Excuse me?'

But then she was gone.

With Hillary's clapping to attention, the crowd shuffled into "lecture" mode in four minutes, thirty-seven seconds, give or take ten seconds. The Minister took his place at the head of the class, raised both hands over the crowd as if either to bless them or acknowledge the applause that didn't materialise as he began to speak with no reference to the notecard Candice had inserted firmly into the book.

'Friends,' he said. 'Let us acknowledge that we meet here today on the sacred lands of the Tk'emlups te Secwepemc – or the Kamloops Indian Band as we used to call them. Poetry, too, is sacred to us, a precious, ethereal language passed down to us from the masters of antiquity...'

'Did you write that for him?' Dylan whispered to Candice, finding her next to him again.

'Only the first part,' she replied aloud. 'He always trips over the pronunciation of the Indian names. But he's in lost-in-space mode now.'

The Minister gave a mercifully short speech then yielded the stage to the author who showed slides of the various flora and fauna that inspired his poems into gems like 'The little sorrows of the ladybird / no more than half an inch beneath the sword...', as Candice, glaring at her watch to make time stand still[107], did her best to nudge the Minister towards the door.

But the Minister would have none of that and made straight for Dylan, all the while shaking hands whenever they were, and even whenever they weren't, offered.

'I know you,' he said, stabbing a finger at Dylan's breastbone. 'You led that wildcat strike years ago down in Penticton during that cold snap, didn't you?'

'I'm impressed you'd remember that,' said Dylan, anything but impressed.

'We weren't in government at the time,' the Minister continued, 'but I recall thinking now there's a good prospect for our party. Have you ever been tempted to run for office?'

Only mildly surprised that the Minister didn't remember

---

[107] http://bit.ly/2EaEOAu

his unsuccessful tilt at the political windmill, Dylan shook his head. 'I'm unpopular enough as a publisher. Why would I want to make matters worse?'

The Minister laughed. 'Fair enough – for now. In the meantime, I want to help you out with your enterprise.'

Dylan roused from his small-talk slumber. 'Really? How?'

'Have you ever applied for an arts grant?'

'No.'

'You should,' the Minister winked. 'I want to break the mould, send a few shivers through the Lower Mainland publishing establishment, decentralise. Get my drift?'

Be still, my heart, Dylan thought. 'Shouldn't we wait until we've got a few more runs on the board, Minister?' he said.

'Maybe you're not cut out to be a politician, after all,' the Minister quipped, finally giving in to Candice's furtive gestures.

Meanwhile, the author, emboldened by applause, fractured as it was, persisted into his coyote epic[108].

Hillary's feet never touched the ground. 'You're saying the Minister offered you an inside track to a grant and you dithered?'

'"Dithered" is such a strong word,' said Dylan, knowing very well what would come next.

'From what you've said, I suspect you actually *super-*dithered,' she pounced.

'No one's ever offered me money. Especially from the public purse.' It hit him then. 'There's a cost, you know.'

'Which is?'

'You get one grant, and then you want another. And another. Pretty soon you're hooked.'

'I fail to see how making friends with a cash cow is a bad thing.'

Dylan held up his hands as though he was stopping

---

[108] http://bit.ly/2C5SLCC

traffic for school kids. 'Freedom of expression – that sort of thing? For instance, if we had made a deal with Angus, it might come back to bite us at the next grant round.'

'Get your snout in the trough in the first instance, then worry about round two. It would make a pleasant change from you being under the tax-free threshold for seven years running, darling. Not that I'm complaining about being the bread winner.'

'*Primary* bread winner,' he said. 'And I'm the sole bread *maker* in this household, so there.'

And so it was that Dylan requested the necessary forms from the Arts Department to apply for a grant. By the end of the process, even with Hillary's skill at fudging figures, he was ready to stick pins in his eyes.

'I make more by the hour publishing poetry,' he concluded, filling in the little box asking how much time he'd spent filling in the application, which came to three days, six hours and seventeen minutes, give or take 10 minutes – which was in fact a slight exaggeration, but it made him feel good that some public servant in a cubbyhole might feel the slightest twinge of guilt over their water torture process.

Weeks later, an envelope arrived, neatly addressed to Black Books Publishing, c/- Mr Dylan Cashew, M.A.

'Formality's good,' he said, noting the "M.A.", carrying the envelope inside and setting it on the dining table while he checked on their stir-fry for dinner. 'I'll wait until she gets home to open it,' he said to the wok. 'Good news comes to those who wait.'

It wasn't good news.

Black Books Publishing
c/- Mr Dylan Cashew, M. A.

Acacia Studio
26 Acacia Terrace
Penticton, BC V2A 5E9

Dear Sir

Thank you for applying to the most recent round of arts grants.

Unfortunately, your application is this instance was unsuccessful because there were far more exceptional applications than our limited funding could satisfy.

We know this news will be disappointing, but we trust you will continue with your valuable work in the arts and do encourage you to apply again in future rounds.

Yours faithfully
E.G.
Assistant to the Deputy Director, Grants

They just stared at each other, as their respective glasses of shiraz grew ever so slightly warmer and their plates of steaming prawn stir-fry grew ever so cooler.

'I thought---' Hillary ventured.

'Look at the signature initials,' said Dylan, poking at it. 'Grade 10 level. Not even the Deputy Director herself but some tepid coffee making assistant!'

Hillary gently swept away his hand. 'Look, there's a number you can ring for feedback.'

'Never mind that,' Dylan snapped, rediscovering his shiraz. 'The *Minister* gave me his card.'

On the dot of 9am, Dylan rang the "Direct" number. It went direct, all right, direct to voice-mail. Dylan groaned heavily into the receiver for a few seconds then hung up, venting his displeasure onto a nearby dishtowel.

Thirty minutes later, he tried again. Same result, more exaggerated response on his part.

He practiced the deep breathing exercises[109] Hillary had

---

[109] http://bit.ly/2lgh85Y

given him to b-a-l-a-n-c-e himself. Then rang again.

This time, there was an actual voice on the other end. 'De la Hunt here.'

Dylan almost hung up. He had no script. What if the Minister didn't recall their conversation? What if he thought him a heavy breathing crackpot who should be referred to the RCMP – or worse?

'Good morning, Minister,' he said, as calmly as someone in stage two panic mode could manage. 'This is Dylan Cashew, M.A., Black Books Publishing.' He caught himself before he continued with his address details from the letter. 'You may not recall our conversation, but---'

'Of course I do,' said the Minister, bouncy as Kanga to Dylan's Eeyore. 'I'm just outside Parliament in the car, but what can I do for you?'

With due diplomatic pacing that impressed even himself, Dylan explained what had happened, taking care to avoid an accusatory tone.

'Ah,' said the Minister. 'I think someone may have fired the wrong pistol, so to speak.'

'Meaning?'

'As Minister I have the last say, which can involve some… fine-tuning of priorities.'

Dylan was all in favour of "fine-tuning".

'Leave it with me,' said the Minister. 'My P. A. will get back to you.'

Doubtlessly the dreaded Candice. She-Who-Will-Not-Be-Disobeyed[110].

'I'll look forward to her call. Thank you, Minister.'

Dylan gave the nearest scotch bottle more than a passing look, but it was barely 10am and he didn't want to distract the Earth on its axis.

Just on lunchtime, the phone rang. Sure enough it was Candice. Who else would not bother to introduce herself

[110] http://bit.ly/2C67QEb

before getting down to gold-platted tacks?

'It seems there's been a... misunderstanding,' she explained. 'The letter you received originated from a support person who recently became surplus to requirements for the department, and this templated communication was mistakenly dispatched by her replacement, who failed to exercise the proper protocol. Needless to say, said support person has been counselled and will be sending you the correct communication, which contains a grant offer that I am sure you will find to your satisfaction. Congratulations.'

Her 'congratulations' was as tepid as day-old tea, but Dylan let it go.

'Thanks,' he said, as evenly as possible. 'Have a nice day.'

For much of that day, the slush pile was neglected as Dylan did his research online about grant amounts publishers could expect to receive. He had only wanted to ask for $10,000 in the original application, but Hillary thought otherwise.

'No one but the Ballet and the Symphony Orchestra gets what they ask for, and sometimes not even they do. Ask for at least twenty grand and maybe, maybe you'll get ten. But don't round to even figures in your proposed budget. The assessors penalise rubbery figures[111].'

'When's the last time you submitted a grant application?'

'Never. But I do lunch all the time with people who have.'

So Dylan had fudged the figures for freight, postage and promotional materials to arrive at a total budget of $20,297.23, but then rounded down to $20,297 since "8" is an even number.

But then the application had succumbed to "templated communication", so he had no idea what to expect. He checked the Arts Department website and found that in the previous round three global publishers had received an average of $30,000 each, while two regional independents had received about $20,000. Obviously, Hillary had lunched

---

[111] http://bit.ly/2t18q1O

with the right people.

When the letter arrived two days later, he ripped it open in anticipation of a luncheon date at the Coffee Club to celebrate. But the offered amount was not $20,297 or even $10,297. They had rounded down to $10,000.

He made the booking at the Coffee Club anyway. Joseph had agreed to join them as their first almost award winner, and there was a fourth chair that D. H. was happy to occupy.

'It's better than nothing,' said Joseph, alternating between the letter and his menu.

'It's *a lot* better than nothing,' said Hillary, checking the wine list after patting his hand.

'I had my heart set on that $297,' Dylan muttered. 'Plus 10K.'

'I predict the service here will be dreadful,' said D. H., glancing around.

'You don't need to eat, anyway,' Dylan said to him.

'What was that?' Joseph said.

'Nothing,' said Hillary, pushing the wine list over to him. 'In times of stress, Dylan talks to his imaginary friend.'

'You know we Mormons don't drink,' Joseph said, pushing the wine list back. 'This... imaginary friend of yours, Dylan. How come you never spoke to him during the strike?'

'Oh, I did,' Dylan said quickly. 'I just kept radio silence[112] – to maintain morale.'

'That's talking on your toes,' said D. H.

'What do my t---' Dylan began before cutting himself off.

'I might have the crumbed salmon,' said Joseph, shrugging it off.

'I'm going to be of absolutely no use here with this bible basher,' said D. H. 'So I might be off. Literary grant, eh? In

---

[112] http://bit.ly/2pRfUTE

my day, publishers actually had to *work* for a living. Spend up big and run, I say.'

With that, he vanished in the general direction of the closest wine bar.

'What I don't understand is why they give the internationals so much and us so little,' Dylan said.

'It's counter-intuitive,' Hillary nodded. 'You'd think that the internationals could hardly be bothered with beer money, so why would they even apply for grants?'

'If the pond is there,' said Joseph, 'why not fish in it? They have people on staff who earn back their salaries applying for grants. And it's also about prestige – who can garner the most government logos for their imprint pages and then crow about it over cocktails at the next industry awards dinner.'

Dylan took a deep breath. 'Have you ever thought it might be time for a career change?'

That went on for a while. Each year at grant time, Dylan would fill out the forms, complete with loglines[113] and promotional summaries written mostly by Hillary after he ran out of keywords he could use to praise his upcoming poetry titles, even with the increased sophistication of Google and online thesauruses. And D. H. always had a different parallel universe to visit as the application deadlines loomed. Dylan grew more creative by the year with his figures, teasing the online budget calculators until they came up with a different odd dollar figure in the dollar's place, anticipating, and then expecting, that the result would be as it always was, precisely $10,000.

Then, just after he'd submitted his latest application, the Government fell. So badly, in fact, that Minister de la Hunt lost his seat, not by a landslide, but just enough. The Conservatives were back in. And the headlines were all about belt-tightening, even though belts had been out of fashion for years, until a hint of arse-crack was all the rage,

113 http://bit.ly/2pTky3m

except perhaps in Parliament where even a suggestion of a show of privates could trigger a Royal Commission.

Like every opposition party before them, the Conservatives ran on a platform of reform built on leggy promises of reducing expenditures through productivity "efficiencies" so as to achieve Nirvana, i.e. a budget surplus. Reform committees were established to investigate, interrogate, conclude and recommend a slate of "efficiencies" from which the Government could pick and choose, not out of alignment with marginal electoral seats. The easiest targets were the softest: welfare services and the arts, not necessarily in that order.

And so it was that Dylan and other publishers were summoned to Victoria by the newly appointed Minister for Tourism, Innovation, Science and the Arts. The Arts Department had been fused into the "Super Ministry" [to reduce assumed duplication and expected inefficiencies owing to the DNA of artists and their vindictive cousins who became administrators] and its position at the string's end[114] was prophetic of its fate as the softest of the soft.

The night before his flight, Dylan received a Private Number call from a muffled voice that reminded him more than a little of the defeated Minister for the Arts.

'A word of warning from a friend,' the voice began.

'Which friend?' Dylan asked. 'Who is this?'

'Never mind that,' the voice croaked. 'Watch your back. I have it from a reliable source that the new minister is sleeping with the poetry editor of a rival Lower Mainland company.'

'Which company? Dylan demanded.

'What else is Google for?' the voice said, less muffled and even more like the recently departed Minister. 'Do your research!'

Dylan had nightmares enough to deal with given printer deadlines with his next three books, which included a Joycean

[114] http://bit.ly/2BNDRN1

stream-of-consciousness verse novel – or what Dylan came to regard as novel verse – by a retired Professor of German from the University of BC about fly fishing in Macedonia for the endangered Ohrid Trout[115].

'Their numbers are going down and down,' the Professor had said in his covering letter, appealing to what he hoped was a distant publisher's ecological sentiment, followed up with a strident phone call during which he listed all the university connections he would hammer for readings, etc., once a release date for the book had been confirmed. The longer the call went on, the more his tone suggested that he was talking about a book for which the contract was signed, sealed and delivered[116].

'Oh, no,' Hillary said that night as he tried to replicate the tenor of the conversation.

'The poor Ohrid Trout?' Dylan nodded.

'No,' she said. 'Poor you – if you agree to publish that lunatic's book!'

'Start local, think global,' Dylan replied. 'Wasn't that your advice?'

'Yes,' she said. 'But here's another fridge magnet for you: start sane, avoid *in*sane.'

She was more than right. The Professor was like a Kaiser in exile: self-absorbed, self-righteous, demanding, and totally unrealistic about what an independent publisher could do for him and his fly-fishing verse novel. Every day a fresh email would arrive in Dylan's box addressed to the "Promotions Manager" with an exhaustive list of foreign contacts at universities and technical institutions that Dylan had never heard of, with texts in translation that said Promotions Manager was expected to transmit verbatim, simply substituting her/his name in the salutation, copied and pasted onto letterhead, promising God knows what to the foreign contact if the Professor's event could be confirmed.

---

[115] http://bit.ly/2G2rHIZ
[116] http://bit.ly/2pMv7oS

Then the flood of emails increased, with the Professor asking how many replies had been logged that day, and when exactly he could expect to receive a spreadsheet of his tour dates updated in real time.

Just when Dylan was about to haul up the white flag or sound a full-scale retreat, the Professor would ring to speak in an uncharacteristic un-Kaiser-like tone to say, 'Tell your Promotions person not to trouble herself with Google Translate. Just forward all replies on to yours truly. Thank you so much!'

Like embracing a sugar-free [exempting alcohol] diet, Dylan swore off anything that smacked of Wikipedia, as if that were even remotely possible, and, with grateful, trembling hands for an excuse to be absent, packed his bags for Victoria.

He had never flown business class for business or otherwise but somehow managed to hug it as his due. Aware that his contemporaries in economy would have to settle for apple juice or even diet Coke-like brand X drinks to wash down their powdered scrambled eggs, he ordered a Dewar's on the rocks before and after his perfectly poached Eggs Benedict with bacon [Canadian, of course]. There was no limo waiting for him outside the baggage collection doors, but then he remembered the voucher they'd supplied for a cab straight to the Chateau Victoria. He was a bit disappointed that they'd reserved him a studio room rather than a suite, but then the Conservatives *were* in charge, and campaign promises had to be kept – at least to some visible degree.

The call from Reception woke him at 8:45 precisely as he'd asked, and a wane young man in a pinstriped suit who looked like he'd been up all night met him in the lobby.

'Right this way if you will, Mr Cashew,' the young man said.

He led the way to a waiting car, which drove them to a pollution-etched sandstone building guarded by chipped gargoyles. Once inside, the young man led him down a Victorian hallway with lighting so diminished that Dylan nearly bumped into a bronze statue of some explorer or vanished Indian chief along the way until his eyes adjusted. Soon they reached the meeting room, at which point the young man held up his hand like a security guard, directing Dylan to sit on a bench against the wall opposite to the room. A middle-aged woman with chaotically curly hair, screaming red lipstick, and a blouse that spoke more than it suggested, slid over to her right, just enough to allow him space.

'The Minister for Tourism, Innovation, Science and the Arts sends his apologies for his absence owing to an extended debate on the Government's first piece of legislation,' the young man whispered as if the oaken door had ears. 'His P. A., Lauren Bide, will be with you shortly. Your patience is important to us.'

With that, he continued down the dark hallway seemingly melding into the carpet.

'Name's Gladys, Abalone Editions,' the woman said, offering her hand with a royal limpness. 'Mr Cashew, isn't it?'

'Yes,' Dylan said. 'Have we met?'

'I very much doubt it,' Gladys said, rolling her eyes. 'I can't remember the last time I set foot east of Burnaby. I hear you're based in Penticton.' She'd nearly run out of breath but managed to add, 'How very adventurous of you!'

Dylan bristled. 'Well, someone has to serve the regions.'

'And what do you publish at...?'

'Black Books Publishing?' Dylan inserted.

'Yes, what a curiously *morbid* name! Genre fiction, I suppose. Horror, feminist dystopia[117] – that sort of thing?'

'Mostly poetry.'

She took a generous breath. 'Admirable. Courageous, as Sir Humphrey would say.'

---

[117] http://bit.ly/2ChHvCp

Dylan had watched and enjoyed more than a few episodes of *Yes, Minister* but didn't want to encourage her. 'Not at all. All of our poetry books return a profit.'

She smiled smugly. 'Before or after the grant you're not going to get next year?'

Dylan was about to answer somewhat rudely, when the heavy door swung open. A slim young woman with red hair so striking that she would not have been out of place on the barricades of *Les Misérables* strode out.

'Gladys,' she said, ignoring Dylan. 'So good to see you again! How long has it been?'

'Monday?' said Gladys, standing up and following her inside the meeting room.

Checking his watch in a reflex, Dylan confirmed that it was in fact Wednesday.

Some thirty-three minutes, give or take 10 seconds, later, Gladys burst out the door, shaken but summoning a composed face for his benefit. Almost as an afterthought, She-of-the-Red-Hair noticed him.

'Mr Cashew,' she said, as if she'd just drawn him from a hat. 'Thank you for your patience. Right this way.'

She walked at quite a clip, and Dylan was just catching up with her when she froze in her tracks. He did bump into her, but only slightly. They entered an outer office.

'Have you been offered a drink? No? What will you have – a latté, perhaps? Long or short macchiato? We can do them all, thanks to our newly appointed staff barista.'

So this is what "productivity efficiencies" are all about, thought Dylan. Well, while in post-Grecian Greece… 'I'll have a latté, double-shot, please.'

'You heard the gentleman, Emily,' She-of-the-Red-Hair said to the receptionist. 'And I know I'll regret it but plunk on another macchiato for me. Artificial sweetener this time – damn the cancer risk. Ring it through and ask Manuel to bring them in.'

She led the way into her office, which was overwhelmingly white in furnishings except for a slender vase next to the albino phone containing a scarlet rose with very apparent thorns. And except for the nameplate, which read

Candice.

Too much of a coincidence, Dylan told himself. The muffled voice had given him a name, but he'd forgotten it. Candice Reconfigured? Better not risk it.

'Oh, that,' She-of-the-Red-Hair said, following his eyes and then flipping it over. 'The replacement nameplate is on expedited order. Five working days, they said, and it's now been eight. But that's what we're on about, Mr Cashew, passing legislation that trims the fat, tames the unions and improves productivity province-wide so everyone benefits. That's where you and Black and Blue... no, Black *Books* Publishing comes in.'

'How so?'

'Will you join us, Mr Cashew,' she breathed.

He hesitated. 'Join us how exactly?'

A light knock at the door cut through the silence between them.

'Come,' She-of-the-Red-Hair said.

Manuel trotted in balancing a silver setting and their coffees together with a plate of slivered almond cookies with an understatement of powdered sugar on top. He actually had an over-sized serviette over his left shoulder. Having served them, he assumed sentry posture in the corner nearest the door.

'That will be all, Manuel,' said She-of-the-Red-Hair.

'Not your luncheon orders?' squeaked Manuel with a Spanish accent. 'The Chef, he say---'

'That will be *all*, Manuel!'

To which Manuel took a practiced half-bow and exit.

Not wanting to repeat himself, Dylan stared at the plate

of almond cookies, willing one to levitate onto his bone-China saucer. Finally, he reached out to the plate.

'By rescinding your grant application,' she said, completing her fragmented thought.

Dylan took one and then a second of the cookies then licked his finger free of the powdered sugar. 'You could just reject the application,' he said.

She took a gulp of her macchiato. 'It's more complicated than that, Mr Cashew. Let me explain. The Government's mandate is to increase productivity by encouraging efficiencies, not only in the public sector but also in private sector organisations that have become... accustomed to grants.'

'Forgive a poor backwoods publisher, but how does having us withdraw a grant application that you are probably going to reject anyway improve efficiency? Doesn't it just create more paperwork?'

'Point taken,' she said. 'That's why you're here. So you can offer to rescind your application, and I can accept your rescindation – all without paperwork.' She picked up the plate. 'More cookies? And how's your latte?'

'Excuse me, but is that even a word?'

'Latté?'

'No, rescindation.'

She smiled. 'The English language is evolving, Mr Cashew, and we must evolve with it. Even as we speak. As a forward thinking government, we pride ourselves at riding the whitecaps of change[118].'

'My latte got cold as we spoke,' he said. 'Even before we spoke.'

She squiggled a finger across her white desk emulating a line in the sand. 'Let me be frank with you, Mr Cashew. There are too many junkies in the arts sector. By junkies I mean organisations hooked on grants. They have forgotten

---

[118] http://bit.ly/2Dtgl37

the thrill of independence. They have forsworn the vitality of a creative voice that only exists when they are free of the shackles of government.'

It was all coming back to him then, the muffled warning, the virtual finger pointing at... 'Where did you say you were working before the election?' he asked.

'I didn't,' she said. 'But if you really want to know, I was a senior editor at Sequoia Books' Canadian sub-office.'

'In poetry, wasn't it?'

She darkened. 'Who told you that?'

'Someone who's already been rescinded.'

'Very funny. I think I can crack that particular nutshell.'

'Thanks for the latte,' said Dylan, grabbing a fistful of cookies as he stood up. 'By the way, will Sequoia Books' Canadian branch be implementing any efficiencies besides seconding you to the Ministry?'

'Fair question,' she said, not standing. 'Why don't you take the whole plate?'

PART 4: LEVITICUS

If you find yourself tempted to have sexual relations with an editorial subordinate, proofread the nearest manuscript – again. I am the Lord your God.

Chapter 14: Rules of E-ngagement

DYLAN LEFT THE OFFICE OF SHE-OF-THE-RED-HAIR WITHOUT HER SILVER PLATE or even any bone China and certainly without rescinding his grant application. Outside, he thumbed his nose at the gargoyles, but he knew the writing was on the wall, in forced rhyme.

There was no car waiting for him, but D. H. was.

'Your driver probably had his orders to dump you in the closest mine tailings pond,' said D. H., 'So I told him to beat it.'

'You let him see you?'

'Of course not. I presented as a doorman.'

'And how did you do that?'

'Art Conan Doyle has been mentoring me on shape-shifting[119]. It took a while, but I think I've got the hang of it.'

'There are no doormen in *Sherlock Holmes*. Not that I can recall, anyway.'

'No, but Professor Moriarty is a man of many vicious talents.'

'Fine. Then let's shape-shift back to Penticton.'

'Easier said than done for you mere mortals. But I've already checked in your bag at the airport. Use your other voucher to catch up.'

Dylan had a head start with his two Dewar's on the plane, but Hillary quickly caught up by means of a very passable red over their seared prawn curry.

'After you texted me, I did my research on the bitch,' she said. 'She worked her way through two husbands, but not before she managed two promotions – from intern at the

---

[119] http://bit.ly/2C8guBW

starting gate, to an assistant editor at the stretch six months later, and then a senior editor eighteen months later. NB: her ex-second husband was, and still remains, managing editor at Sequoia.'

'Very intelligent, and/or an expert at Kama Sutra?'

'I vote "or",' said Hillary. 'You'd better let me check your back for scratch marks.'

Dylan actually lifted his shirt and assumed *The Thinker* pose. 'Maybe it's time to cash in my red pens and beg for my old job back?' he sighed.

'I wouldn't give Browbait the satisfaction. Besides, so long as I'm the chief breadwinner, I have first dibs on the remote.'

And so it was that Dylan worked on for seven more years, including nights, and in the eighth year Amazon cast its eye over the earthly fog and decided it was missing something, so it would launch into books as one minor cog in its determination to tame the ozone [economy] layer. And so the eBook was born. While the big publishers fortified their bunkers, Dylan decided to go for broke and learn the rules of engagement for publishing online, so he registered BBP with Amazon, and then Apple, and then Google, and then, behold… the list of distributors grew and grew.

He learned to speak a new language tagged with keywords like ePub [scotch-free], mobi, iBooks, Kindle [matchless], and eventually "fixed layout[120]" [optional pause here while some of you resort to private googling, or simply click on the generously provided link]. Soon he became known as the eBook guru of Penticton, largely because no one else could be bothered with all of this.

Meanwhile, back in the world of wood chips and glue, authors made an unconscious effort to ignore the spectre of eBooks like a quasar against a night of interstellar space. This, despite Hillary's best effort to position BBP as an

---

[120] http://bit.ly/2pTl7t2

"innovator," "an early adopter of new technology," even a "Stellar brand." No, the authors who sought out BBP were overwhelmingly bricks-and-mortar in bias, and none as stridently so than Ivan Smirnov [not to be confused with the vodka].

As legend [or, rather, Dylan's daydream] has it, Ivan arrived in Canada by husky-powered sled over the Bering Strait in a climatic year that broke all previous records for sea ice between Siberia and Alaska. It must have been a "Super" sled, even grander in concept than the raft of "Super Ministries" vogued in BC around that time, because he would have had in tow his wife Katarina, who would not be seen, even in a blizzard, dressed in anything more casual than Prada designs, or at worst Gucci, not to mention their six children, Inga, Inessa, Izolda, Iskra, Kiril and Konstantin, who had probably never been east of Lenin's tomb.

More likely, the Smirnov family arrived by private jet one dark and misty Vancouver morning to escape interrogation by the FSB, formerly known as the KGB, for decidedly capitalist activities that were the envy of Kremlin wannabe plutocrats[121]. It's anyone's guess what happened to the jet, but Smirnov somehow managed to bankroll Penny Lane Real Estate in Vancouver, which specialised in managing vacant apartment suites for overseas arms-length developers. Charging a premium rate of 15% of assessable value on these properties, Smirnov quickly became a millionaire several times over. He and Katarina bought their way onto the A-list of Vancouver society where the landed gentry patiently listened to many hours of his exploits in Russia after the breakup of the Soviet Union, including several poker flirtations with Vladimir Putin that he generally managed to lose at despite the vagaries of Chance[122]. Smirnov's broken English was a bit hard to follow, especially several Black Russians into the evening, but the gracious and always stunningly dressed

---

[121] http://bit.ly/2Ec6V2n
[122] http://bit.ly/2Cjw1vC

Katarina helped to colour in the blank expressions of the male listeners, whether they were heterosexual or not.

It was no surprise then that the real Smirnov sent his wife alone to Penticton to meet Dylan, who Smirnov had chosen to publish the memoir of his struggle from pauperdom on his arrival in Vancouver to Number 17 on the city's most wealthy list. Dylan had hesitated [he almost never met with prospective clients in his modest studio, which seemed grander as described by Hillary with liberal if not poetic license on the BBP website landing page], but Smirnov's offer of a $500 consultation fee for 'just a few minutes of your time' heightened his curiosity just enough that he agreed to the session.

He spent the appointed morning tidying his In and Out trays, clearing away spent scotch bottles, consigning the many rejected manuscripts to plastic garbage bags in the garage, even vacuuming and then waxing away the stains on his desk.

When the doorbell rang at 9:15am precisely, he glanced around with satisfaction at the job he'd done, forgetting that he was still in his pyjamas.

As he opened the door, Katarina looked him up and down and smiled. 'I like your dress code,' she said in a slightly tantalising accent. 'Shall we get down to it?'

'Excuse me a second,' said Dylan, heading for the bedroom. 'I forgot to feed the goldfish.'

'You keep goldfish in your pyjamas?'

'They're... shy,' said Dylan, slamming the door behind him then shaking a fist at the full-length mirror. 'You could have told me,' really directing it at the absent D. H., before slipping on clean shorts and the only business shirt and unwrinkled walking shorts he could find, then brushing his teeth in a nanosecond.

'Now, where were we?' he asked, emerging, finding her poised on his chair in the studio.

'Aren't you going to introduce me to your goldfish?' she teased, staring below his belt and smoothing her skirt over her crossed legs.

'Maybe not,' he said, drawing up a spare chair. 'They're excitable.'

'I thought you said they are shy.'

'The two states of consciousness aren't mutually exclusive,' he said, straining for formality.

'Very well. Perhaps after we have sighed the contract?'

'You mean *signed*?'

'Yes, of course, that's what I said. I have a second degree from Stanford University, so I do not make mistakes in the grammar.'

'Shall we get on with it, then?'

She fetched a cheque from her Gucci bag. Sure enough, it was already made out to Black Books Publishing in the promised amount. 'It is all in order, then?'

'Very much so. Thank you.'

'Then we will want at least 5,000 copies for the advanced reviews, then reprints of 10,000 to coincide with the major book reviews. This is all possible?'

The numbers were dazzling. Dylan's largest print run to date had been his vastly optimistic 500 for *Arctic Secrets*, 293 copies of which remained in the garage as verified during his most recent stocktake[123].

'Of course, he said, 'but we have first the matter of the manuscript, which I've yet to read.' It struck him that he had echoed her idiomatic expression with an awkwardness of his own – *we have first…* – what was he trying to prove?

She reached into her bag and pulled out a gold-plated – he had no doubt by then that it was a real rather than an imitation, since nothing about Katarina was synthetic – flash drive, stuck it into the USB slot on his keyboard and shook her head when his virus scanner commenced to do what it was paid for. 'Is there no way to override this waste of time?'

---

[123] http://bit.ly/2pRSvRW

'Oh, that,' he said. 'Norton will be finished in a few seconds.'

A few minutes later, Norton was.

Katarina slid her chair to the right ever so slightly. 'You will like to scan a few pages to be sure?'

He eased himself into the available space in front of the iMac, which she gradually compressed until there were only millimetres between her left knee and his bare right.

Chapter One wasn't Pulitzer-winning, although Smirnov's early obsession with the conspiracy theories[124] surrounding the escape of Anastasia, daughter of Nicholas II, during the unsightly royal purge by the Bolsheviks and whether or not she survived due to her jewel-studded bullet-proof vest did slow the pacing. Still, the writing was polished enough to bear witness to the hand of a hired-gun professional editor.

Scrolling down, he was distracted by her hand transitioning to his knee and only when her pale cheek touched his shoulder did he comprehend that she was about to faint.

With her eyes rolling back, it was certainly pointless reading on into Chapter Two.

'Anas… I mean Katarina, what's wrong?' he asked, putting an arm around her to prevent a total collapse.

'I… am… sorry,' she murmured, coming out of it only slightly. 'My anaemia is what first attracted Ivan to me. "The royal affliction", he still calls it. The Canadian specialist prescribed drugs…' [at which point she gripped his knee again for balance] 'that mostly work.'

'Would you like to lie down?' Dylan asked, hastily adding 'on the couch?'

'No, I must have a bed,' she said. 'The space between cushions on a couch aggravates my circulation…'

He helped her into the bedroom and onto the bed, doing

---

[124] http://bit.ly/2pRHiRp

his best to keep his feet on the floor. She pointed vaguely over his shoulder.

'The goldfish,' she whispered. 'Place their bowl as close as possible to me on the bedside table – it will help the dizziness to pass.'

Of course, there were no goldfish, and especially no bowl, but Dylan fetched and placed the closest thing – a rounded perfume bottle of Hillary's from her dressing table, which almost immediately seemed to relax Katarina, if not him.

'Thank you, Mr Cashew,' she said, eyelids drooping. 'Now, I must sleep for an extended period. Perhaps you will have a nap as well?'

'No, thank you,' Dylan said, extricating himself, fearing one of the glimmering jewels in her necklace might be a spy cam[125] to exact a higher royalty figure. 'I'll keep reading – while you rest.'

It defies fiction, Dylan thought, eyes glued to the screen on Chapter Two and then Three, taking in only the gist of it.

'What the hell are you doing?' smirked a familiar voice behind him. 'You'd better ring Hillary, and quickly.'

It was D. H., sporting the wings of a guardian angel.

'You're taking this shape-shifting game too far,' said Dylan. 'I've done nothing wrong here. I'll find the smelling salts soon and call a taxi for her. Hillary won't be home for hours.'

'So naive. I suspect she's already been tipped off. You'll have just enough time to check your collar for lipstick, print out the contract and waken Sleeping Beauty with something slightly more abrasive than a kiss.'

Dylan had just hit the print command when he heard their car pulling into the drive. Thankfully, the printer was doing its job as Hillary burst in the door.

'Are you OK?' she said, breathlessly. 'They said it was an emergency – someone fainted?'

---

[125] http://bit.ly/2lowch8

'That would be Ms Roman---, I mean Smirnov.'

'You've been drinking *and* cleaned the house? It's never looked so tidy!' She peeked into the bedroom, and then did in fact check his collar.

In a reflex he started to unbutton his shirt.

'Not now,' she said. 'Too kinky by far.'

He shook his head. 'I thought you wanted to check my back for scratches again.'

And so it was that Black Books Publishing added an imprint, Big White Press, with a logo that resembled a glaciated mountain scrawled in free-hand overprinted with BWP in the same font as its parent company, for the purpose of publishing "assisted" works such as Ivan Smirnov's *Musings of a Homesick Oligarch*. It became a first in more than one respect. The initial print run was in fact 5,000 copies, paid for in advance by Smirnov, who had already pre-booked its printing by a company in a distant province of China that Google Maps hadn't translated let alone charted, air-freighted to Penny Lane's Coquitlam warehouse at an address that Google Maps hadn't discovered by 2D let alone 3D rendering, though Dylan had no reason other than this to doubt the existence of the printer, the warehouse, or even the freight company that freighted the books by air in less time than it took the parcel containing ten sample copies of the book to arrive in Penticton from the warehouse.

It hardly mattered that the books were printed on stock of marginal thickness, or that Dylan's token copies had to be prised gently from each other due to packing too hot from the press, but the gilded, raised font on the Getty stock image that echoed a 19th century High Tea that would have made Charlotte Bronte blush was sure to impress jet lagged browsers at the airport shops.

'Never mind,' said Hillary some evenings later, as they toasted his luck, and especially the sizeable cheque in the

BBP account that hadn't yet bounced, at the best [and only] Ukrainian restaurant Penticton had to offer. 'I could get used to the occasional vodka with cranberry chaser.'

'I thought you meant the paper stock,' said Dylan, sticking out his tongue at the tartness of the cranberry as if it were his penance for compromise. 'I still feel… violated, somehow.'

'Get over it,' said Hillary, refreshing their glasses from their diminishing BYO vodka bottle. 'Besides, with a ten book elevation, your virtual goldfish will have a stunning view of our formal garden with its tri-coloured fountain.'

Dylan gave her a funny look. 'You really are enjoying this, aren't you?'

'Not as much as that rejigged *Kirkus Review* that appeared in the *New York Times*, syndicated in L. A. and in *The Washington Post*, *The Guardian*, and the———'

'Yes,' said Dylan. 'But it's a good thing that irony and sarcasm don't translate well from English into Russian.'

With the Smirnov-fuelled boost to BBP's cash flow, Dylan was able to upscale his patchy website and add an ecommerce store to showcase his growing list of titles – or rather, hire an Indian company to do so. It happened that now even the poets on his list were getting switched on to the digital space and questioning why their flowable ePub files weren't available for instant payment and download "24/7". The last straw was when one of them asked if the BBP site was properly optimised for SEO by means of targeted keywords, hashtags, etc., etc. and why the "http" in the URL didn't have an "s" at the end. To Dylan, at first this seemed like just a minor editorial oversight until he did a little digging and found out that his site wasn't "secure'" for payments, which only happened when data coming in and out were automatically encrypted. Worse, he discovered that lately the internationals were venturing out from their bomb shelters to set up premium direct-to-consumer platforms run by a chorus line of geeks who had been lured from their happy hour hacking by grey-haired Digital-VPs who didn't know a byte from an extra-curricular bite but who were feeling the pressure from parent companies located in Germany, Switzerland or even Shanghai to deliver the virtual goods to out-drone Amazon – or else.

The Black Books brand was in real and immediate danger of being trampled by a new breed of international publishing "evangelists[126]", so, not to be outdone, Dylan made his first move by paying attention for a change to the numerous Indian website creators who had been tap, tap, tapping at his e-mailbox for attention like persistent woodpeckers.

Like most independent publishers who distrusted cause-and-effect on principle, Dylan believed in fate: things happened for a reason and at a preordained time, and so forth ad nauseam. So, when a pitch came just at the right conjunction of stars from a chap named Aryan of flashsite. com[127], in reasonably articulate English, Dylan took note:

> Leave the Hachettes hacking for air. Lay waste to the Penguins. You don't have to worry yourself about coding, you don't have to stress about how to make your website actually appear online and stand out on the Internet. Our website builders take care of all that technical stuff for you until your site is one for Google to love.

While Dylan thought a virtual drag race with the Hachettes and Penguins might be a tad unrealistic, he replied as noncommittally as possible with his "specs" and a wishlist of desired "functionalities", ending with terse request for a flashsite.com's 'best price', making it clear that several other companies were in the running for BBP's business. He then picked out two other companies at random from his junk mail box to send almost identical emails to because one piece of business advice he remembered was to get quotes

---

[126] http://bit.ly/2Incu5n
[127] http://bit.ly/2IfKCRw

from a minimum of three.

As if to confirm that flashsite.com was a rising meteor rather than a fake UFO, Aryan's quote came in a few hundred dollars lower than the others, accompanied by an angel shower of testimonials:

> our business tripled within weeks…

> Aryan will stop at nothing to satisfy…

> Thank God we found flashsite.com…

It went on like that for screens. Dylan knew enough to distrust testimonials, especially those invoking God and ending with just a first name and a last initial, but Aryan assured him that he wouldn't have to pay a cent until he was "utterly content" with the draft redesign and its functionality. Even then, there was PayPal's "money-back" guarantee on the advance, which would leave him with "absolutely no out-of-pocket risks".

Dylan took the punt.

Aryan even offered to redesign the BBP logo for free, which Dylan declined after musing on what a Bollywood-inspired logo might look like, finally deleting that message lest Hillary see that he was even considering it.

He was about to send off a digitally signed copy of the contract when D. H. tapped him on the shoulder.

'I hope you're paying in loonies, not bitcoins,' said D. H.

'Bitcoins? I thought the Indian currency was the rupee.'

'It is, but all the dystopians are insisting on bitcoin payment.'

'PayPal doesn't list bitcoins as an option. What the hell are they?'

'The imaginary tulip bulbs of the 21st century.'

'Have you been into my scotch?'

'Not at all. Just as long as you're paying in loonies.'

'Well, no, Aryan only accepts greenbacks. But that's OK – Paypal saves.'

'Jesus saves, PayPal converts?'

'You *have* been into my scotch!'

'I trust you bargained with him?'

'I didn't have to. flashsite.com had the lowest price.'

'He doesn't know that. The Indians love to bargain. They don't respect you if you don't bargain. So bargain.'

'He only wants a thousand bucks.'

'Then offer him $700, and then meet him halfway at $750.'

'That isn't halfway.'

'Yes, but it will be if you stand your ground for two rounds. He comes down to $900, you offer $700 again. He comes back with $800, and you offer to meet him halfway. Done deal!'

Dylan had his misgivings, but it was worth a few bottles of Dewer's to give it a try.

It went exactly as D. H. predicted.

Within a month, the new BBP site was up, and soon after the eCommerce site was under construction with the money Dylan had saved by bargaining. To save money, Dylan only required Aryan's team to create templates for each type of book they published. In theory, then, Dylan would work from the templates, do a little cutting and pasting, and voilá, the other mid- and backlist titles would appear.

It wasn't quite that simple.

It wasn't even *quite* that quite that simple.

Eventually, Dylan worked out a workflow: coding + scotch + scotch = product page.

He and D. H. became a sight for sore eyes. Dylan would have the template up on his screen, which D. H. would replicate on his holographic version, shuffling, cutting and pasting, fine-tuning with a speed that made Dylan negatively [as opposed to positively] dizzy.

'There!' D. H. would exclaim.

'Where?' Dylan would reply, eying the melting cubes in his scotch glass.

'No, I mean finished. Copy 'n paste time.'

And so it was done. And Dylan cast his eye over the digital horizon and declared that it was good – at least good enough.

'Now all you have to do is buy an encryption certificate,' said D. H.

'A what?' Dylan said, feeling the sudden impulse to vomit.

'A block of code you buy and send to your web host, who applies it to your domain so each of your pages displays a tiny green locked lock with "secure" to the right of it.'

'I thought you said we'd be done, D. H., when we finished the coding.'

'We were,' said D. H. 'But unless you want to keep this virtual work of art to yourself, it needs to be encrypted by means of a certificate.'

'Paid in bitcoins, I presume?'

'I wouldn't advise that,' D. H. said smugly. 'They've increased 30% in value since we last spoke about them.'

'That was yesterday.'

'Time to sell.'

'Sell? I didn't buy any.'

'More fool you!'

After his vomit, Dylan had forgotten all that he didn't know about bitcoins but felt much better about what he didn't know about encryption.

Two weeks after the new site launched, Dylan visited the "back end", as Aryan called it, and noticed that they had registered only three "hits" to the Store, two of them from Aryan testing it, and one by Dylan ordering a copy of *Arctic Secrets* to ensure it had "bestseller" status – at least on the BBP site.

'It's not working!' he grumbled that night, only managing to make baked pasta and cheese with an afterthought of bacon bits for dinner.

'What's not working,' Hillary said, pawing at her pasta with a fork. 'The oven? This cheese isn't half toasted.'

'No, I meant the web site, the Store – everything. I've spent $750 US and earned $17 Canadian for my own book, less the PayPal fee.'

'There, there. These things take time.' She got up to zap her dinner in the microwave.

'I could have earned more by now with my $750 US in a term deposit – or by buying a tenth of a bitcoin.'

'I heard that bitcoins dropped 50% in value yesterday,' she said, showing him her plate, with the cheese properly melted.

'Long live the loonie,' he said.

She explained then that it wasn't enough to simply mount a new website and even encrypt it if nobody knew about it. There was Facebook to face, Twitter to tweet on, LinkedIn to fuse with, Instagram to execute book and author "selfies" on, YouTube and Vimeo to clip with, and WhatsApp to transmit his every move and mood.

'Never mind,' she said, seeing how his pupils rolled back and didn't return. 'I'll get you started.'

The cheese on his plate melted itself.

Chapter 15: Divest and Diversify

SO THE POETS KEPT COMING. KEPT COMING AND COMING. They kept at it because there were fewer and fewer places for them to submit elsewhere, and even the elsewhere places were getting ruder by the day.

The elsewhere places had been polite in the days of manual ink. They would send back typewritten and even hand-written submissions with a rejection that could be read by depressed eyes as encouragement, especially if the few lines of the photocopied rejection slip was signed by a real person, and even more so if the signature was more than "H. Y." or an "F. O." but actually a full name. It seemed that stationery supplies were in short supply at the elsewhere places because manuscripts were never returned now with spelling errors circled with red pen, let alone whole paragraphs annotated with remarks like "show, don't tell!"

This had something to with the fact that poetry editors at the elsewhere places had metamorphosed with the change in season into copyists of romance, memoir, horror, or, as befitting their change in mood after drying their wings, editors of sci-fi and dystopian novels predicting the triumph of "self-publishing apps" over an industry in geometric decline.

But it had more to do with the fact that the elsewhere places were being run by proxies of conglomerates who were well-meaning about their sub-sub-sub-sub enterprises but more interested in survival than syllable count, profits than pentameters, marketshare than message. In short the value of poetry wasn't to be measured by performance indicators or charts with anything but the most minuscule of scales: the generic rejection slip. It was to be the Tasmanian Tiger[128] of literature, respected, even secretly revered by those editors who had published so much as a chapbook of it or wished for even more, but then freeze-dried behind thick glass for a retro age of enlightenment when human delegates colonised a planet with fewer digital distractions and more opportunity for poetry to regenerate as an transworldly form of expression.

And so it was that Dylan as one of the few remaining publishers of poetry now achieved the status of national as opposed to local guru, although he himself had only published his preciously thin volume about subjects that Southerners could hardly relate to except in the dead of winter by the enforced crackling of a simulated fireplace. He made it onto the festival "circuit" of celebrity speakers who were actually paid to reassure any who would listen with hearing aids at full volume and those too young to have shed their ideals that there might be a future for literature amidst the din of modern media and millennial attention spans[129].

It was a good opportunity, as Hillary reminded him, to hawk the "brand" and so he did by alluding to the many [actually only several] awards that Black Books had achieved over the years. When introducing BBP to a crowd that had never heard of the company but should have – the percentage always astounded him – he would rely on pat line – 'I don't have a death-wish; it was never my intention to be *just* a publisher of poetry'. Rather than decrease the number of poetry submissions, it had quite the opposite effect because people tended to read irony into his humour.

The turning point came at the 63rd Bi-annual Squamish Literary Festival when the token session at 5:30pm Sunday that had been scheduled to feature BBP poets had between six and thirteen people in the audience, five of whom were

[128] http://bit.ly/2ChQyDi
[129] http://bit.ly/2zJDelR

poets waiting for their turn to read. Really, there were only eight at best since five of the starters left within the first five minutes either because they hadn't expected it to be all about poetry or because the modest refreshments had run out by then; and the other two from their wane expressions had only stayed on because they were too embarrassed to leave while someone was reading from the heart.

Dylan should have seen this minor disaster coming. During his morning reconnaissance of the festival bookshop, he couldn't find any BBP books face out on the shelves, or even spine out for that matter. When he distracted the clerk at the till from texting her boyfriend – or perhaps girlfriend if her spiky hair was any indicator of gender preference – she replied as if in the midst of a breakup.

'Black Books Publishing? No, I don't recall unpacking any books from you.'

Dylan pointed to his business card. 'Our boxes carry this distinctive logo. Are you sure you haven't seen it?'

The woman's phone beeped a notification just then, and she just shrugged and turned away.

'Bad news, I hope,' Dylan muttered, spinning on his heels.

He decided to take matters into his own hands by riffling through boxes under the shelving units, leaving them strewn along the aisle as a few early bird browsers shot curious looks at him. No luck. Then he spied a pair of boxes scrunched in under a unit at the far end of the shop. Sure enough, there was the logo, the boxes clearly unopened. He ripped open the seal on each box, pulled out five copies of each title, and deposited the books on the counter in front of the clerk who had resorted to actually talking on her phone. He finally had to tap her on the shoulder to show her the books, which she acknowledged with a breathy 'sorry'.

Taking nothing for granted, he returned at lunchtime to check on the welfare of the books to find them exiled from the front counter to a haphazard pile off in a vacant space in the "life writing" section. Finding no poetry section elsewhere in the shop, Dylan decided on lateral tactics, doubling up face-out copies of books by the same author to free up space for his authors. There were two clerks now, the spiky one at the till and a second even younger one, with amazingly platinum Abba hair, replenishing stock for celebrity authors at the signing table. Neither noticed Dylan at his subversive best.

On his way out, he took note of a display unit at the front of the shop labelled "Feature Authors Now in Session!" and later returned to stack the celebrities behind the unit as he replaced them with his authors' books. In this historic moment, he felt a pang of emotion not unlike that felt by the Greek soldiers waiting inside their Trojan equine piñata[130].

Back in the BBP session, he found that the Trojans had been tipped off and the town evacuated. There was nothing left to do but smile encouragingly at his authors as they took their place at the lectern and read out their work as if to a stadium of devotees. Afterwards, after even they had slipped out of Troy, and he was left to help clean up the jetsam of paper plates licked clean of mini blueberry muffins, Dylan decided to diversify into something more commercial than poetry and more uplifting than Russian ex-pat memoirs about how to make a fortune in real estate.

He asked a cracked mirror in one of the Festival bathrooms: 'What's the fairest genre of them all, one that I can be proud of?'

The stench from a nearby cubicle reminded him of diapers, not that it should have since he and Hillary had decided via The Pact not to add to the world's problem by adding any offspring whose DNA would be inevitably scarred by their addiction to scotch reveries, but it did, and diapers inevitably suggested an answer from the arrogant

---

[130] http://bit.ly/2EakMXc

mirror: children's books.

'You're crazy,' Hillary told him that evening when he floated the idea of a children's imprint. 'Sure, there's a market for children's books, but the majors have it cornered. Every primary school has a book club, right? And it's run like a monopoly by one particular publisher I'm sure you know of.'

'When's the last time you set foot in a primary school?' he said suspiciously. 'Are you thinking of breaking The Pact?'

She reddened ever so slightly. 'Not at all. But we can't always afford to choose our clients, and some of them end up being politicians, and politicians are fond of promoting their primary instincts[131], if you get my drift.'

'I mean, if you want to break The Pact---'

'You're beginning to worry me now. I'm sure you know who the publisher is.'

He shook his head. 'Winnie the Pooh?'

'Begins with "S" and has three syllables. Come on!'

'Scribners?'

'That's *two* syllables, dummy.'

'I give up.'

'Rhymes with "plastic".'

'Oh. OH.'

It was clear that Dylan had a lot to learn about children's literature, not to mention publishing it, and he suppressed the thought that his impulse to create a new imprint might have something to do with some unresolved childhood hang-up, but he was willing to let his inner child[132] tip-toe into what Hillary described as a minefield. He flooded BBP's social media channels with the announcement of a new imprint: Black Books for Kids. To his surprise, the announcement effectively killed two birds with one tweet because the more dour poets began to shy away from submitting to a company

---

[131] http://bit.ly/2E5U95w
[132] http://bit.ly/2lhSjqj

that would water down its commitment to the esoteric by publishing trivia.

The slush pile faucet grew an extra spigot, and soon a dribble of children's submissions were coming in. By then, of course, wired authors had learned that they could save on paper and postage by appending an attachment to their pitch. This provided welcome space on Dylan's desk for a scotch bottle in waiting and even a seasonal Venus Flytrap, which had to regenerate regularly since the few flies that ventured into the Studio had inherited a genetic aversion to spines not unlike Dylan's aversion to paper submissions that arrived without a self-addressed-stamped-envelope or at least a discount voucher bribe that could be redeemed in a liquor chainstore.

The submissions were often accompanied by testimonials from children with a generic first name and an initial who claimed to have conquered dyslexia after a first reading of the author's polished draft, and even clipart by some Taiwanese-born disciple of Miró offering to submit her portfolio upon request.

And then it arrived: The Dog Who Slept With Newspapers.

The story was simple enough, and set in those byte-free times when newspapers were still delivered by hand instead of in plastic-shrouded missiles. The synopsis was to the point:

> A young boy, living alone with his mother in a dismal
> basement apartment, has a paper route with over a hundred
> customers. He has to wake in the dark to deliver the papers
> before school, dragging them along on his sleigh through
> snowdrifts that obscure the sidewalks. One morning, he finds
> a puppy asleep between bundles of the paper at the collection
> point. At first he shoos it away, despite the puppy's large
> pleading eyes, but the puppy follows him the whole way and
> is there the next morning in his cubby between the paper
> bundles...

Dylan tried it out on D. H. even before Hillary.

'It's timeless,' D. H. said, his eyes somehow misting holographically. 'It reminds me of my youth in Eastwood. The dog is a symbol of the boy's lost innocence, even the spirit of his dead father----'

'You're going Freudian on me again,' Dylan said. 'But would such a book *sell*?'

'With the right illustrator.'

'And where will I find the *right* illustrator?'

'I'll ask E. H. the next time we go sky-sailing.'

'E. H.?'

'Shepard. The illustrator of Winnie-the-Pooh? Master of anthropomorphic characters. He'd know. Might even do them himself, if you don't mind a nom-de-plume.'

'Sky-sailing?'

'We go in a threesome with J. M. Barrie[133]. You don't think Disney got the idea by himself, do you?'

And so it was *The Dog Who Slept With Newspapers* was born, lavishly illustrated at the right price by an artist with a very Polish sounding last name, and, though the author was curious to meet the mysterious he or she signified by the J. M. initials, Dylan deflected this by saying that the illustrator was so famous in her/his native country that s/he could not have been seen as involved with the work of an unknown author until the book had sold a minimum of ten thousand copies. Given that the first print run was a mere thousand, Dylan believed that this would be a waterproof excuse.

As it happened, the author was well connected and the launch and its immediate aftermath sold well over a hundred copies. There was good chatter on social media among the children's groups, and the initial book reviews were positive, even from the snooty Lower Mainland dailies. The Black Books Store even scored a flurry of sales online, so *The Dog* soon swept past *Arctic Secrets* as BBP's first 30 days bestseller.

---

[133] http://bit.ly/2CjzX2c

Soon after, though, the momentum was lost.

'You need to get your author into the schools,' Hillary advised. 'In between book club days hosted by you-know-who.'

'She's keen,' said Dylan. 'But she's allergic to lice at any distance. They set off her asthma.'

'Make sure she brings a puffer, then,' said Hillary. 'And a phone to ring an ambulance.'

Hillary managed to organise readings at three schools in Nanaimo, the author's hometown, as a warm-up for the Big Smoke. Then, only days before the tour was to begin, the author rang from somewhere with the clatter of bedpans in the background.

'I'm sorry about this,' she said, sounding very congested in voice as well as outlook. 'I had a relapse yesterday, and it's serious enough that they won't let me out until at least Thursday.'

Of course, the tour was scheduled for Wednesday.

As soon as she found out, Hillary announced Plan B. 'You'll have to do it.'

'What?'

'Hang up and let me book your tickets.'

'But I'm a poet, not a children's author.'

'You're also a publisher with a recurring cash flow problem.'

'I've never even been to Nanaimo.'

'Take a fishing rod and make a holiday of it, then.'

'The only thing I hate more than eating fish is fishing for them.'

Not only had she booked the plane, hotel, car and fishing charter for him, mostly from her own frequent flier slush fund, she'd also set up directions to each school for him on Google Maps.

He arrived at the first school ten minutes early but was

spotted by the groundskeeper the instant he set foot out of the car.

'Can't park there, bud,' said the man with the tone of an ex-lumberjack. 'Prince and teachers only.'

'But I'm your guest author,' lied Dylan, to keep things simple. 'I'll only be here for thirty minutes or so.'

'That's what they all say,' said the groundskeeper, pointing to a distant lot. 'Shift your shiny new coupe over there.' Looking him over, he added. 'You don't get out much, do ya? Walk'll do ya good!'

Dylan knew better than to admit to the fact that the car was a rental.

Once inside, slightly puffed from the brisk uphill walk, he fronted reception.

The middle-aged woman at the desk seemed impressed. 'I thought you were a woman,' she said. 'But that's wonderful – men are in such short supply around here!'

A teacher's aid showed him up to the library where several classes were waiting. As soon as she opened the door, he was greeted by excited "woofs" and a floor space covered with wall-to-wall children wearing furry masks. The "woofs" were a dead giveaway.

'I hope you don't mind,' the teacher in charge said. 'We find that role playing keeps them off their smartphones.'

Yes, thought Dylan, doing his best to acknowledge, with a regal wave, as many woofs as he could, school has certainly changed.

There really must have been something magnetic about having a man in the classroom because, as soon as he sat down, the students edged forward. One particularly brazen boy managed to balance on his knee to 'help him turn the pages'. As he read, Dylan felt sure he felt the creep of moisture from the boy's trousers, which was confirmed by the dark patch left when the boy dismounted.

It was some consolation that most of the children came with pocket money, most of it in small coins, to buy books. Not to disappoint them, Dylan forged what he reckoned to be the author's true signature, until his fingers were cramped.

With no purse to contain the proceeds, Dylan's pockets weighed him down with coins. As he tried to make a graceful exit, he noticed several children pointing and giggling at the pocket with the most coins, almost directly above the dark patch on his leg.

Two schools later, all proceeds and expenses considered, not counting the dry cleaning bill for his slacks and the fruitless fishing trip, Dylan had cleared $23.75 on the day. An inauspicious start, but slightly better than BBP had done from poetry sales at the 63rd Squamish Literary Festival.

There was a spare seat next to him on the flight back from Nanaimo, and D. H. was in it, despite his aversion to single-engine aircraft.

'Rome wasn't sacked in a day,' he said, taking a sip from Dylan's second drink.

'I think you mean Rome wasn't *built*?' Dylan said, snatching the glass back from D. H. lest one of the other passengers noticed it floating in mid-air beside his head.

'I was being ironic.'

'You really think I should give it up, don't you?'

'Well, I never thought you should have started in the first place. Prose Styles of D. H. Lawrence still has an enduring ring to it, don't you think?'

'Nope. Time to give it away, and find some other starry-eyed master's student to haunt.'

'Write you off?'

'Unintended humour[134]?'

'Hmm. Well, I can't just leave you in the lurch. What would my fifth dimension happy hour comrades think if I let you fail?'

---

[134] http://bit.ly/2CjecwH

'I see. So there's some kind of competition between you spirits, eh? The Holographic Academy Awards, and all that jazz?'

'Nothing quite so material as that,' said D. H. 'You get used to being a high achiever, making your mark, seeing your name in the spotlights. After you pass on, the beams have an annoying green tinge to them, but you are always tempted to bask in the glow, however intangible it might be.'

'OK, well, what would you have me do to get Black Books Publishing into the spotlight?'

'Hitch your bicycle to a star.'

'Like E. T.?'

'No, I mean like Harry Potter.'

'That's been done, D. H. By J. K. Rowling.'

'Of course. But she was a nobody when she started with a book that nobody wanted to publish, but she stuck with it until she found a publisher with a vision.'

'She's an author, I'm a publisher. Your point is?'

'Harry Potter Healing – it's a manuscript midway down in Slush Pile 2. It's still pretty rough, but with a steady but firm editorial hand---'

'J. K. Rowling is a *brand*, D. H. She's the ninth best selling fiction author of all time.'

'Which means there's still plenty of room at the top to use her brand to your advantage.'

'You really are up in the clouds. She has law firms in every developed country in the world to defend Harry Potter from unlicensed use.'

'And to defend *her* against claims she lifted the *Goblet of Fire* from another book.'

'Oh, so you've heard about the infamous Willy the Wizard[135] case?'

D. H. nodded. 'It kept us out of boredom for months. The clouds were virtually seeded with opinion on either side.'

---

[135] http://bit.ly/2CivVof

'It was a sham, D. H. *Willy* was a sixteen-page book, devoid of substance. The *Goblet of Fire* is more than 700 pages and full of moral wisdom as well as having a stunning plot.'

'Which is why you need to look at Harry Potter Healing before the author sends it anywhere else.'

'We don't have a legal slush fund. We don't even have a lawyer.'

'That's putting the cart before the broomstick. Just read it, OK?'

Dylan put it off for exactly six hours, 43 minutes, give or take 10 seconds, even after he'd ransacked Slush Pile 2 to find Harry Potter Healing. Finally he was sick of skimming children's picture book proposals with text that was too long or short or too self-absorbed to be feasible for illustration by any self-respecting artist, or poetry manuscripts with sing-song rhymes by nurses wanting an alternative vocation to shifts in the emergency ward. Dylan had paused for at least six minutes, give or take ten seconds, on a memoir by an ex-hippy who claimed to have seen The Light, dim as it was, during his ten-day retreat to the Hare Krishna ashram in Prince Rupert where he had learned to hum relentlessly and atonally the mantra for the "True Way" similar to that popularised, but – as posited stridently in his synopsis – only partly understood, by the Beatles years before.

Finally, he turned his attention to the Harry Potter Healing manuscript, which seemed to have an otherworldly aura about it, perhaps due to residual radiation left by D. H.'s scan of it, or more likely the dying semi-chords of *Krishna, Krishna* as they dissipated in his head. The author, one Dr Imelda Psycle, who claimed to be an online contract lecturer in developmental psychology at Chilcotin Community College somewhere in the Cariboo [not to be confused with the more Arcticly inclined cari*bou*] District of BC, with a PhD in psychology from the University of Thunder Bay, ON and a list of publications as long as Dylan's sleeve [on those rare occasions when he wore a long sleeved shirt] in journals he had never heard of but found to be alive enough in a randomised Google search.

Not once was there a mention of Harry Potter, or even Harry, in the titles of Dr Imelda Psycle's articles, but Dylan was willing to give her authority the benefit of the doubt at least until he had skimmed a chapter or two.

Her headings were telling:

Animal Subtraction

Beasts Supercharge Power

Top Creature Cuddles

Free Your Inner Beast

Heal With Nature

and she had clearly immersed herself in the Series, deriving from it lessons for troubled youth and even more troubled parents and time-challenged school counsellors looking for ways of appealing to a child's subconscious without invoking detention, suspension, expulsion or even the strap[136], which had been outlawed in the BC public schools for as long as anyone could remember but which persisted in the folklore of principals inclining to retirement about the "good old days".

Dr Imelda Psycle seemed to be writing for those people, and, aspirationally, many more.

It was 4:30pm, and well past the time it would take to make pizza dough rise for their evening meal, before Dylan realised he had been reading for more than three hours with no more than melted ice cubes left in the glass on his desk.

---

[136] http://bit.ly/2BR6qt8

'Damn you, Mephisto!' Dylan declared, wincing at a thigh muscle in spasm mode as he stood up. 'You've offered me a poisoned chalice.'

Rubbing his thigh back to conformity, it hardly mattered that he was accusing D. H. of shape-shifting into Lady Macbeth.

Hillary was uncharacteristically bullish about his prospects with Harry Potter Healing.

'You're right about the risk of litigation,' she said, having speed-read the entire manuscript in half the time it took him. 'But think of the publicity. National, global, even!'

'Aren't you afraid of us losing the house?'

'We're renting, Dylan,' she reminded him. 'With no greater prospect of home ownership than keeping a muskox as a pet.'

'We could be evicted, then. With no garage to our name, our stock of *Arctic Secrets*, etc. etc. would be homeless.'

'It'll never come to that,' she said. 'J. K. has much bigger warlocks to impale. And even if she decides to make an example of you, we could crowd-fund a barrister, or maybe find one to represent us pro bono so Dr Psycle's reputation could go viral.'

'These psychologists,' said Dylan, passing a finger slowly above the candle she'd lit to create an occult atmosphere for their only slightly burnt crust poutine pizza, an experiment so named by Dylan to describe the flourish of leftovers employed when he realised he had run out of standard toppings. 'They're all mad as hatters, you know. They ride under-powered motorcycles and wear excruciatingly tight denims[137] over their cowboy boots.'

'She writes in a very sane fashion,' Hillary said. 'Look at this paragraph. And that one.'

'This is her list of references,' Dylan said, edging their second bottle of Shiraz subtly closer to him.

[137] http://bit.ly/2Dt1nzj

She looked more closely at the page. 'Point taken. It's so dark in here – who turned off the lights?'

'You did,' he said. 'So as not to see what you're eating.'

'Well, get in contact with her. Immediately, if not sooner. For an appointment, or something. Remember what happened with Angus. Make any excuse.'

And so it was that they drove up to Williams Lake in the Cariboo [not cari*bou*] District to visit with Dr Imelda Psycle because the good Dr did not have a car, not because she couldn't afford one, or even two, but because she was convinced that car ownership, let alone car 'drivership', was contrary to her environmental code, which she, exfoliating in great detail during a long distant call at Dylan's expense, always favoured *less* over *more*, *conservation* of energy over *waste*, and so forth. Dylan was reassured to learn that she was just as down on motorcycle ownership and drivership, if not more so because they invariably radicalised[138] molecules from stasis, e.g. silence, into combustion, i.e. noise.

It took a while for them to locate Number 12, 1008 Williams Lake Duck Road, because they could find no addresses at all on Williams Lake Duck Road until they'd reached a trailer park at 1008. The trailer homes were arranged in a prudent circle like a wild west wagon train[139] at the furthest point of which was Number 12, distinctive from the others by the fat satellite dish fastened to its roof. There was a short flight of three stairs up to the door at Number 12 on either side of which were matching rat traps, one of which sported a recently decapitated victim. Above the rusty doorbell was a sign:

I. L. Psycle, PhD
Office Hours: 9 to 5 daily
or 24/7 as emergencies dictate

---

[138] http://bit.ly/2Bj88Cq
[139] http://bit.ly/2ClCvu6

'The Dr must be IN,' smiled Hillary as she rang the bell.

Dr Imelda Psycle had made an effort. Freshly washed dishes sparkled on a drying rack. A dusting cloth wavered in the breeze from a strategically bent TV antenna. Dylan was a bit worried by the unfamiliar brand of Moscato wine poised on the coffee table, but the selection of cheese and crackers seemed safe enough.

'Thank you so much for driving all this way,' Dr Imelda Psycle said, in a rather grating high-pitched voice as she ushered them to a section of couch that had less worn cushions than the others. 'Will you stay the night? I have a two-person tent out the back. It's only semi-waterproof, but---'

'That won't be necessary,' said Dylan, trying to repress the scent of peaches drifting his way from the Moscato. 'We've got a room at the Lakeside Inn.'

'Very nice,' said the Dr. 'I could afford to stay there for a holiday, but it would be such a *waste* of resources on a single person. Moscato?'

Hemmed in on the tight side of the coffee table, there was nothing for them to do but hold up their smudged glasses warily as she poured. The cheese and crackers were borderline stale.

'I can't tell you how much this would mean to me, being published,' she said, tossing back her first glass as if it were a shot. 'The *Tribune* wants to do a full-page spread on me before the launch, but I've told them nothing is certain in these things. Like depression, and anxiety.'

Just when Dylan thought she had settled into common sense about media coverage, she had to tar it with the mental stuff.

'I think you handle those disorders particularly well in the book,' Hillary ventured, glancing sideways at Dylan as if to say take it from here, baby. 'With the exercises, and all?'

'Yes, quite well,' Dylan said, chewing on a bare cracker to

mute the taste of over-ripe peach.

'I've validated each and every one of them,' the Dr said, 'with our local Warthog Readers Club.'

'What a clever name,' Hillary said, gently pushing away her unfinished glass of Moscato and reaching for the cheese knife. 'Inverting Hogwarts?'

The Dr looked slightly confused. 'No, Warthogs,' she insisted. 'Our club predates Harry Potter by decades, but they were happy to adopt the Series when it chuffed into Williams Lake.'

'So you've trialled these exercises on real teenagers?' asked Dylan.

'A few,' the Dr ventured. 'After all, there *is* a shortage of youth around these parts, with the unemployment crisis, and all. But everyone in the Club knows a teenager, or at least remembers what it was like to be one, even before this obsession with screen culture took over, so it was easy for them to... role-play.'

Don't ask, Dylan thought, staring at Hillary, with her university elective in statistics. Please don't ask about control groups!

'And who did you use as a control group?' Hillary asked.

'Very good question,' the Dr said. 'I'm glad you asked that. We crowd-sourced our controls. We started with open trials, of course. Then, having tweaked our methodology, we moved onto single-, double-, and even triple-blind trials[140].'

Dylan was so relieved that he gulped down the rest of his Moscato and reached for the bottle, but the Dr headed him off at the pass. 'Pacing,' she cautioned, 'is a virtue. Especially among those who are tempted by car keys!'

Despite Hillary's temptation to flirt with the paparazzi[141] and litigation, Dylan held off on the Dr's contract until he heard back from Bloomsbury, the publisher of the *Harry*

---

[140] http://bit.ly/2ClR4hj
[141] http://bit.ly/2C6u2y1

Potter Series. He described the book in exhaustive detail and provided them everything suggested by the *Dummy's Guide to Copyright,* including a chapter breakdown and samples from the draft with exercises, the initial print run, the Dr's credentials, eBook versions planned, and so forth. While he waited for a reply, he kept the Dr dangling by suggesting a tightening of language in this particular chapter, or more appropriate examples from the Series in that chapter. She seemed more than happy to comply, and he didn't hear back from her for weeks.

Finally a crisp email arrived from London, to wit:

> Mr Dylan Cashew, Esq.
> Publisher
> Black Books Publishing, etc.
>
> Dear Mr Cashew
>
> Thank you for your comprehensive letter requesting permission to reference substantial sections of our *Harry Potter* Series in your upcoming title 'Harry Potter Healing'. Given the socially important aim of your proposed book, we are prepared to grant permission for you to do so, without costs, assuming that the usual acknowledgements and credits to us as publisher are provided. We have also consulted with our colleagues at Warner Bros., who hold the exclusive film rights to the Series, and they are also prepared to grant permission, again without cost.
>
> We wish you every success with this venture.
>
> Yours faithfully,
>
> Prudence K-W.
> Rights Dept.

'Be still my heart,' Dylan murmured. At the very least I would have thought they would have insisted on a title change to protect their trademark, but, no, here is a publisher with a social conscience[142]. Praise be to the Almighty Arbiter

---

[142] http://bit.ly/2ClZo0g

of Copyright, wherever he might reside.

'Not so fast,' came a familiar voice behind him. 'There must be a catch.' Of course, it was D. H. 'This Prudence character seems rather casual about your acknowledgements. I'd ask her for the exact wording.'

'But she said---'

'It could be a trap,' D. H. insisted.

'What ever happened to the "gentlemen's agreement"?'

'Prudence is no gentleman. She may not even be a human being. I've heard that publishers are now using bots for this sort of thing – and more.'

'You've heard of bots?'

'Some of my best friends are – or were – bots of sorts. How do you think all those serial novelists like Dickens got by?'

Dylan shook his head, not because he thought D. H. was having him on but because he might have a point about the wording for the acknowledgements. 'OK, I'll follow up with Prudence,' he said.

'Keep it simple,' said D. H. 'Bots may be as intelligent as your average assistant editor, but they do have a limited repertoire of answers.'

Dylan kept it simple all right, and Prudence K-W's reply came back within minutes.

Mr Dylan Cashew, Esq.
Publisher
Black Books Publishing, etc.

Dear Mr Cashew

Thank you for your comprehensive email requesting exact wording for the credit you wish to place in your upcoming book. I'm sure that the usual industry wording for such credits will suffice. Once again, thank you for making contact with us, and our very best wishes with your venture.

Yours faithfully,

Prudence K-W.
Rights Dept.

Dylan interrogated every word for evidence of a bot at work, and he had to admit that the reply showed signs of intelligent repetition.

'Never mind,' he said aloud to the nearest stained coffee cup. 'I've got it in writing, and that will be that.'

And so it was that the Dr's contract was prepared, sent out by registered post to her Williams Lake post box [Dylan had noted that the post box outside her trailer had been fused shut by rusty neglect], signed in two copies, witnessed [by a signature that looked suspiciously like the Dr scrawling with her left hand] and returned by normal post two weeks later. Then began the structural edit in which Dylan tried to cull repeated instances of Harry's encounters with her favourite wizards[143] and beasts, suggestions to which she always replied gratefully, allowing the cuts in that round but then sneaking them back in later in the chapter or even in a different chapter. Dylan was no psychologist, and had good reason to suspect anyone who was prone to self-medication, particularly at times of stress. For example, a sequence of editorial comments in red ink could, in the mind of such an individual, take on an animated presence, not unlike a laser-armed Transformer[144], thereby triggering an irrational if not a paranoid response.

Since Dylan had noticed that the Dr seemed more calm when fixated at her laptop screen to show them her top ten preferences for body fonts, which grew to twelve when she couldn't cut the cord from Luminari and Chapperal Pro, he decided to use the thought bubbles[145] in Microsoft Word as a less confronting approach to suggesting changes. Though he repeatedly asked her to turn on 'Track Changes' before she began working on the draft he'd returned to her and saw that the file she sent back did in fact open up with Track Changes on, a quick comparison of random paragraphs between their

---

[143] http://ti.me/2zKwNPv
[144] http://bit.ly/2n0EEUy
[145] http://bit.ly/2EbA7qr

versions revealed that she turned Track Changes on and off only when it suited her, especially when she wanted to slip in something he had already cut in a previous draft.

He got so frustrated by this subterfuge that he finally had to ring her.

'It's been six months now,' he said, after they'd dispensed with the small talk about how many rats she'd decapitated that week and shipped to the local high school pro bono for student dissection practice. 'And we still seem months away from a polished draft.'

'Two steps forward?' she giggled in that high-pitched voice.

'Something like that,' he said. 'We really do need to buckle down if we're to release this book before the Christmas sales.'

'Oh, yes, of course,' she said. 'And I'm grateful, *so* grateful for all the work you've done, which is why I've accepted all your changes to each draft, and---'

'Not quite all,' he corrected. 'In fact, not even close to all.'

There was silence on the line, as if she was peeking out the trailer window to check her rattraps yet again. 'Oh, dear,' she said, finally. 'I have been naughty. Maybe you should drive up here right now and… and give me a *spanking*?'

She had the drop on him. 'I hope that won't be necessary,' he coughed.

'You're my editor,' she said, 'and my publisher. Do whatever you feel is necessary. I'm but wet clay between your fingers!'

'Track Changes,' Dylan said, hearing a slight tremor in his voice. 'Keep it on, please.'

'Anything you say, my captain. Until we meet again.'

The Dr did actually behave herself, for the most part, from that time on, and three months later, Hillary was doing the final proofreading of the text while he layered on a few choice magical stock images for the book jacket. The background was a brooding blue, with a rising half moon casting a lightning-struck tree and surrounding forest scene into silhouette. Poised on a limb, and slightly interfering with the title font, was an owl that vaguely resembled Hegwig in its snowiness but slightly more barney[146] to avoid upsetting J. K. and hence Prudence K-W.

'Spooky!' Hillary declared over his shoulder. 'I'll make a designer out of you yet.'

'dreamstime.com did most of the work,' Dylan confessed. 'But what do you think of the font – too Harry-ish?'

'It'll do,' she said, tracing it with her finger. 'Did you remember to put in the disclaimer on the imprint page?'

'Yes, of course.'

She took the mouse and scrolled down. 'I love some of the testimonials. Like this one from Heather, the fruit picker: "No matter what happens, good or bad, you can make good choices. Never give up." Sweet!'

'I like this one from that former president of Animal Liberation Victoria: "Animals have so much to teach humans". He's clearly heard about the Dr and her rats.'

'It's refreshing to see so many non-academics here – a nurse, bar attendant, there's even a cleaner.'

'Yes, but she does have psychologists, homicide victim support groups, psychiatrists.'

'Relax,' she said. 'I'm sure it's headed for top of the charts.'

'There's no soundtrack to it,' he smiled. 'Where is John Williams when we need him?'

And then the very day he got the word that the presses were running Harry Potter Healing, a very official letter addressed to The CEO, Black Book Publishing, etc., arrived by post.

---

[146] http://bit.ly/2zJqEDe

Mr Dylan Cashew, Esq.
Publisher
Black Books Publishing, etc

In Confidence and for Immediate Attention

Dear Mr Cashew

This is formal notice of our claim that your book entitled
Harry Potter Healing is in breach of the copyright held by
our client and the licences granted to the first rights holders
of the book and its adaptation into film and other forms.
We hereby demand that you immediately cease and desist all
actions related to the publication, launch, distribution and
sale of this book in any form or via any media. Your failure to
confirm your intention to comply will result in court action
taken against you for damages and costs incurred.

Regards,

Alison B.
Contract and Rights
Hollingsworth & Hollingsworth, etc.

It was after 3pm, certainly well within the parameters of
a scotch docking break, but Dylan wasn't the least bit thirsty.
'"Regards" indeed,' he said, aloud. 'D. H., where are *you*
when I need you?'

'You only need to rub my lamp,' D. H. said, appearing on
his usual landing spot, Slush pile 1. 'Where's the fire?'

When Dylan showed him the letter, D. H. nodded sagely.

'Don't just nod sagely,' Dylan said. 'What am I supposed
to do? The book's already in print. The Dr's already ordered
three cases of Moscato, anchovy canapés and a special
canopy to keep out the rain, not to mention that made-to-
order snowy owl cap[147] she'll wear during her reading.'

'Nothing to worry about. You've kept Prudence's emails?'

'Of course.'

'Admit nothing, concede even less. Send this Alison

[147] http://etsy.me/2C4h7MW

227

character a tersely worded reply to the effect that's she misinformed, that you hold the necessary clearance from the first rights holders and that, her letter notwithstanding, you intend to exercise your rights as granted. Append your disclaimer, Prudence's emails, and that, I suspect, will be that.'

'I can't remember all that,' Dylan said, sliding the keyboard his way. 'Here, you write it.'

D. H. sighed. 'Do I have to do *everything* around here?'

Alison B was nothing if not tenacious. In reply to his, she emailed back to say that the wording of his disclaimer was 'at best, inadequate and misleading' and her initial warning stood.

'It seems,' he said, showing her reply to D. H. and Hillary, who was so excited by the prospects that she feigned a sore throat so she could conspire with them for the day, 'That that was certainly not *that*, as far as Alison is concerned.'

'This is great!' Hillary declared. 'I'll work up a press release, fire it off tomorrow, and then book a room in the Sheraton for the national media conference. It might even get syndicated and go international. *The Guardian*, yes the Guardian – I'll put them at top of the list!'

'Cool your heels for a second,' D. H. said. 'We need counsel. The best of the best. Hmm.'

'What are you up to?' said Dylan.

'Leave it with me,' said D. H. 'I'll be back before sunset, PST.'

And so he was, with a crusty chap in pinstripe slacks held up by suspenders.

'Don't tell me,' gasped Hillary. 'Clarence Darrow?'

'The same,' Darrow said in a thick Southern accent.

'Clarence... who[148]?' said Dylan.

'Never mind my hubby,' Hillary blurted. 'He doesn't get out very much.' Turning to Dylan, she added. 'Only one of

---

[148] http://nyti.ms/2zJ9y8F

the most famous criminal lawyers ever. Don't you remember the Scopes monkey trial? Spencer Tracey, and all that?'

Dylan's jaw dropped. 'He defended a… monkey?'

D. H. stepped in. 'It's a long story – you can do your research later. The long and the short of it is, the *real* Mr Darrow – or should I say the genuine facsimile of the real – whom I've known since *Lady Chatterley* was banned and then released in the USA, has agreed to defend us by proxy – if it comes to that – for free.'

Darrow shook his head. 'Copyright is more a pastime for me than a specialty, but this is an open and shut case,' he muttered. 'Nothing to answer. This Alison character is clearly a bounty hunter, and you're the prey, but I'll let her know that she's just firing blanks, and that we've got the live ammunition.'

'Don't be too hard on her,' Hillary said. 'I still want my press conference.'

Whatever Darrow said, it was short and sweet, and perhaps he came to Alison as a fit of irritable bowel syndrome, but soon she offered a compromise: he was to print a disclaimer on the front cover making it clear that Harry Potter Healing was not endorsed in any way by J. K. Rowling or any of her licensees world-wide. There was no mention of Darrow anywhere in the email, but her tone had an intangible awe about it.

'Case closed?' Darrow said. 'I do have a pressing cold case cocktail date… up there.'

'Not quite,' Dylan said. 'The book is already printed, cover and all. We'd have to reprint, which is effectively what Alison wanted us to do in the first place.'

'It's against my better media judgement,' said Hillary, but we can get your disclaimer printed on unobtrusive labels – light blue on dark? – and stick them on only as needed.'

'She's a keeper,' Darrow said of her, vaporising before their eyes.

And so it was that a roll of light midnight blue labels was produced by Pentiction Rapid Printers with a six point disclaimer and attached to all copies of the book bound for public spaces like bookshops, libraries, offices of counsellors, psychologists, psychiatrists and especially the stock to be sold at the much-anticipated *Harry Potter Healing* Costume Party And Book Launch to be held outside the Dr's trailer at 11:30pm for a precise midnight start on 31 October, which even Dylan knew to be Halloween, but true Harry Potter aficionados would recognise as the death date of Lily and James Potter.

Word of the launch spread as far as bytes could travel by satellite and dozens of people of marginal Druid[149] lineage pitched tents in a crop circle around her trailer from sunset on 29 October. In the absence of port-a-potties, no one seemed to notice the lurid scent of decapitated rats amidst the off-pitch strains of the *Harry Potter* theme song[150] that echoed well into the wee hours. So crowded were the grounds that Dylan and Hillary had to walk most of the way in, elbowing away a swarm of fans from clawing at the boxes of books they had to lug in.

Someone had already set up a half-moon of trestle tables outside the Dr's trailer, the legs of which were strewn with the sticky spider webs one expects to avoid on Halloween, the tops of which were covered with black crepe paper weighted down with assorted Harry Potter figurines of various sizes, some of which were slightly animated in the breeze by concealed spring works in their bodies, and it was all that Dylan and Hillary could do to breach the trestle table redoubts without ripping away their paper façade. Overhead were strings of Chinese lanterns whose faint glow grew stronger with the darkening sky.

'Look at them,' Hillary said of the figurines. 'I'll bet she's measured the distance between them with a ruler.'

[149] http://bit.ly/2Eg7sAo
[150] http://bit.ly/2Eel6mn

'Or with stale ballycastle bat wings,' Dylan quipped.

'You're really getting into this, aren't you?' she said.

'Yeah, pass me my cape, please.'

'It's not midnight yet.'

Having unpacked and set up the book display with minimal intrusion on the figurines, Dylan knocked on the trailer door while Hillary kept watch over the books.

'Too early,' called the voice inside. 'It's only ten past the hour.'

'The plebs are growing restless,' he said. 'They want you to sign their books.'

There was a pause. 'You mean you've sold some – BEFORE THE STROKE OF MIDNIGHT?'

'No,' Hillary called over her shoulder. 'He's lying. They're only browsing – respectfully.'

'Just as well,' came the reply, in a horror filmic low voice. 'I would have had to call the whole thing off.' But then the high pitch returned: 'Only joking, my captain!'

'What did she mean by that?' whispered Hillary.

'I think she thinks of me as a kind of Severus Snape[151] to her Hermione,' Dylan whispered back.

With her snow owl cap, black cape and cheeks smeared with combat charcoal, at the soundless stroke of 11:30pm, the Dr was hardly visible even under the brightest Chinese lantern as she distributed plates of Double, Double Chocolate Cauldron Cakes, Peppermint Toads, Golden Snitch Butterbeer Cake Pops and Weasley is Our King Cupcakes – all apparently prepared by hers truly. Given the oversized rave crowd[152], these all disappeared quicker than anyone could have intoned *Dumbledore and The Deathly Hollows*.

Probably the only one out of costume, a psychologist from the Williams Lake Crisis Centre, gave a nervous but emphatic launch speech, referencing Bruno Bettleheim, the

---

[151] http://bit.ly/2Capx5J
[152] http://bit.ly/2CapDKD

neo-Freudian who most in the mob assumed to be a minor wizard, then yielding the floor – or rather the ground – to Dylan who provided minimal details about the Black Books Publishing Mission lest some of them submit their over-wrought Druid haiku[153], adding to Slush Pile 3.

No one seemed to mind that his right cheek was smeared with the remains of Double, Double Cauldron Cake.

Then it was the Dr's turn. She had notecards that she squinted at for a few seconds before hurling them over her shoulder like spilt salt and smashing her papier-mâché wand on the ground to gain attention along with a piercing stare that even unsettled Dylan.

'Friends,' she began, before lowering her voice nearly a throaty octave. '*Friends*. The book you see before you is my magnum opus, dare I say my life's work. Countless nay-sayers littered the pathway at its genesis, but I regarded them as nothing more than cracks in the pavement because this work *had* to have its being through me, not as author, but as a channel for its timeless message. Night after night I communed with them, the hopeful voices of transformation, redemption and, yes, deliverance. Our age is overwhelmed with the swords of negativity, the brass knuckles of self-destruction, the faked fake news of politicians. We must lead by example, lend our youth the stamina of wizards, and, yes, the resilience of Harry Potter. Through this book, and your purchase of it in multiple copies, will its message be heard and all of us saved. The time for action – and book signing – has come!'

At the end of it all, Dylan and Hillary had only empty boxes to carry back to their car, after settling the good Dr to bed with her dose of herbal medication. Dylan suspected that a significant number of books were stolen under their noses in the rush, but then there was something to be said

---

[153] http://bit.ly/2DyObsX

for word of mouth freebies[154] that might get the attention of Amazon algorithms and copycat blog reviewers.

'Damn,' Dylan said, starting the engine of their emblem of waste. 'Where do we go from here?'

'Beats me,' Hillary sighed. 'A broomstick cruise? And a very long one.'

---

[154] http://bit.ly/2DyQ7BJ

PART 5: GENESIS YET AGAIN

And so the Lord said, to a sleepy congregation,
'in a world of snakes, agents, and over-ripe fruit,
it is not good for authors or even publishers
to be alone.'

Chapter 16: All that Glisters

HARRY POTTER HEALING WAS THE NUMBER 1 BESTSELLER IN THE CARIBOO [NOT CARIBOU] DISTRICT FOR EIGHTEEN WEEKS RUNNING. Even in Williams Lake's only surviving used bookshop, it earned an eye-height shelf of its own above the label of "almost new – mint condition" copies. The book was harder to place in the various Okanagan shops who had never heard of the Dr, though they invariably lifted their brows at the key words in the title wondering if they dared stocking it, even with the disclaimer on its front cover.

'We're haemorrhaging to Amazon as it is,' one bookseller said, tremblingly. 'We can't afford litigation with J. K.'

'Clarence Darrow says it'll be fine,' said Dylan.

'Clarence... who?' asked another bookseller, doubtlessly an intern in worldly wisdom if not by age.

'Pull the other one,' shouted another. 'You think I've never heard of Spencer Tracey?'

Bookshops had always been something of an untested ground for Black Books Publishing. They had no space, let alone shelves, for poetry. And if a memoir didn't involve a celebrity, preferably with a sporting pedigree[155], or a bare-clad political scandal, they weren't interested. Even literary novels provided no more than a short runway for BBP if they hadn't been at least long-listed for the Man Booker, the Pulitzer, or at least an Arctic District Commonwealth Writer's Prize, never mind a Governor General's Award. Dylan soon came to believe that most bookshop owners fantasised about being promoted one day to airport shop managers where books came and went in the hands of jet lagged passengers as profusely and predictably as Mexican fruit flies.

---

[155] http://bit.ly/2pS3c70

The Lower Mainland shops were the worst. They ignored email pleas. Their nipples were unhardened by seductive voicemails. Even when Dylan spent a week down there "cold-calling" where he couldn't land an appointment, the manager was reported to be on lunch until an unspecified time, in a stock take crisis meeting, busy as a UN secretary, on maternity leave – or a join-the-dots combination of the above. On those rare times when he tripped over a manager who wasn't on his way to Burnaby, Toronto or Shanghai, s/he had a toolkit of excuses:

'Canadian poetry/fiction/non-fiction doesn't sell, I'm afraid.'

'Can you come back after our Christmas/Easter/Mother's Day/School Holidays stock take?'

'We don't deal with [holding her nose]… vanity presses.'

'We don't have an account with you.'

'Central office does all our ordering from Seattle – or is that Tokyo now?'

'There was an earthquake last week – or one is forecast for tomorrow. Can't you see we have no shelf space?'

'I was/am/hope-to-be pregnant and need to refine my breastfeeding technique.'

It got to be so predictable after a while that Dylan could and did finish or at least mime their sentences for them. If he was at his flirtatious best, a manager – regardless of his/her/genderless non-specific sexual orientation – might invite him to stop in the next time he was in Vancouver/Victoria.

'I've decided to give up on bookshops,' he told Hillary after yet another fateful sortie.

'Why?' she asked, as if it were a foregone conclusion.

'I think Revenue Canada just might disallow my expenses if I can't show any income from these trips soon.'

'We could move to the Lower Mainland,' she offered, 'Then you could make a pest of yourself daily.'

'It's depressing enough to hear "no" on random trips. What makes you think living there would make things any easier?'

'It probably wouldn't. But *my* prospects for promotion would be much improved, and, as we have already established, she who bread-wins controls the set top box.'

That was the lowest cut of all, but he took it under advisement.

As fate would have it, the very next day, an email arrived for him from Arts BC. There had been a provincial election a few weeks earlier, with yet another change of government, which Dylan hardly noticed even as he cast his ballot in a semi-scotch induced state. It seemed that his former champion, ex-Minister for the Arts, Frank de la Hunt, had narrowly won his seat back, and, in recognition of his precarious victory, had been resoundingly appointed Minister for Science, Innovation, Casinos and the Arts. The email of course didn't come directly from the Minister but rather none other than his faithful private secretary Candice Blunt, who hadn't missed a beat[156] in his absence.

The bottom line was that the Party, and her minister in particular, had learned their collective lesson while in Opposition and were therefore determined to be more "proactive" in ministering their ministries, that is, junketing out of the Province more often and visibly to 'promote BC First'. It was a catchy slogan, and Dylan found himself scrawling it on a mini notepad he'd lifted from the counter of the most recent Lower Mainland bookshop at which he'd been rejected, just so he didn't go away completely empty-handed.

A pang of guilt shook him out of his reverie long enough to prompt him to read the rest of Candice's message. The gist of it was that the Minister was proposing a trade mission to China for select "innovative arts entrepreneurs" and was

[156] http://bit.ly/2pWS0pQ

inviting Dylan, as a "respected" regional CEO to come along, all expenses paid, to Beijing, except for accommodation, a "few" meals and a "modest" fee for crowd-shared translating assistance.

Dylan was so excited by the prospect that he ordered in a lavish Chinese banquet for them that night to create the right atmosphere for dropping the news to Hillary.

'Who have you offended this time?' she asked, seeing the spread.

'No one,' he said. 'It's about what I *might* do.'

'You mean *we*, don't you?' she said, with that look the import of which he understood immediately.

And so it was that Hillary called in a few more favours and redeemed yet more frequent flier points to, as she put it, 'tag along in business class' to ensure Dylan wouldn't careen off the Great Wall in some jet lagged stupor, which really meant she had done her research on the best places to shop for bargain clothes off the 'beaten path'[157] with or without a translation app and was content to leave him otherwise to his own devices and boring trade delegation meetings throughout the day. Adept as she was at "multi-tasking" and sign language, she also managed to chart the best places for their evening meals in several shopping districts she visited the first day.

Meanwhile, sipping more green tea and less scotch than he ever had in eyes-wide-open memory, Dylan found himself tapioca in the hands of his designated translator who, in showing his sample books to the speed-dating Chinese publishers, seemed to be bit-coining undecipherable jokes with them. As the day wore on, he interrogated his mind about this, deciding instead that Chinese publishers and translators only affixed happy faces[158] when in the company of foreigners, especially when their mood was being tracked

---

[157] http://bit.ly/2Ediq9R
[158] http://bit.ly/2BTGWep

by the CCTV cameras that seemed to be everywhere – in the hotel lobby, from the corners of the meeting room ceiling, and probably between the polluted blades of every air filtration unit as well.

His translator, Wang Fang, whose name in Mandarin was pronounced nothing like it looked on paper, was a slender, pale-skinned, rouge-cheeked Senior student from Beijing University, who confessed she'd signed on for translation work so she could save for an iPhone 10, or whatever edition it would be succeeded by in the seven years she estimated it would take her to make it her own, because she was convinced it would be wired with the chutzpah of Steve Jobs[159]. When she and Dylan first met, she excitedly browsed through the pile of books Dylan had brought with him in hopes of landing a rights deal, but she parked at the Dr's Harry Potter book.

'Oh, Ha*rr*y Potter,' she said, making a concerted effort not to stumble when pronouncing her "r's". 'You will have many, many Chinese publishers interested in this book.'

She was right. Each publisher they met dove into the book, chattering excitedly with Wang Fang. They were more somber about his children's books, and pushed away the poetry ones as if they had been touched by the Dalai Lama.

Finally, at tea and pastries break, Dylan could contain his hopes no more.

'What happens now?' he asked Wang Fang. 'Will any of them make an offer for the Harry Potter book?'

'I am not a… publisher,' said Wang Fang, 'but, if it was me, then, yes, most certainly I would be doing so.'

Dylan was so upbeat about his prospects for a sale that he hardly looked at his menu that evening at the restaurant Hillary piloted him to, which hardly mattered since it was in finger-smudged Mandarin. The decor was very retro with circular tables with florally embellished tops and polished

---

[159] http://bit.ly/2DxUlnN

chrome trims and legs. He was disappointed not to find an *Easy Rider* poster on the wall.

'If any of the publishers ask about the author, I might give them her Tinder profile.'

'What Tinder profile?'

'The one I'm going to create for her this evening.'

'We don't have a VPN, Dylan.'

'So? Are you going all geek on me again?'

'A Virtual Private Network is the only way you can do Tinder, or even Google for that matter in China.'

'Well, can we afford one of these...VPNs? Instead of dessert, perhaps?'

'There's no way I'm letting you lose on a VPN, darling. Enjoy your wonton.'

He slurped for a while.

'The Dr might do all right on a tour,' she said, finally. 'She has an instinct for cheap Chinese lanterns.'

'And she might be OK with the owl headdress,' he added, looking distastefully at his lonely green tea cup. Have you ever heard of Jai Yi?'

'No, should I have?'

He had the drop on her for a change. 'You'll have to get in The Zone if you're going to organise her tour. Jai Yi was a Taoist politician in the Hin Dynasty, who was very much pro-owl, despite the views of others. He even put words into their beaks, as it were.' He pulled out his phone and linked to a web page. 'Ah, here it is.'

> Be free and have trust in your fate
> and be a man who seeks what's true
> and though the thorns and weeds may scrape,
> what can such trifles mean to you?

'That owl must have been hooting for you,' she said. 'But forget spending your royalties before you have them[160] – I've

---

already done that on dresses and silk scarves. What will you have for your main course?'

He glanced at the menu front and back. 'It's still in Chinese. I should have brought Wang Fang with us. She looks like she needs a good feed.'

'Never mind that,' said Hillary. 'On the menu outside the restaurant, all the dishes have pretty pictures. You're lucky I have a visual memory.'

They ended up with a squid dish and something that looked like a cross between pulled pork and stressed chicken in a dark but translucent sweet and sour sauce.

'I thought you were ordering vegetarian,' he said, teasing a lump with his chopsticks then easing it into his mouth. 'To avoid a stomach bug?'

She was already well into it. 'This place is jammed,' she said, her mouth full. 'And the Chinese have come a long way with hygiene since Mao.'

By then, he was too hungry to worry.

After dinner, they wandered out onto the street to promenade with the locals. On every street corner, it seemed, hawkers were in their face with selfie poles, or strafing them with drones armed with red-eyed cameras, And then there were the swarms of fake Rolex and Apple watches, not to mention offers of "massages for two" with free "happy drinks". The night was alive with colour, commerce, a meteor shower of conversations – and sultry lovers.

'We should have come here on our honeymoon,' Dylan said.

'And have passed up on Big White?' laughed Hillary.

On the last night of the trade delegation, Dylan was obliged to wear a suit and tie for the closing cocktail party, and, to his and Hillary's pleasant surprise, there was plenty of scotch whiskey to be had. They had fortified themselves by the time the trade ambassador wandered up.

'Good choice,' she said, breathing in the aroma from Dylan's drink. 'For many years, the Chinese avoided scotch, before Diagio moved in.'

'Haven't heard of that one,' said Dylan. 'I thought this was good old Johnny Walker.'

'But of course,' the ambassador said. 'They're the parent company, and they've handled distribution so well that demand far exceeds supply, and a bottle can go for £400 or more.'

'That's more than a box of poetry books,' Dylan mused. 'At full retail price.'

'Don't mind him,' Hillary said to the ambassador. 'He's hoping that some day poetry books will replace bitcoins as the next crypto currency.'

'Yes, well,' said the ambassador, tolerating the joke. 'At business meetings here, the host will generally take his clients to a special restaurant where they sit around huge round tables and then place several bottles of premium Johnny Walker in the centre of the table to "save face", as they say.'

'So why isn't that happening here?' sniffed Dylan.

'You must be *patient*,' said the ambassador. 'The Chinese are a patient people. Relationships in business can take years to develop. First they must get to know you, and maybe later---'

'Does that mean we might not sell rights on this trip?' Dylan interjected. 'Even with Harry Potter... Healing?'

'I wish I could say you never know your luck[161], Mr Cashew, but there are more years than luck involved.'

'Well,' said Hillary, pointing her empty bottle at the bar. 'Let's make a start, shall we?'

'Speaking of which – where's Wang Fang?' said Dylan. 'She's supposed to be translating for us.'

As if on cue, he spotted her at the entrance door and

---

[161] http://bit.ly/2ltJN74

waved frantically to get her attention. She bobbed and weaved her way, docking with them at the bar. Her make-up had the potential to transform her from university student into socialite, but her cocktail dress was at least one size too large, as if she'd had to borrow it from a friend, or even her mother.

'So very sorry to be late, Mr Dylan,' she said, breathlessly. 'But I have been meeting with Mr Chou about your Harry Potter book, and I am pleased to report that he wants to meet you at his offices tomorrow first thing.'

'Mr Chou?' said Dylan, forgetting to introduce her to Hillary.

'Yes,' said Wang. 'He is very important man. President of China First Publishing Group.'

'We'll accept "important",' said Hillary, elbowing Dylan.

'Oh,' said Dylan, 'Wang Fang, this is Hillary.'

'His *wife*,' Hillary said, extending a 3rd person hand to her.

Wang offered a bow, but seemed slightly confused. 'Very nice to meet you, although most publishers who come here choose to leave their wives at home.'

'But we're not most publishers,' said Hillary, 'and I wouldn't have missed your beautiful country for the world.'

'I am so very pleased that you like what you have seen so far,' said Wang, glancing nervously at Dylan. 'You will do tour afterwards, then? China is so much more than Beijing. I know this company. Very reasonable rates.'

'Maybe next time,' said Hillary. 'Especially if Mr Chou is in the buying mood[162].'

Dylan rediscovered his front foot. 'And when do we meet this Mr Chou?'

'Tomorrow morning,' said Wang. 'He will send a car to pick us up from the hotel lobby. At nine a.m.'

A limo? wondered Dylan. BBP + CFPG: that has a nice ring to it!

---

[162] http://bit.ly/2Ca1hQV

They took the lift down to the lobby floor restaurant next morning with a good half hour to spare. At breakfast, Hillary had announced that she'd decided to sacrifice her morning visit to the Malls at the Oriental Plaza.

'Seen six Parisian plazas, seen them all, I suppose,' she said, as they waited for Wang Fang. 'Besides, you might need back-up with Mr Chou.'

'How so?' asked Dylan.

'I'll play Bad Cop; you play Good Cop.'

'You've been watching too many crime thrillers,' he said, spotting Wang Fang coming in the revolving door. She was wearing a smart embroidered blue blouse, stretch black denims and stacked heels. Smart casual certainly suits her more than cocktail attire, thought Dylan.

A white Mercedes coupe arrived at precisely 9am, complete with a uniformed driver. No sign of Mr Chou. After the driver and Wang Fang exchanged a few animated words in Mandarin, she got in the front seat while they got into the back. The leather seats exuded a fresh scent as if the car were straight from a showroom, or at least resprayed to smell so. Each front seat had an embedded screen, not unlike a business class airline. Dylan resisted the temptation to browse away from the latest *Kung Fu Panda* episode that was already playing.

It took nearly half an hour to arrive at the headquarters of China First Publishing Group. It was a glistening office block of at least twenty floors, Dylan estimated, straining his neck to look up as they got out of the car. The lobby was vast, with marble floors and walls enhanced by what looked to be traditional Chinese sculptures and paintings. The lift was glass-encased, and smudge-free, giving them a commanding view of the smoggy city as it accelerated whisper-quiet up to the top floor, No. 26, Executive Suite.

They were ushered into a boardroom with wall-to-ceiling glass and a round oak table with plush burgundy upholstered chairs. At opposite ends of the room were gilt-framed portraits of Mao and Xi Jinping, the latter being tactfully larger than the former. Dylan tallied ten male executives and one female seated around the table, with four spare seats – one for each of them – plus one, they were soon to find out, reserved for Mr Chou, who arrived fashionably late[163]. From his crisp attire, and slicked back greying hair, he would not have looked out of place in the front row of a meeting of the Chinese Central Committee.

Dylan leaned over to whisper to Hillary. 'I hope they didn't mistake us for someone important, like a Random Penguin.'

'All the better I dressed you in black and white,' Hillary whispered back.

Mr Chou spoke in slightly accented Oxford English, which Dylan guessed had something to do with the fact that he had graduated from there during an earlier Dynasty. Soon after welcoming them with a deference Dylan thought more appropriate to foreign diplomats, Mr Chou snapped his fingers once, almost silently, but, as if by spell, several waiters animated to pour green tea and serve lavishly iced pastries into/on delicate bone china. Then there was a brief hush in the room as the waiters backed up to their respective corners after which Mr Chou gave the subtlest of bows as a signal for those seated to partake of their refreshments.

'At China First Publishing Group,' Mr Chou began, as his associates froze in mid-bite or sip. 'We seek strategic partnerships with foreign friends so that our two great peoples will be able to partake the very best work from our cultures.'

There was a silent chorus[164] of nods and smiles around the room, so Dylan joined in as he imagined any assenting Random Penguin executive might. All eyes in the seconds following were on him, as he vacillated between the

---

[163] http://muse.cm/2BSfb63
[164] http://bit.ly/2Cp2yjZ

alternatives of raising his teacup in a toast or actually saying something.

'Thank you so much, Mr President,' he said to break the fortune cookie silence. 'On behalf of Black Books Publishing, we are most grateful for the opportunity to meet with you and your... esteemed staff.'

The remark went down well, if the almost identical chorus of nods and smiles around the room could be an *X Factor* measure.

Mr Chou proceeded to introduce every person around the table in a blur of log lines that included their names, imprint and a brief catalogue of bestsellers featured in *The China Times*. Dylan of course took in very little of this and understood even less, but he was somewhat relieved to note Wang Fang taking profuse notes in Mandarin, or whatever shorthand script system she had at her disposal.

Finally, the time came for Dylan to introduce the BBP list, which of course was headed by *Harry Potter Healing*. He added in several children's picture books, then delved into a sci-fi chapter book series about extraterrestrials and animals that had won a minor environmental award, but cut it short when Wang Fang scythed a sour look at him.

'Of course our list is growing rapidly as our brand becomes better known,' he concluded. 'Which is why we are here to discuss rights sales – with your esteemed company.'

That seemed to be that, for morning tea, at least.

The rest of day was regimented into stops at the imprints on various floors of the high rise where they were met with polite staff ushering them to somewhat more modest boardrooms but no less sumptuous tea and pastries, during which this or that publisher or chief editor would pass around a slurry of titles none of which were in English but all of which had high production standards that Dylan could with all sincerity show admiration for while secretly wondering if they had been assembled by hand in distant sweatshops.

At the refilling of the teacups, it was Dylan's turn to pass around his sample copies at which various staff members gesticulated their admiration at the cover of *Harry Potter Healing*, although he noted few of them ventured beyond the back cover. Each stop was like a recurring daydream[165] of the previous one, until, by late afternoon, Dylan was tempted to surrender with a serviette pirouetting on a chopstick.

D. H. squeezed between them in the car on the way back to the hotel. Or rather, Dylan and Hillary automatically allotted space for him as if he weren't a holograph of his former or present self.

'You should have brought a doggy bag,' D. H. said. 'Not that I have the munchies.'

'I didn't want to encourage them,' said Dylan. 'If I had accepted one of their books for possible rights sale, it would have been impolite to refuse the rest.'

'So you didn't take any?' D. H. scoffed. 'You have a lot to learn about protocol, my boy.'

'Not that you have any China connections.'

'*Au contraire.* There's a whole auditorium named after me at the Ningbo campus of Nottingham University.'

'That's here – in China?'

Dylan noticed Wang Fang casting curious looks in the mirror at his disjointed conversation – or at least at the bits directed at D. H. – but she managed to distract herself with a typical millennial defence, browsing her phone.

'Yes, it's south of Shanghai. I'm in good company there, with their Tian Yi Ge Library, which dates back to the 16th century.'

'Congratulations,' said Dylan, lowering his voice for Wang Fang's benefit, 'but what does that have to do with me violating protocol?'

---

[165] http://bit.ly/2pV3k5E

'The Chinese are all about not losing face[166]. If you had taken some of their books "on approval" they would have done the same. You would have a rights deal by now for *Harry Potter Healing* at the very least.'

'But I don't speak Mandarin.'

'So you could have judged one or two of their books by their cover and gifted the rest to the lovely Wang Fang as a thank you.'

'It's done and dusted now,' sighed Dylan. 'Why weren't you there when I needed you?'

'I was,' said D. H. 'But I don't get iced biscuits very often.'

And so it was that Dylan, Hillary, and presumably D. H. flew back from China with nothing more to show for it than the memory of powdered sugar on their lips yet with a green tea hope that something would materialise after they landed. In all, they had met with ten Chinese publishers during the delegation, including the CFPG, but Dylan decided to adopt a glass half-empty approach[167], assuming that the outcome would be no worse than the arthritic MasterCard report from Hillary's clothing extravagances and the catalogue of selfies she took, backdropped by as many Parisian stores she could find.

Something clearly snapped in his mind between the airport and home about the wish list of becoming an international publisher with offices in Beijing or at least Shanghai, and with Wang Fang as his executive PA. Suddenly it all seemed a chore – the entire independent publishing racket, working his feet raw, and for what? A bank account that trended below the minimum wage, media outlets that ignored his pleas for attention, bookshops that thought they were doing him a favour by even stocking his books on consignment, and a growing cast of authors who were disillusioned to find that his best efforts didn't earn them the outside lane on the

---

[166] http://bit.ly/2IjMLMf
[167] http://bit.ly/2CpQLID

highway to bestseller status.

Am I getting jaded? Dylan asked himself, hoping D. H. was in a different zone at his moment of self-doubt. Was it those prolonged days of scotch-deprivation, or the abundance of scotch on tap, that had droned him into this crevasse of indecision? "Moderation in all things" suddenly made sense.

Keep busy, he exhorted himself. *Detox by proofreading some poetry.*

With uncanny timing, an email from none other than Minister Frank de la Hunt was waiting for him the next morning. Well, more likely from Candice, who had an instinct for bureaucratic speak that meant he only had to read every other line, if not every third. But this one had a fetching subject line:

Acquittal Report – China Delegation, For Immediate Attention

The sheer number of questions confronting him for answers plunged him into a jetlag depression, especially the penultimate one asking not only for 'outcomes' but for specific details on what they might be worth in royalty dollars, and inviting him to append 'extra sheets' of information as required.

In his enthusiasm over his ascension back to Cabinet, Frank had again made the mistake of giving Dylan his new direct phone number, and, as star-crossed meteors would have it on this occasion, he actually picked up.

'About this acquittal report, Minister---'

'Oh, it's you, Dylan. I take it you enjoyed your junket[168] to Beijing?'

'Yes, but---'

'And the delectable Wang Fang? I pulled out the stops to get her for you – as translator, I mean. Still, not a bad sight in the no-go zones between conversation?'

---

[168] http://bit.ly/2q1ihn5

Frank had the drop on him. 'No, she was very nice. And *professional.'*

'In every respect?'

'In *every* respect!'

'Well, you *would* have to go and take your wife with you, Dylan.'

Dylan had to admire Frank's skilled detour from the topic at hand. Doubtlessly a master during Question Time.

'I think Wang Fang has a boyfriend, Frank.'

'Oh, these university boyfriends come and go, mostly go, when there's a shot for a bright, attractive girl to emigrate to a prime destination like Canada.'

'What are you suggesting, Minister?'

'You're not recording this by any chance, are you, Dylan?'

'Of course not. I may be an author and a publisher, but I'm loyal to my… friends.'

'And obviously your wife. Most commendable. Everything else is strictly off the record.'

'Could we get back to the report?'

'Oh, that. You're a wordsmith, right? So just wordsmith in some words to fill the respective spaces and send it in.'

'What if there's just a huge gap where the answers should be?'

'Dylan, Dylan. No one actually *reads* these reports. Unless there's a royal commission or some random Freedom of Information application. And when's the last time we had a royal commission into expenditure in the arts[169]?'

'So a work of fiction will do?'

'Your lovely wife's in PR, right? She must know how to string clichés together. I'm confident she can splice in all the necessary words like "promising", "impending contract", "potentially lucrative" and "game-changer for the industry".'

'Exaggeration's one thing, outright lies are quite another, Minister.'

'Are you *sure* we're not being recorded? I thought I just

---

[169] http://bbc.in/2FcjkaM

heard a faint beep.'

'Not at my end, Frank. Maybe the Opposition has targeted you?'

They went on like that for quite a while, until Dylan was convinced that he could report almost anything, and his acquittal report would be harmlessly archived, or even shredded by an untraceable robot, if push came to shovel[170].

He was surprised at how willing Hillary was to play along with this, as he verbally blacked out the Minister's intimations of immorality with respect to Wang Fang, who Dylan had rewound as if by video track to detect any undercover flirtations. Now that Frank mentioned it, there had been instances of "come hither" in her eyes that Dylan could not dismiss as refractions of sunlight, not to mention her Parisian dress and expensive perfume that she wore throughout the delegation meetings but more subtly on the day Hillary accompanied them to CFPG.

'You'll just have to kowtow,' Hillary said.

'W-what?' Dylan replied.

She held up the form. 'With this, silly. It's no different than that form you have to fill out at Customs asking if you've been trekking in Africa. They always overlook your muddy hiking boots – unless you make an issue of it. So let's just bend the truth and give them what they want: yellow brick roads of an outcome.'

'You're wasted in PR,' said Dylan. 'You should go into politics.'

'No, thanks,' said Hillary. 'In PR you let other people wear your lies, or, rather, exaggerations. As a politician you're under scrutiny all the time and have to have the talent to spin awkward truths into confusion or lies into evasive eloquence until no one knows what you meant in the first place.'

Dylan handed her a pen. 'OK, musical theatre, then.'

---

[170] http://bit.ly/2Dx2cam

Chapter 17: Waiting for the Drones

AFTER THE CHINA ACQUITTAL REPORT WAS FILED WITHOUT A BLIP OF ACKNOWLEDGEMENT – Dylan wondered if any being physical or robotic actually read them – life at Black Books Publishing gradually settled into normalcy. To make matters worse, or even more normal if that was possible, the dreaded Statement of Accounts time had arrived. Red pen, slush piles, and editorial mark-ups on real manuscripts might sink into the quicksand of industry yesterdays, but Statements of Account were forever. On some tablet it had been and still was writ that these should be compiled every six months and reported on to every creator that had a stake in this or that creation.

Back in the prehensile age of publishing, Amazon was no more than a river that would inspire *Heart of Darkness* remixes, an apple was something you took a bite out of after washing it free of pesticide memories in lieu of a sleeping tablet, and a google was a typo for goggle. But now these had not only shed their skins for virtual 3D wear but also spawned a host of "start-up" distributors and online shops with smoke and mirror techniques suggesting they had stock of this title or that when, in reality, they had no more physical stock than a chat centre.

Back in those mildewed ink and paper days, publishers simply had to account for sales of physical books either directly from their stores or via the snake oil reps who went from shop to shop hawking their wares in the hope that some droplets would stick. But with eBooks, almost everything changed. Suddenly there were dozens of start-up and up-start distributors that publishers could partner with, each of whom had their own commercial-in-confidence method of recording and reporting sales. There was a lot of one-way trust required in dealing with these distributors by independents like BBP, but it was like dealing with the big banks – either you took the plunge or hid your cash under a CCTV-monitored straw bed.

And so it was that Dylan immersed himself in the Brave New World of "multi-channel" publishing – with DIY tools of accounting for sales and royalty payments due to authors since there was no margin to hire even a part-time bookkeeper, let alone an accountant. It was hard enough when BBP had only a handful of titles to report on, but now it was taking several days, and a blur of scotch bottles, to get through. As the ratio of scotch sips to statements increased, so too did the number of errors, and the extra time to sort it all – or to hope it would just go away.

Something had to give – and something did: what was left of Dylan's sanity.

D. H. found him face down one 3am, dribbling into his keyboard. If iMac screen-savers could snore, Dylan would be singing along.

'T. S. was right,' said D. H., blowing nanographically into his ear until he woke.

'T. S.?'

'Eliot, of course. As in "Hurry up please its time" Tom.'

'I'm only halfway through the statements,' Dylan moaned.

'Of course he was talking about pulling teeth not paying royalties,' D. H. continued.

'Same thing – but with less local anaesthetic.'

'Good night, sweet authors, good night.'

'That tolls a familiar bell, too,' said Dylan, managing a grin. 'What am I going to do? Don't answer that.'

'Exit Stage Left?'

Dylan smiled. 'I never know which way that is – my left or right? Maybe I could just subdivide what I have in the company bank account between all my authors, post them a cheque and be done with it. Do you think anyone would notice?'

'The ones you were underpaying would get grumpy, and the ones you were overpaying would be delighted. Chances are they would average out in any X-Box game, and equilibrium would be restored. But not until your iMac had been ransomed for scrap. Third Law of Thermodynamics[171], right?'

'I think you'll find that it's the First,' said Dylan, amazing himself at his random power of recall. 'But who's counting? I do find myself approaching absolute zero. *To sleep, perchance to dream?*'

'I stand corrected,' said D. H. 'But don't go all Shakespearean on me. I reject everything I ever had to memorise – and so should you! Time to call in the big guns.'

With that, another holograph swung in at D. H.'s left. The figure was vaguely familiar but not so much so that Dylan could hang a name on it.

'What you need is a good accountant, Pilgrim,' winked the arrival.

Dylan blinked more than once. 'John Wayne?' he ventured.

'Wrong,' said the stranger. 'I'll give you three clues. And if you don't figure out who I am by then, I'm off.'

'Meaning he'll be offended,' D. H. whispered in Dylan's ear. 'Ready? *The Pelican Brief.*'

Dylan scratched his head. 'Sorry, I'm not a bird-watcher.'

The stranger narrowed his eyes. 'Nor am I. Let's try again. *The Client?*'

Dylan took an extra deep breath. 'Now *that* rings a bell.'

'And?'

---

[171] http://bit.ly/2BX3IST

Nothing more than a sigh from Dylan.

The stranger grimaced. 'Are you *sure* you're a publisher?'

'Niche,' Dylan said, apologetically.

'Short for Nietzsche?' D. H. offered.

'Last chance, Pilgrim. *A Time to Kill?*'

Dylan's synapses sparked. 'Oh, my God. Grisham. John Grisham?'

'The same,' said Grisham, extending a hand, which, as Dylan shook it, had an impressive physicality for a holograph.

'But how do you know---?'

'D. H.? Well, we go way back,' said Grisham. 'Not that we ever met – in physical time, as it were. I was intrigued by the case at the Old Bailey, where *Lady Chatterley's Lover* went on trial.'

'And my literary virtue with it!' affirmed D. H.

'As you should know,' Grisham continued, 'though I trained as an accountant, I was first and foremost a lawyer, and this watershed case has always intrigued me, especially for the brilliant defence mounted by one Gerald Gardiner.'

'Assisted by me, of course,' said D. H.

'Awkwardly so,' said Grisham, 'Since you'd been dead for thirty years!'

'It took me nearly that long to find a way to materialise notes from… beyond to here, as it were,' muttered D. H.

'I love it when you talk transcendental[172] to me,' chuckled Grisham.

'I only wrote what others wanted to conceal,' said D. H. 'That is, we are first and always physical beings, desperate for love.'

'You really should go back to the Prose Styles of D. H.,' Grisham said to Dylan, scanning the BBP online see-through catalogue. 'A fat backlist here – and what do you have to show for it?'

---

[172] http://bit.ly/2zO2IPb

For an instant, Dylan could imagine what Julius Caesar must have felt on the steps of the Forum: a hundred stab wounds and no *Times* bestsellers to show for it all.

He turned to D. H. 'Is that why you invited him here? You never give up, do you?'

'*Never* is more achievable,' D. H. smiled, 'once you've graduated to the After-life.'

'You never cease to amaze me,' Dylan replied. 'How did you come up with the power to transmit a *living* person from Oxford, Mississippi to here?'

'Well, well,' Grisham answered for D. H. 'You didn't recognise my books, but you know where I live?'

'Only by accident. I wrote my Master's on William Faulkner, and that's where he's from. You came up in a footnote.'

Grisham snorted. 'Bill was a bit of a show-off. All that stream-of-consciousness[173] crap. A master of the verbal fugue. I suppose he deserved the Nobel for sheer tenacity, but I always preferred Steinbeck for his biblical sub-texts. Don't get me started.'

Dylan sighed. 'If you must know, Black Books fills a niche. We publish those who don't have a chance with the majors but who still deserve to be read.'

D. H. clapped his hands in mute mode. 'Here's to the mid-list. But, still, publishing never was meant to be a charity.'

'So you invited Grisham here just to prove Black Books isn't worth doing?'

Although, in his current immaterial state, D. H. didn't really need to, he mimed a deep breath. 'Someone has to bring on... how do they put it now – your reality check[174]?'

'Don't get me wrong,' Grisham intervened. 'I wouldn't write if I didn't enjoy it. But, at the end of the day, there's got to be a buck in it – something more than a rusty tin cup. But busking is *so* last century.'

---

[173] http://bit.ly/2DxiLTx
[174] http://bit.ly/2CaXK59

'True,' Dylan said, pointing at the computer. 'But see for yourself – we're solvent!'

As they looked over his shoulder, Dylan opened his accounting program, ran a report to the end of the previous month, then pointed at the screen. 'See? A clear profit!'

'Wow,' said Grisham. '*Almost* three thousand dollars. Hardly enough to keep up the loan payments on your Mercedes.'

'We don't have a Merc.'

'Precisely,' said D. H. 'Eventually, you have to spit out the dust and abandon the coal mine.'

'And do what?' snapped Dylan. 'Write my Lawrence dissertation? It's probably been done by some Oxford don.'

'A few times,' said D. H. 'But so dry and tepid – because none of them had the insider knowledge[175] I could give you.'

'The boy has a point,' said Grisham. 'How would he have referenced all that? "Personal interview with the author" wouldn't pass muster.'

'No credit necessary,' said D. H. 'The nitpickers would have to put it down to pure inspiration, or something like that.'

Dylan brought his fist down on the desk so hard that his keyboard bounced. 'The point is, I'm doing it because I enjoy it, and I don't have to answer to anyone.'

'Sounds familiar,' said Grisham. 'Why not become an author instead?'

'I *am* an author,' sniffed Dylan, bracing for it.

'Of *one* book,' tut-tutted D. H. 'Which sank like a pebble.'

'I believe the expression is *sank like a stone*?' said Dylan.

D. H. smiled. 'No, *prose* sinks like a stone; poetry sinks like a pebble.'

'Never mind,' said Grisham, clapping him on the shoulder. 'I can respect the uncertainty, the fear.'

'What fear?' said Dylan.

---

[175] http://bit.ly/2zNl2qc

'Of failure. You can be an editor, a publisher, or even a lawyer, and hide behind other people's circumstances, but, when you're an author, you're out there with a reputation naked to the cat o' nine tails – apologies to Jeffrey[176] – of criticism.'

'You should be taking notes,' D. H. said to Dylan. 'Grisham's on a metaphorical roll.'

'More of an allusive one,' said Grisham. 'But, seriously, I like you, Dylan. More than that, I feel for you. Here's my card. If there's anything I can do to make the transition easier for you, ring me. I've never had a Canadian as a ghostwriter, but there's always a first for everything. Just off the top of my head, Terror on the Tundra has a certain frigid twang to it. Does it do anything for you?'

Dylan stared at his empty glass. 'Not at the moment.'

'Not that I'm boasting, but I'm at 400 million copies in print world-wide as of COB yesterday,' said Grisham. 'Amazon adores me. I've heard they're delivering my novels by drone within minutes after the buyer clicks Buy Now.'

I may be easy, but I don't come cheap, thought Dylan, lifting the glass. 'Maybe we can discuss all that after a refill?'

In a flash, D. H. produced a vintage scotch out of not-so-thin air. 'Here's to bestsellers!'

Chance has a way of bringing even the dimmest bent light of space into focus, and so it was that Dylan was determined to prove Grisham and D. H. wrong about Black Books Publishing's supposed backwater status. But he had no idea how to do it.

A home-cooked gourmet dinner was always a good start for lateral thinking, especially if he wanted to get Hillary's opinion. He dipped into his *epicurious* recipe archive and found an article "The Creamiest, Dreamiest Way to Cook Pasta", which seemed to capture the mood he was after – a creamiest, dreamiest way to publish a bestseller. Sure enough,

---

[176] http://bit.ly/2zN6lzn

the recipe encouraged a creative leap[177] by suggesting the cook treat his pasta more like a risotto rather than boiling it to death in roiling water as salty as the Dead Sea.

'This is just what we need,' said Dylan, holding the bag of pasta aloft, as he sped-read the recipe, only to find he was missing one key ingredient, some fresh greens to stir into the dish once it reached *el dente* status.

'Don't move,' he instructed the pasta, setting it down on the stove and grabbing his car keys. 'I'll be back before you can say *Quill and Quire*... fifty times.'

The pasta maintained a starchy doubtful silence.

Of course, this could not be a normal grocery store sortie. One could only guess where chain store greens were from, and where they had caught their breath along the way. So Dylan drove straight to the Penticton Farmers Market, which not only had the reputation of being *the* best farmers market in Canada but also had the only clerk who had attended the Penticton launch of *Arctic Secrets* and hadn't yet pawned off her autographed copy to The Book Shop. How did he know she hadn't? Because Dylan numbered each and every autographed copy inconspicuously at the lower left corner, knowing that anyone who wanted to sell their copy wouldn't dare to tear off the corner of the most conspicuous page.

Her name was Karen [that was all he knew: he hadn't harvested her last name], she was old enough to be his mother, but she had looked after herself [Lower Mainland botox[178]] and had sculptured brunette hair that reminded him more than vaguely of Anne Bancroft's coiffure in *The Graduate*. They'd had a harmless flirtation over peaches and nectarines for months, even years, but she usually left him on his own when it came to the greens.

Today, though, it would be different. He needed just *the* greens to go with his special recipe – and needed help. So he

[177] http://bit.ly/2CmdWzw
[178] http://bit.ly/2BUSYo9

lingered among the baguettes and loafs of rye until she was free from customers.

'Dylan, my dear!' she exclaimed, kissing him Italian style on both cheeks. 'What brings you out to the markets on a weekday?'

With tremulous fingers he showed her the recipe. 'I need your opinion,' he said, 'on something less ordinary than my usual spinach.'

She nodded, reading through it then pointing at the small print. 'Yes, kale is what you're after.'

'Kale?' he said. 'But isn't that more tune-out food than top drawer?'

'Ah,' she winked. 'Don't tell me you're still a kale virgin?'

Dylan felt himself go beet-red, but maybe that was just from his empathy with the subterranean vegetables. 'If it's exotic, I'm willing to try it. But isn't kale supposed to be bitter?'

'Think of brussel sprouts sans farts,' she said. 'Kale is far more trendy – and versatile.'

There was something sensual in her "versatile", but Dylan managed to overlook it with 'I'm not after trendy, just persuasive.'

She narrowed her eyes. 'And you need something more… intense than a poem to set your romantic scene?'

'Yes and no,' he said. 'But mostly yes.'

She led him down the aisle, picking up ingredients along the way. 'My advice would be to first sauté the kale in butter, with a shy spring onion and some assertive pressed garlic. You do have a garlic press?'

'Is an editor ever caught without a red pen?' he smiled.

'Then this recipe will do fine,' she said, sniffing the garlic like a perfume sampler. 'But remember to stop off at the Bench 1175 Winery on your way home. You'll want a first-class red to set the right atmosphere.'

The reds were breathing like a vintage movie star by the time Hillary got home, just as he was introducing his pasta risotto to his slurry of creamy, simmered kale.

'New Zealand!' Hillary announced, holding up the first bottle. 'How did you know what was on my bucket list for our next holiday?'

'We might have to settle for a taste until BBP produces its next bestseller,' Dylan said.

'Did I miss something?' she laughed, polishing the rims of two wine glasses. 'What was our first?'

He smiled. 'I'm glad you said "our".'

Her lips formed the characteristic upturn at the corners that meant she was on to him – as usual. 'It might be easier if I just bankroll our holiday – yet again,' she said, holding each wine glass up to the light in turn.

'I'm rapidly becoming a kept man[179].'

'Nonsense. My mother always says *a kept man is an ungrateful man.*'

'So she's never... kept your father, even in his retirement?'

'Only teasing,' she said, pouring the wine. 'I'm not my mother's daughter in that respect, and I look forward to supporting you in your dotage.'

'Which may come sooner than you think – though I'm only three years older than you.'

She nodded. 'You've been talking to D. H. again, haven't you? That man's obsession with your dissertation-not-to-be would send him to an early grave – if he weren't already there.'

'He brought along reinforcements,' Dylan added, mentioning Grisham.

Hillary shook her head. 'What does D. H. have in common with an airport novelist?'

'A love of money, it seems. They both think I'm wasting my time on wannabes.'

---

[179] http://bit.ly/2zPQp4Y

'You probably are,' she said, toasting him. 'But there are far more boring ways to be employed.'

They'd mulled over this more frequently of late. A few drinks in, Hillary would talk about how she was getting a bit stale with her current client list. There were only so many cheery things you could say to promote Penticton as a tourist destination, or pumping up the local wine industry, especially when the current face of Penticton, the mayor, had a Costco dress sense, and the boutique wineries had only a cask budget to promote their premium products.

'Maybe D. H. is right. We could toss it all in, buy round-the-world air fares and refresh, rethink, remix at random *castillos* along the way.'

She kissed him square on the lips. 'I love it when you talk Spanish to me. I'm in!'

He gulped down half a glass. 'You're serious? You'd just up and go?'

'Watch me,' she said. 'Watch *us*! Of course, I'd have to give my partners two or three weeks' notice so they could bring in a temp, but it will take at least that long for me to organise flights, etc., etc.'

'What about BBP? I don't know of any temps I could just slot in there.'

'Haven't you heard of email auto-responders and bots? You can do all of your banking online, and let your POD print companies process the orders. Anything truly urgent you can handle via wi-fi from whatever castillo we're at. Simple as.'

He reached for the wine bottle and divided the remains between their glasses. 'I wonder if D. H. had a problem with Franco lookalikes.'

Fate has a way of shattering your best wine glass just when you thought you had the rest of your life – or at least the next month – sorted out.

The very next day, an email arrived from a certain David O., novelist, based in Montreal. The message was so extraordinary that Dylan had to read it several times to absorb it all.

> Dear Mr Cashew,
>
> I have, for many years, been faithful to P___ as my publisher who have, up until my last two novels, sold them into the six figures even before foreign rights were sold. Now, it seems, since they were bought out by B___ and then ruthlessly con-verged into P____R____, as a mere Canadian I have been consigned to the ranks of the mid-list and have even been deprived of my long-standing promotional person there. I could have signed with M____, and know from my agent that H____ has been sniffing around, but I am a great believ-er that all things happen for a reason, and that there was an omen of change in all this. Which is why I write to you.
>
> Some years ago, I ran across a remaindered copy of *Harry Potter Healing* in Librairie Drawn & Quarterly, my favourite bookshop. Of course it was the key words in the title that drew me to pick it up, and I was fascinated by the fact that J. K.'s shock troops hadn't quashed it before you could let it see the light of day. So I made a mental note of your imprint before settling the volume down between its dusty fellows as someone to contact in the future if the need arose, which, as you may have gathered, it has.
>
> Would you care to consider the first volume of my latest tril-ogy: *What the Under-Secretary Knew?* I've taken the liberty to attach it here.

Ah, political intrigue, thought Dylan. That would make a pleasant change from our memoir list. If it's not written in terza rima[180], it might be worth a look.

And yet, there was his agreement with Hillary not to sign any more authors until they'd returned from their trip.

---

[180] http://bit.ly/2mZQNKh

'Clear your desk,' she'd said, in dot points. 'Vanquish the slush pile. Immediately trash all messages that don't have "remittance advice" in the subject line.'

He'd agreed, but then what was he to do while she cleared her desk for her replacement? You could only spend so much time in make-believe mode on Expedia before your brain turned into oatmeal.

If a tree drops in a forest[181], and no one save a few squirrels are there to see it fall, who can bear witness that it ever stood upright in the first place? If he read the first few chapters of David O's novel, with no squirrels stickybeaking, it would be between him and Time Machine©, right?

Just then, the phone rang. It was a private number, which he usually ignored because it was bound to be someone selling cheaper electricity or the latest overpriced premium wine discount deal, but for some reason he answered it.

'Yes?' he said, with minimal tonality.

'Black Books Publishing?' drawled a woman, with a hint of Texas in it. 'Mr Dylan Cashew?'

'Yes… and yes,' said Dylan.

'Well, I'll be,' said the woman. 'Straight through! I'm used to dodging private secretaries running interference for their bosses, but yours must be on lunch break!'

'Excuse me – you are?'

'Beatrice Compson. David O's agent. He gave me to understand that he has sent you his latest manuscript for your personal consideration. True?'

'It is,' said Dylan. 'But I haven't read it yet.'

'Don't bother, sweetie.'

'You're his agent, yet you're telling me not to read it?'

Beatrice laughed the laugh of two tequila sunrises[182] and counting. 'Naw, you're getting me all wrong. I meant there isn't the time to read it, because if you take the time there won't be any manuscript left for you to accept – if you get

---

[181] http://bit.ly/2lm2ydn
[182] http://bit.ly/2CoeDGf

my drift.'

It was a bit too early for scotch, even for Dylan, but he just had to pitch himself and glance around for hidden cameras. 'Tell me… Beatrice. Does David O. know that you're ringing me?'

'Thank you for that question, Dylan. I presume it's OK to call you Dylan?'

'Yes.'

'Well, now, let's just say that he knows as much about this call as I knew about his email to you – before I intercepted it.'

'You *intercepted* his email?'

'And do so on a regular basis, sweetie. When you make 15% on each deal, you want to be sure you're the deal maker – or breaker, as the case may be.'

'How do you do that – I mean, intercept his emails?'

'By having friends in Homeland Security. Never trust your smartphone to keep mum – or your TV, for that matter.'

Dylan held his iPhone at eye level and examined it for signs of micro forced entry[183].

'Don't bother,' said Beatrice. 'We don't need to touch your phone to tap it.'

'You can see what I'm doing?'

'No, silly. Now *that* would be invasive. I'm just out to protect my interests, and, if you take my advice to offer a contract now, yours as well.'

Just then his iPhone and iMac beeped in unison.

'Did you just send something?' he asked.

'Our contract, of course,' she said.

'You sent *me* a contract?'

'Yes, sweetie. Now don't take this the wrong way, but I've studied some of your current contracts via my Shared Desktop app, and they leave much to be desired for both parties. Since time is of the essence, I thought---'

---

[183] http://bit.ly/2FSDF22

'Thanks, but no thanks,' said Dylan, tapping the hang up button.

A microsecond later the phone rang again. Even Beatrice couldn't ring back so quickly, he thought. It's a physical impossibility.

He answered it.

'I thought Canadians were a friendly people,' Beatrice said. 'At least let me lead you through the negotiable clauses and answer any---'

He hung up again.

She rang again. It was if she'd found a way to initiate a recall and then pause it until he hung up. Another Homeland Security trick, no doubt.

This time he didn't pick up.

After the call went to voice mail, the Mac Mail app on the iMac went berserk, flooded with messages with the subject line in all caps: PICK UP, PRETTY PLEASE? PICK UP, PRETTY PLEASE? PICK UP, PRETTY PLEASE? PICK UP, PRETTY PLEASE? PICK UP, PRETTY PLEASE? PICK UP, PRETTY PLEASE? etc.

It was Jack Nicholson in *The Shining* all over again, only this time with a digital axe, hacking away at the screen.

Dylan had the force of mind to quit Mail and then connect up with his ISP to block Beatrice's address and block-delete all her spam messages. For almost a minute, the guns fell silent over his trench, but then the messages started coming again – from a different address.

He resorted to his Autoresponder function, filling the window with NONONONONONONONONONONONONO etc. before turning off his phone and switching the iMac offline. He extinguished all of Beatrice's messages in his inbox before selecting David O's original message and, after only a nanosecond's pause, deleting it as well.

'There!' he declared to the iMac. 'The nightmare is over!'

'Not quite,' said a familiar voice behind him.

Dylan wheeled around. 'Did you have anything to do with this?'

D. H. smiled. 'Let's just say I had an inkling that it was coming. And I must say you handled it very well – not to mention with integrity.'

'Was any of it real?'

'Some bits,' said D. H. 'David O. is what he says he is, though his legacy is no more permanent than a tub of cheap ice cream. Beatrice, on the other hand…'

'So this was a test? To see if I'd take on a manuscript sight unseen on the chance it could make a bestseller?'

'Mozart says he's proud of you – and more than a little amazed – that you've managed to resist.'

'And if I hadn't?'

'No matter. I might have taken it on as a challenge, ghostwriting it to a polished version to see if we could make the *Times* list, or at least buy a star or two rating from *Kirkus*. And, if you made your fortune, I would have bowed out gracefully, leaving you to your next eon of publishing.'

That might have been the end of the story, except that, at 7:02 from the digital read-out on their clock radio, the phone rang. Hillary was in the shower, and so, bleary-eyed and more than slightly hungover, Dylan answered it. It was David O.

'Apologies for ringing so early,' he said. 'But I wanted to catch you before you got caught up in your daily routine. Have you read the manuscript?'

'Yes,' Dylan lied, hoping the brief synopsis and critique D. H. had given him was on the mark.

'Impressive, no?'

'No, I mean, no, sorry, it wasn't.'

The intake of breath on the other end of the line could only be compared to a leopard's before it leaps from a tree onto its prey. 'WHAT?'

Rubbing his forehead, Dylan rattled it off from memory. 'Diffuse plot, too many characters, painfully long exposition… Need I go on?'

'How dare you?' snarled David O.

Dylan imagined yellowed fangs, stale blood streaks. 'I'm afraid so. And we don't have the resources to---'

Just then Hillary emerged from the shower, towelling her hair, then miming Who Is It? In answer to which Dylan drew imaginary concentric circles around his phone-less ear.

'I've worked with some of the finest fiction editors in Canada,' David O. seethed on. 'Never, EVER, have I been subjected to such a string of creative writing workshop clichés.'

'Judging creative work is a subjective exercise,' said Dylan, adding another concentric circle in reflex mode, and vainly motioning to Hillary to stifle her giggles. 'Other publishers may well disagree.'

'What? Who's there?' David O. must have overheard Hillary. 'Do you have us on speakerphone, for Christ's sake?'

'No, not at all,' said Dylan, switching the phone onto speaker. 'My wife just showed me the latest *New Yorker* cartoon.'

'I see now,' said David O. 'You checked up on me at P___ R___, didn't you? And of course you took their views at face value – the ungrateful bitches!'

'I'm sorry to disappoint you, David.'

'You remember Bloomsbury? They were nothing before they took on J. K. I could have made your company the Bloomsbury of Canada. But you're not worthy of that. You're so immersed in the second-rate that you wouldn't have a clue of what makes for first-rate fiction.'

Hillary was practically doing somersaults by this stage.

'I can feel your pain,' said Dylan, barely holding it together. 'But, again, I have to say no – and good-bye.'

And with that, he hung up – and turned off his phone.

As she was getting dressed, Dylan gave her all the sordid details about David O. and the eavesdropping by Beatrice and her Homeland Security mates.

'You don't really believe all that cloak-and-dagger shit?' she said.

'I believe she *thinks* she has a contact, but I wouldn't put it past D. H. to have impersonated J. Edgar Hoover to get her onside.'

'We really must cut back on the scotch, darling,' she said, with more than a hint of mint jelly in her tone.

He flung off the sheets and stared down blankly at his limp penis. 'Maybe I *should* have taken him on. The man has supposedly sold more copies of his novels than all of our backlist combined.'

'Sight unseen?' she said, sitting on the bed and trying hard not to notice the penis. 'You did the right thing. Besides, next month we'll be in Spain, throwing rotten eggs at Franco's statue in Hemingway's memory!'

'Wait,' he cried, jumping out of the bed and, still naked, heading straight for his iMac. 'Let's see what Dr Google has to say about David O.

He fired up the computer and keyed in the name in the search window.

Nothing came up.

'Try Wikipedia,' said Hillary.

He did – still *nada*.

'That bastard!' cried Dylan. 'This time he's gone too far! Lawrence, where the hell are you?'

They waited a few seconds, but there was no sign of him.

'He's more of a cat than a dog,' Hillary observed. 'He doesn't come on command.'

'Miaow,' murmured a voice before D. H. emerged in a costume that reminded Dylan of Old Deuteronomy from the Vancouver production of *Cats*. 'Do you like it?'

Hillary couldn't stop laughing. 'What does T. S. think of it?'

D. H. struck a pointer pose. 'You mean Andrew L. W. – or more likely John Napier, who is just old enough to make a deal from his wardrobe to stay in the Land of the Living[184]?'

Dylan and Hillary glanced at each other, confused.

'Don't change the subject,' said Dylan. 'You owned up to inventing Beatrice, but you said David O. was real. Why?'

'It's a wonder what they can do with 3D printers and robotics now,' said D. H. 'You'll see the day when authors, as you know them, will be no more than avatars in some publisher's AI menagerie. I never expected Black Books Publishing would be the pioneer in this area because you have too many principles. And you proved me right.'

'And your point was?'

'You'll see… tomorrow.'

'We'll see what tomorrow?'

'It's a surprise.'

Dylan suddenly remembered he was naked and made an awkward attempt to cover up himself without making a scene of it. 'You mean you're going to go one better than David O. and Beatrice?'

D. H. placed a sheathed claw over his heart, or where his heart would have been if he weren't in costume and a holograph underneath it all. 'I swear by George Washington and his cherry tree that *I* have had nothing to do with tomorrow.'

'But you know what is about to happen?' Hillary piped in. 'How convenient!'

'I sense a certain lack of trust in you, Dear Lady,' said D. H., with his customary slight bow. 'But tomorrow will be what it will be, and I shan't be here to colour it in any fashion.' He paused for effect. 'If you must know, I have a new recruit, a DPhil candidate at Oxford who is 101% committed

---

[184] http://bit.ly/2zQ4krK

to complete the work you only started. I've agreed to be a dissertation examiner in the guise of one Dr Rebecca Beasley, who underplays my contribution to the modernist cause to a shameful degree. It will be an awkward scenario, having to divert the real Dr Beasley to a cruise on the Black Sea at the appointed time, and---'

'Enough!' said Dylan, with his privates now throughly covered by an out-of-date Photoshop manual. 'Can you give us any clue as to the nature of this final surprise?'

D. H.'s whiskers twitched. 'Let's just say the initials W. F. will figure prominently in the proceedings. Arrivederci!'

Chapter 18: But a Whimper

DYLAN HAD NO IDEA HOW "TOMORROW" WOULD BE DEFINED IN THE AFTERLIFE to which D. H. subscribed, so he and Hillary signed yet another verbal pact not to drink anything with the slightest content of alcohol in it past 22:00 hours for the next twenty-four.

As the digital clock in their living room bleeped toward midnight, Hillary offered him a mint.

He sighed before taking it. 'Why do I feel like Don Giovanni teetering on the edge of the orchestra pit?' he said.

'Oh, don't be so melodramatic,' said Hillary, shooting their mint wrappers into the fireplace. 'Anyway, I don't know of any initials for Satan that involve "W" and "F".'

'You may be right,' said Dylan, feeling his arteries narrow as the clock ticked over to 23:58.

'I'm always right,' she said, polishing a corner of the glass coffee table with a tissue, 'about things that matter.'

And so it was that the clock reached midnight, and then a few minutes on for good measure, and no brimstone or even smoke appeared in the fireplace. Dylan could ease up on the pranayama and then the kapalabhati breathing techniques Hillary had taught him to survive the final stages of Statements of Account.

'Let's make the most of your unresolved tension[185],' Hillary said, pulling him up from the couch, 'in the bedroom.'

Uncharacteristically sober as he was at this time of night, Dylan was equal to the challenge. 'But wait – Beatrice might be watching.'

They buried their iPhones under the couch pillows.

---

[185] http://bit.ly/2zOvMWA

Dylan woke once or twice during the night to do a wee, and the second time he thought he saw two faceless, schematic figures heading toward him from the ensuite. When he froze on one foot, afraid to advance to the one suspended in midair, the figures vanished. It took him a while to urge his penis into action at the toilet.

It was just another working day for Hillary, so when dawn and then breakfast came and went, she kissed Dylan at the doorway.

'D. H. was probably just having yet another laugh,' she said, rubbing the back of her hand against his cheek. 'But you can text or even ring me if and when W. F. Lucifer rolls up.'

He cleared away the breakfast dishes. Nothing.

He checked his emails. Nothing.

Polished his outdated profile on LinkedIn. Still nothing.

Nothing is with thee: *pues nada*.

Just when he was about to fling his autographed copy of *Lady Chatterley* into the fireplace, the doorbell rang. Which was odd because their doorbell hadn't worked for days or even weeks as it waited for him to replace the batteries that were never in stock at the local hardware because the mechanism was, as the hardware clerk put it, part of the capitalist plot to ensure we had to replace an entire device for the sake of a minor element – in this case a nonconformist battery – that was nowhere to be found in this forgotten shard of the universe.

Dylan had suspected she had Stalinist tendencies and so he declined to buy a replacement unit until he'd checked eBay. Sure enough, the batteries were available from several suppliers somewhere in China for less than a dollar each, including free postage, so Dylan had ordered six when he only needed two, and waited, and waited, for them to arrive.

He was still waiting at the point in question when the otherwise unmuted doorbell rang.

On his way to the door, he considered texting or even ringing Hillary with an update but decided against it. It was probably just another silly D. H. prank teleported from Oxbridge.

Two figures were smiling at him at the front door, and he recognised them instantly: Wang Fang, the translator, and Mr Chou, CEO of China First Publishing Group.

Always the skeptic, especially when sober, Dylan's first impulse was to reach for the doorbell, but he resisted.

'Wang Fang! Mr Chou! What a pleasant surprise!'

'G'day, mate,' said Wang, in a practiced accent.

'No, no,' Dylan replied. 'That's Aussie. You're in Canada now. "Hi" will do just fine.'

They looked past him as though he was concealing a diamond stash.

'Oh,' said Dylan, eying the doorbell again for signs of tampering. 'Please – come in.'

They gathered around the still-polished coffee table while Dylan tried to think of a delicate way to ask them why they were here.

'Coffee? Tea?' he asked, thinking of no better way to break the ice than with caffeine.

Mr Chou crossed his hands in perfect symmetry. 'A Regular Coffee,' he said. 'New York Style, of course.'

'Let me help you in the kitchen,' said Wang energetically.

'O.K.' said Dylan. 'It's just… over there.'

Once there, she leaned over to him conspiratorially. 'Mr Chou always orders a Regular Coffee when he attends Digital Book World.'

'Straight black, then?' Dylan said searching out their airtight coffee can from the freezer.

'No, no,' said Wang. 'New York Style is drip-filtered and then you add in cream and sugar.'

'Filtering and sugaring I can do,' said Dylan, putting the kettle on to boil. 'But creaming might be a problem.' He patted his stomach. 'Have to watch the cholesterol, you see!'

'Oh, but why?' she smiled. 'You look so... how you say, *fit?*'

'Gracias,' said Dylan, arranging cups. 'But apparently *the look* has nothing to do with the health of your arteries, and mine are stressed enough from my love of alcohol.'

She laughed. 'Very naughty. If I looked after you, you would live to be at least a hundred years.'

This was the perfect opportunity for Dylan to drop in Hillary's name, but for some reason he didn't.

'So you are working for Mr Chou now?' he asked, papering the filter and spooning in their best Arabica.

'Yes,' she said, then adding under her breath. 'And that is all thanks to you and the introduction you gave me to China First Group.'

'I really didn't do much,' Dylan said, pouring in the boiling water.

'Oh, but you did!' she insisted before patting him on the back of his free hand. 'In China, introductions from trusted friends are everything.'

'True,' he said, getting desperate. 'My wife is in PR, and she's always going on about networking, and how I need to get out more into the sociosphere.'

'Sociosphere? What is this sociosphere?'

'I just made it up,' he smiled. 'Sort of a place where you meet people in the virtual as well as the real world.'

She laughed. 'You are so clever, Mr Dylan. So *very* clever.'

The coffees poured, and the flattery half-digested, his thoughts returned to the cream. 'I don't suppose Mr Chou would notice a teaspoon of vanilla ice cream stirred in?'

She giggled. 'Probably not. In private, he really prefers green tea, but has asked for coffee just to impress you, the host.'

As the deed was done, he just had to ask. 'Wang Fang, why are you here?'

'Oh,' she said, going all shy again. 'That is not my place to say. You must be genuinely surprised when Mr Chou makes his proposal to you. And promise me that you won't turn it down without thinking about it.'

So he was no more the wiser for asking.

Back in the living room, Mr Chou was flipping through *Arctic Secrets*.

'I hope you don't mind my taking the liberty of reading your book,' he said.

'Not at all,' said Dylan. 'It's only an apprentice work.'

'You are too modest,' said Mr Chou. 'Poetry is the highest form of written expression, do you not agree?'

'Yes, of course,' said Dylan. 'But no one reads it here.'

Mr Chou tutted. 'That is a self-fulfilling prophesy. Your Robert K. Merton[186] coined expressions such as *anomie* to describe divergent expectations – in this case, that poetry should not be sold because no one is buying it, so the assumption realises the outcome.'

Dylan was glad he was not hung-over for once – he got only a fraction of what Mr Chou was getting at. 'So we should publish more poetry in spite of what we expect to sell?' he said.

'Precisely. And that is what brings me here today. Your company publishes much poetry but sells little, is that not correct?'

Dylan gritted his teeth. 'Look, *Arctic Secrets* was the springboard for Black Books. And once you publish one book with high production standards, others inevitably follow.'

'After so many of your poets were left stranded by Penguin Australia,' Mr Chou nodded.

Obviously, Mr Chou's trolls had been doing their research. 'I don't really hold that against Penguin. I've learned that

---

[186] http://bit.ly/2oQ4U5g

you do what you have to do to survive in this game. And publishing poetry didn't make sense for them any more.'

'And it does for you?'

Dylan took a long sip from his cup and hoped that the lingering taste of vanilla wasn't a giveaway. 'I wouldn't do it if I didn't love it.'

Mr Chou cocked his head. 'And do you really love it?'

For some reason, Dylan felt like Will Kane being faced down by Frank Miller in *High Noon*. 'Most of the time,' he conceded.

Mr Chou cleared his throat. 'I have been in this business all of my life, Mr Cashew. My father was a publisher, and his father before him. I have been at the core of every decision that gave birth to the many imprints that make China First Group today. There must be more than love, even *pure* love, for an enterprise like yours to not merely survive, but to thrive.'

Dylan glanced over at Wang Fang and was surprised to see her taking notes. It was like they were in a boardroom discussing international trade relations.

'I agree with all that,' said Dylan. 'So why, Mr Chou, are you here today?'

'Thank you for that question,' said Mr Chou. 'I was just coming to that. But since you have raised it, let us get to the point. I mentioned my father and his father, but not my son Hu Yang. He is a very accomplished boy, a graduate of Cambridge, and, like you, Mr Cashew, a lover of books. In less than five years he has risen to be publisher of one of our children's imprints and he is leading us into the digital world. Soon China First will have its own flip books application and animation studio, and so it goes.'

'That's all impressive, but what does that have to do with me?'

'Hu Yang is as ambitious as he is accomplished,' said Mr Chou, 'and he wants me to step aside as CEO.'

Dylan looked him straight in the eye. 'And you're not ready to retire, are you?'

'Not at all. But the winds of fate have brought Hu Yang and me to this point, and something must give way – old age to youth.' He paused, but only briefly. 'I love this country, Canada. When I was younger than Hu Yang, I was offered a visiting teaching post at the University of Toronto. In those days, it was easier to gain permanent residency, especially if you had – how can I put this diplomatically – the financial resources to seem a likely prospect for permanent settlement. Which I had. So I stayed on and worked here for three years before *my* father called me back to take the path that Hu Yang is now on.'

'I get it,' said Dylan. 'You want to move here?'

Mr Chou glanced at Wang Fang and spoke a few words in a tone that transcended linguistic boundaries. She stopped taking notes and closed her notepad, then cradled her cup of coffee.

'Yes,' said Mr Chou. 'And to take up a fresh challenge, one that involves you.'

'You mean Black Books Publishing?'

'You and Black Book Publishing. Or, if you prefer, Black Books Publishing as an entity on its own.'

'Go on.'

'You are familiar with the Bloomsbury Books?'

'Yes,' he said, suspiciously, remembering yesterday's conversation with David O. Was this just D. H. shape-shifting yet again?

'There are those who say it was pure luck that Bloomsbury ended up with the Harry Potter series.'

'A bit of judgement, too,' said Dylan. 'A dozen or so of England's best editors had turned her down.'

'And he would have done so, too. Except for his daughter Alice who loved it with the eyes and imagination of a child and then pestered him until he agreed to publish it. Do you know how many copies he printed in the first run?'

'Never mind all that. I don't see the connection between Black Books and Bloomsbury – unless you're planning to buy us out.'

Mr Chou shook his head. 'I prefer to invest in companies that are yet to achieve their potential.'

Dylan pinched himself. 'Are you a fan of D. H. Lawrence, by any chance?'

My Chou narrowed his eyes. 'Oh, yes. I too was very fond of my mother. But what does that have to do---'

'So you've never met him?'

'Impossible. I was only a child when he died.'

It was time to put all of his cards on the table, and to see who was bluffing[187] with Jack high.

'Mr Chou, would you still be interested in… investing in Black Books if you knew the owner, namely me, believed in multiple universes in which authors like D. H. Lawrence can meddle in the affairs of the everyday world?'

Wang Fang's pupils were as dilated as black olives. 'Do you need me to translate this for you?' she asked Mr Chou.

'No, thank you, child,' said Mr Chou, before turning back to Dylan. 'My people retain their beliefs in Confucianism, with its spiritual connection between ancestors and the living, and of course Buddhism speaks of the wafer-thin barrier between the here and the after-here, but I have never had the good fortune to be visited by an author of such poetic insight.'

'And you swear he hasn't put you up to this?'

Wang Fang's fingers tightened into anxious fists, pressed against her face.

Mr Chou stared at him for what seemed like minutes before his expression curled into a smile, which gave way to a Confucian belly laugh. 'You can be assured that what I am about to offer you comes from no one but me and was confirmed in my mind only minutes ago as we spoke.'

---

[187] http://bit.ly/2BjJuBs

If a Confucian-come-Buddhist former conglomerate CEO could gush with sincerity, that, in the uncharacteristically sober view of Dylan Cashew, was what seemed to be happening.

'Out with it, then,' said Dylan, about to prick the bubble of whatever parallel universe hovered between them.

Dylan had already ordered a bottle of Mission Hill Family Estate Bordeaux when Hillary flashed in the door of Theo's Restaurant, which was all but deserted since it was, after all, only 5:30pm on a weekday.

'I got your text,' she said, sitting down and checking the label of the wine. 'Mission Hill? You didn't even spring for that on our honeymoon. What's the occasion?'

'I've just had an extraordinary day,' said Dylan. 'And that calls for an extraordinary wino!'

'Yes,' she said. 'But you could have given me time to freshen up, straight from work. So who was the mystery guest?'

Dylan gave her the 500-word synopsis – which stopped short of the punch line and made no mention of Mr Chou and Wang Fang, so it really had nothing to do with the earlier chain of events at all.

'And? And?' she said.

Dylan pointed to her menu. 'The Artichoke Salata and Prawns Skaras come highly recommended. Or, if you'd prefer vegetarian---'

'Later,' she said, fists on the menu.

'I, on the other hand, will have the Gluten Free Oreteka, followed by the Salmos Sto Phylo.'

'Dylan Cashew, what have you done?'

'Nothing much – just sold BBP?'

The waiter came over just then and poured their first glass of wine, as Hillary was poised with all the patience of an Antarctic ice shelf about to self-destruct into bergs.

'You SOLD Black Books?'

Dylan held up his glass in a toast. 'If this wine sells for $120 including GST and we have three glasses each, what does that make it per glass?'

'Answer the question!'

'$20.'

'Don't be stupid – you know what I mean.'

'Oh, about BBP. Well, I didn't exactly sell it, although there are those who would say that sell[188] is probably the most appropriate word in the circumstances.'

The waiter returned. 'Are Madam and Sir ready to place their order?' he said, with a French accent.

'Are you from Quebec?' Dylan asked, with an almost sincere tone.

'Oh, no,' said the waiter. 'Although I have been at Theo's for nearly eighteen months. My home is in Lyon.'

'Ah, Lyon,' Dylan said. 'We know it well.'

'No, *we* don't,' said Hillary. 'I've been to Lyon, but you've never even been to France.'

'Time is irrelevant when galaxies collide,' said Dylan, closing his menu. 'Isn't that the country just north of Spain?'

The waiter looked over at Hillary as though it might be a trick question.

'Humour him,' Hillary muttered. 'He hasn't had enough wine yet to be serious.'

Dylan closed his menu. 'Since Madam is still making up her mind, I'll have the Gluten Free Oreteka, followed by the Salmos Sto Phylo.'

'Very good, Sir. And Madam?'

Hillary closed her menu with tense fingers. 'Do you recommend the Artichoke Salata and Prawns Skaras?'

'Oh, yes, Madam. Both received five stars on the Trip Advisor.'

---

[188] http://bit.ly/2Du1Zcl

'I like that waiter,' Dylan said in his wake. 'I think we should give him a big tip.'

'What is wrong with you, Dylan? He hasn't even brought our food yet.'

'Sorry,' said Dylan. And then 'sorry' again as if to emphasise his newly found sincerity. 'I was getting ahead of myself with France. We'll have to get bored with Spain first.'

'Will you please tell me WTF is going on?'

'I love it when you speak in acronyms.'

'WTF is an abbreviation, not an ac---' She caught herself. 'But you knew that. Go on.'

'All right, there were actually two mystery guests, and it had nothing to do with buying an investment property at Whistler[189] – though it could now, if you want to.'

'We've had this discussion before,' she reminded him. 'And you told me you were happy running Black Books, and---'

'No,' he said. 'I *said* there was nothing at that moment in Earth Time that I could think of that I would rather do.'

'Except retrace Hemingway's steps through Spain?'

'Yes, but that was only to get my mind off of D. H.'

'But then our mystery guest changed your mind?'

'You remember Wang Fang?'

'She was one of the mystery guests?'

'Yes, but she was only taking notes for Mr Chou, the CEO of China First Publishing.'

She shook her head. 'You're telling me that the head of one of the most powerful publishing groups in China is interested in buying Black Books? That's ridiculous!'

'The contract's being drawn up, even as we speak.'

She shook her head even more vigorously. 'No, you're making it up. This is pure fantasy!'

He grabbed the bottle of wine, divided the remains between them, held it high in the air until he caught the

---

[189] http://bit.ly/2BjXuet

waiter's attention then mimed that they wanted a second bottle.

'There,' he said. 'Would I do that if this was just make-believe?'

She leaned across the table and eyeballed him. 'You *are* telling the truth. Oh my God. How can that be? No more Black Books?'

'There is to be a... transitional period,' he confessed. 'During which I'll act as consulting editor, curating the final choices on our poetry list. Mr Chou and his team will do the rest. And from Toronto, it seems.'

'For how long?'

'Until we win our first Governor General's Award, or at least the Griffin. Or until I tell him I don't want to do it anymore. Even then, the name, and even perhaps the logo, will live on.'

The waiter brought over their first course and the second bottle of wine.

'I just realised how hungry I am,' said Dylan, tucking in. 'I've been off the scotch all day – funny what that does to your appetite!'

'We don't have to move back East, do we?'

'No,' said Dylan, his mouth mostly full. 'As you said, Dear Lady, have wi-fi, will travel. Just as long as I check in every few days, and fly to Toronto for board meetings two or three times a year.'

'You'll have to buy a new suit,' she said, before breaking into laughter.

They were so full after the main course that they opted for just coffee and a Bailey's to finish off.

'End of an era, I suppose,' mused Dylan.

'Yes,' she said. 'But what will you do when we get tired of travelling?'

'Stained glass,' he said. 'I've always wanted to make a tiffany lamp.'

'Stained glass?' she said. 'You've never mentioned that.'

He smiled. 'Let me tell you about D. H.'s style in "A Fragment of Stained Glass".'

'Oh God,' she laughed. 'OMG!'